Of Chains
and Shadows

Lauren Duell

OF CHAINS AND SHADOWS

Copyright © 2021 by Lauren Duell.

ISBN: 9781737877905
LCCN : 2021918734

First edition, 2021

For Grandpa Jim.

Thank you for all of your wild stories. You would have thought this was so cool.

PROLOGUE

Reina's mother dragged her by the wrist down streets filled with people setting up stands for the festival later that day. Joyful music spun through the air and made Reina desperately wish to be among those who were dancing. The brick buildings on either side of the stone walkways made the air feel warm as they emitted the sunlight they had absorbed all morning. Reina tried to tug away from her mother's grip, but her mother held firm and shot a disapproving look over her shoulder.

"There'll be time for activities later, Reina. If we stop now, we will be late to the ceremony." Reina stopped struggling and settled for staring in awe at the statues and fountains that littered the kingdom. The sunlight made the world look golden to Reina's young eyes, and the crowd filled her with an aching excitement. Her mother pulled her past an opening to a small alley where a woman led her plump pig toward where the auction would be held that evening. Reina reached out with her loose hand and lightly tapped the animal's rump. It jerked its head around and snorted at her. She chuckled gleefully as the pig disappeared from view, and she looked to the dancers who lined the streets.

Reina had always thought the dancers were otherworldly. The acrobatics they could accomplish while clad in colorful dresses that hung to their knees, as well as their graceful spins and dips, made Reina fiercely wish to become a dancer someday. One of the dancers shot her a wink, extended their hand, and gave the young girl a white rose. Reina grabbed it out of the dancer's hand in passing and twirled it in her fingers as she ran behind her mother.

"Thank the gods," her mother said, pulling Reina up and into her arms. "We have yet to miss it." Reina looked out from her new viewpoint and recognized the town square around her.

Carts stocked with food lined the cobblestone square, and the merchants screamed out in search of anyone willing to buy from them. Buildings stood proudly around the edges of the crowd, and the shops inside were all closed down for Albur don Gracos, the Day of Thanks. Stairs at the front of the gathered people ascended to a plateau raised slightly higher than those who stood waiting. On that plateau is where Reina's father stood proudly. He stared back into the crowd with a soft smile on his face. His blonde hair was pulled back out of his kind blue eyes, and he had on his finest clothes.

Even at eight years old, Reina recognized how significant an honor it was for her father to be up there. He was nothing more than a coal miner by day and a family man by night. The days spent in the mines were grueling, but many men worked in the tunnels to put food on their tables. Reina would meet her father at their door when he arrived home at night, and he would scoop her up in his soot-stained arms and spin her about their foyer. Reina would scream and laugh as her mother scolded them both to clean up and prepare for dinner. Her father had never done anything out of the ordinary, nothing worthy of being honored on Albur don Gracos. Not until the day his mine collapsed earlier that year.

Nobody told the miners the part of the mine they were moving into had been deemed unstable. So when the miners entered the shaft to begin their work, it collapsed. Soldiers were sent out to clear the debris and rescue those trapped inside. After days of digging through the rubble, it was deemed nobody could have survived the wreckage.

Reina's father had been in that mine, and when the news arrived, she couldn't understand the severity of it. Her mother sank deep within herself over the days that passed, and Reina sat and stared blankly at the walls in her room. Her father had been her hero, and she refused to believe he was gone. It felt too impossible to wrap her head around.

The following days in the kingdom were dark, and many sympathies arrived at Reina's doorstep. A vigil was held in the town square five days after the mine had collapsed. People who hadn't even known the miners cried as candles were lit in their memory. Reina had been angry at the strangers who attended the vigil. It was unfair that they could go home after shedding their tears, and their worlds would ultimately be unchanged. Reina couldn't escape the loss of her father. Her tears would stay with her as she prepared for bed that night. The sorrow would weigh heavily on her heart forever.

Then one day, a shout echoed across the kingdom and brought people to their doorsteps in search of what news the cry carried. The men had escaped the mine. They had trekked farther back into the dark tunnels until they had found a small opening. For days they dug and had eventually managed to make the opening large enough to escape. The idea had been created, and the journey had been led by one man: Reina's father. He ensured even the injured were not left behind and helped everyone trapped make their way to safety. He was no longer a hero to only Reina but a hero to the kingdom as a whole. He was up on that stage to receive the highest honor the king could bestow upon a commoner: The Medalle don Herosta, the Medal of a Hero.

The crowd erupted as King Speranta made his way to the top of the steps and faced the crowd. When he signaled for silence, his people quickly complied, and everyone listened for the king's words. "People of Crieda," he shouted into the hundreds of onlookers. "I would like to thank you all for having made your way out here today to celebrate Albur don Gracos. Every year we start the festivities by honoring people within this community who have done spectacular things for their kingdom. You likely all know the faces of each man and woman up here with me today, but I would still like to honor them each by name. When they are called upon, they will step forward and claim their Medalle don Herosta. This medal, given to only the bravest Criedans, signifies that these men and women have helped this kingdom in its prosperity and good fortune. Without them, we would not be where we are today. Therefore, it is my honor to be here today, recognizing these brave Criedans as the heroes they are." The crowd gave another cheer and quieted down as the king began to call each person to his side to place the medal around their necks. When Reina's father was called, her mother screamed so loudly that Reina's ears began to ring.

He looked so big up there as he stood with the king, his chest stuck out with pride and his chin held high. He was so sure of himself and looked ready to take on the world. Reina smiled and cheered along with her mother. For a moment, everything was beautiful. Then it wasn't.

The ground shook beneath the crowd, and everyone froze in confusion. People looked around, unsure of what to do when the earth stopped trembling. Nervous laughter filled the air. Then the ground shook again, and someone shouted, "The wall!"

Immediately everyone's attention locked on the wall which surrounded the kingdom. Reina squirmed in her mother's arms and began to cry out in fear. Her mother tried to soothe her when someone screamed, and everyone watched the southern wall collapse. The crowd started to panic and pushed north, away from the fallen wall. Reina was thrown from her mother's arms in the commotion, and they were separated within seconds. Reina screamed for her mother, trying desperately to dodge the legs that ran by her. She thought she heard her mother call her name, but it was hard to discern what direction it came from as screams echoed through the air around her.

She caught a glimpse of her father, still at the top of the stairs beside the king, and Reina started toward him. She thought if she could get to her father, then they could find her mother together. As she moved forward through the panic, her father's eyes found her. He looked relieved, and his mouth opened to yell her name. Before a sound could escape him, soldiers crowded the stage. Reina looked on in confusion. The soldiers weren't Criedan. Blue plates adorned their chests, and golden helmets reflected the sunlight. The colors clashed with the red and silver armor of the Criedan soldiers, who moved toward the king in a panic.

Her father spun as the men came from behind him, and he seemed to yell something Reina couldn't quite hear. Before Reina could comprehend what was happening at the top of the stairs, a soldier plunged his sword through her father's chest.

"Daddy!" She screamed, but she couldn't even hear her own voice over the cacophony of noise that surrounded her. His body fell unceremoniously to the ground, and Reina watched as the soldier who had taken his life simply stepped over him. As if he were little more than a doormat.

A lump rose in Reina's throat, and she found herself unable to breathe. Her hand was still clenched around the white rose given to her earlier, and a thorn tore into her skin. She looked to the king through his frenzied guards and found him staring at her. Sadness was evident on his face as he looked at the small girl at the base of the stairs. His armed guards vigorously tried to fight off the invading soldiers around him, but the king seemed to know he would not be able to escape the hell that had come to his kingdom.

Their way had never been war. Crieda had no enemies, no quarrels with the outside world. The Criedan soldiers had been given no real training. Never had they needed to raise their swords, which likely hadn't been sharpened in decades. Crieda never stood a chance.

So as his guards fell around him, he held Reina's gaze. There was so much said within those few seconds between them, and Reina felt as tears fell freely from her youthful eyes.

When the last guard fell, a soldier stepped forward and slashed his sword through the king's neck. His head fell from his shoulders and rolled down the stairs to Reina's feet. She looked in horror to find the king's eyes stared up at her, but there was no more to be said between them. Her king was dead.

She dropped the rose from her hand and watched as running feet crushed the petals. She took a step back, but someone ran into her side, and she fell to the ground. Reina tried crawling from the scene which had taken place on the plateau, but she was being crushed under the stampeding people. She felt her ankle snap as someone stepped on it, and she cried out into a world that she knew wouldn't hear her. She realized she would die on the cobblestones beneath her, and nobody was around to care. Her father was dead, and her mother was gone. She was going to die all alone. A sob tore through her body.

Just when she was about to give up and accept her fate, a surge of energy filled her. A warmth started at her left collarbone, then quickly turned into searing pain. She reached up to her shirt and ripped it aside to see a glowing circle on her skin.

She reached for it, unsure of what it was. Her eyes looked to see if anyone saw, but everyone still ran from the soldiers as they descended the stairs. Nobody noticed the small girl on the ground. She felt her ankle mend itself slowly, and she was able to pull herself to her feet. When her ankle was healed, the burning sensation disappeared, and she looked back under her shirt to find that the mark was gone.

Her chest rose and fell with uneven breaths, and she looked around to find that most people had been able to escape the town square. A soldier stood before her and looked down. His golden helmet was alive with sunlight, and Reina swallowed the fear that rose to the surface. She stared back at the man. His green eyes clashed with her blue ones. She knew there was no point in running. She knew he would catch her before she made it anywhere safe. So she stood her ground, a young girl before a conqueror.

His vice-like grip clasped around her arm and dragged her off in the direction of the fallen southern wall. She pulled against him, but it was no use. Reina looked back to her father, the king, and the other heroes from that day, dead upon the plateau. The stairs leaked red and pooled around the king's head at the bottom.

She realized how many people had been crushed to death under the very feet that almost took her own life. Bodies scattered about, broken and nearly unrecognizable. Reina began to shake uncontrollably as the soldier pulled her out of the square and through the kingdom.

She saw other people being taken by soldiers. Some fought back while others followed with haunted expressions plastered on their faces. Soldiers carried out limp bodies, and Reina couldn't tell if they were unconscious or dead.

As she was pulled through the collapsed wall, Reina tripped over her own feet at what she saw. There were thousands of soldiers and hundreds of Criedans. The Criedans were chained together, most covered in blood and bruises from whatever they had been through in the city. Reina tried desperately to slip from the man's grip, but she couldn't do anything as her hands were forced in front of her and chained to the other Criedans who stood broken and lost in line.

1

REINA

ELEVEN YEARS LATER

Reina was jolted awake by the sound of a guard running his keys along metal bars. As he unlocked her cell door, he sneered in at her lying on the cool dirt. She felt a dried trail of drool on the corner of her mouth, and she wiped at it aggressively as she pulled herself to her feet.

When she met the guard's gaze, he tilted his head back and yelled down the cell block, "All of you, to the yards! Line up and be prepared for your assignment." He gave a tug on her door, and it creaked open before he disappeared up the stairs.

Her back ached in protest of how she had slept that night, and she stretched her arms above her head to try and pull out the kinks. A soft sigh escaped her lips in satisfaction as her muscles loosened up, and she rolled her head to crack her neck.

"Stay in there any longer, Rein, and they'll take the whip to you for disobedience." Keane's voice startled her, and her eyes darted open to see his brown gaze peering at her through the bars. She smiled ruefully at him in response.

"That they would," she breathed as she walked past him. Keane's cell was next to Reina's own, and over the years, that had helped develop a friendship between them. They had grown up together in their twisted reality. Reina had watched him turn from a boy into a man. He had a brown-eyed determined stare, dark brown hair that had grown out to his waist due to their inability to cut it, and olive skin that stretched over his broad chest and adorned the muscles he had gained from years of grueling work. He had, in turn, watched Reina grow over the years.

She couldn't imagine what he saw when he looked at her. With her golden hair fiercely knotted about her head and her prying blue eyes that always seemed to trail back to him. Her frame was thin from malnourishment, and her skin was prematurely weathered from the sun. She wondered why it mattered to her what he thought of her, but for some reason, it did.

Reina walked over to the base of the stairs and looked back to ensure Keane followed. There were three levels of cell blocks at Den Zei, and their cells were at the bottom. Down there, it was often cool and damp, but they appreciated the environment after long days in the hot sun. Each level had a group of guards assigned who had their own living quarters in the back of the cell blocks. They originally made their nightly rounds to ensure no escapees, but after a few years, they became more of a cleanup crew for bodies of people who had taken their own lives.

Reina shuddered at the memories of the dead passing by her cell in the dark aisle, back when there used to be multiple a week.

That number had slowly dwindled over the years to one every few months. The guards didn't make their rounds as often anymore; they had the slaves of Den Zei trained too well to even entertain the idea of escapees. Den Zei had become a place of broken souls.

As she made her way up the stairway, she made sure to hold the handrail. The steps were slimy and slick, and a fall down those steep stairs promised a broken neck. Reina watched from her periphery as Keane held his arm out and knew that although it looked as if he were preparing to catch himself in case he fell, he was doing it for her benefit. Throughout their time in Den Zei, she had learned to deal with Keane's attempts to protect her. Though that never stopped her from reminding him she could take care of herself.

"I see you back there," she pointed out and watched Keane's mouth curl in amusement as he released the railing.

"Being careful has never hurt anybody." The words made Reina turn her head so she could see him better, and her eyes flashed mischievously.

"Maybe not," she drawled, "but it does tend to make people excruciatingly boring."

"Did you just call me boring?"

Reina shrugged, her head turning back around to watch her steps as she ascended. Keane's soft chuckle behind her made her smile quietly to herself.

Keane would always look out for her. She knew no matter how many times she tried to point out his attempts as being ridiculous, he would always brush them off. He worried about her; she knew he did. But she couldn't help herself. In a way, she would always be the little girl looking up into the soldier's eyes in defiance.

When she stepped out of Den Zei and into the yard, her eyes burned in protest of the light. Her skin began to itch and burn under the relentless sun rays, and she breathed in the unbelievably dry air. It hadn't rained in weeks, and the only damp place to retreat to was her cell. When her eyes adjusted, she took in the Criedans lined up within the yard and found a spot to squeeze in.

"Final reminder, line up for placement!" The captain of the guard stood above the yard in a tower which the Criedans had made. A mixture of metal and stone spiraled up and into an open room at the top. The captain would make his way up the stairs every morning and look down on the slaves below. He ensured everyone was lined up in an orderly fashion and would call out orders to guards below if there was dysfunction. Reina had always hated the man and even had the honor of having had his whip grace her back when she was a child. She had cried when a stone slipped from her back and crushed her foot beneath its weight. Her punishment had been three lashes, and she hadn't cried in front of the guards since.

When the Criedans all fell in line, guards moved out to give them their placements for the day. Reina's eyes searched the crowd of people for Keane. They had learned from a young age never to stand beside each other in line. If they wanted any hope of having a shared placement for the day, they always had to stand far away from one another.

She found his back facing her, and she stared holes into his shirt in hopes the gods would hear her prayers and place them together. She deflated when a guard came up to her and told her she would be in the stone yard. Keane's broad back was making its way to the wagon that would take him to beams.

In her disappointment, she had stood in her spot a second too long and caught the guard's attention. "Is there a problem with your assignment?" He asked, his voice laced in false authority and vague threats. Reina looked up at his youthful face and had a brief moment where she realized the man could not have been much older than she was. His dark skin was smooth with faint black stubble that lined his jaw. His eyes were clear, and his hair showed no sign of graying. Yet, he looked as if he had been a guard at Den Zei for years. His stare was mean and unforgiving, and his hand rested at the hilt of his whip.

"No, there's no problem." Reina disengaged the situation, squared her boney shoulders, and marched toward the wagon that would lead her to the stone yards.

The wagon was nothing more than rotten wood barely held together. No rails lined the sides, so they huddled in the center to avoid falling off and getting crushed by the wheels below. It used to be challenging to fit everyone in the wagons, and people falling from the sides was a common occurrence back then. Throughout the years, it became easier. There were fewer slaves than there used to be. Too many of them had died.

As Reina climbed onto the wagon, the rotted wood creaked in protest. She sneered at the thought that they would likely be having the slaves craft new wagons in the future. The irony was not lost on her that they would be building something designed to take them to their torture. Although she spared a thought that maybe they could put rails on the new wagons.

The wagon took off with a hitch and jolted everyone who sat within. The old wooden contraption drove them past the dreary houses of those who lived in poverty. Reina watched an older woman who was clad in nothing but rags chase after a young boy who was without any form of clothing at all. She screamed after him, but he still ran through the dried grass and paid her no mind. He laughed into the air, and Reina recognized that moment could have quite possibly been freedom to him.

She smiled when their eyes connected, but he was startled at seeing the slave wagon go by and quickly ran back to the old woman. She gave him a swat on his naked bottom and sent him back to their crumbling shed. Reina stared at the building until it disappeared from her view.

When they arrived at the stone yard, Reina felt a pang of unease deep in her gut. She hated the stone yards, and she hated what they were building. As she climbed off the wagon into the knee-high dried grass surrounding the area, she looked up at the wall in front of her. The wall was made of thick, heavy stone, which the Criedans were tasked with carrying to the top. Building a wall for the kingdom that knocked theirs down.

She made her way to where the harnesses were given out and lifted her arms so a guard could strap one around her torso. Her back cramped at the thought of what was to come, but still, she made her way over to the large pile of stones and let another guard hook one to her back. She had to hunch forward to adjust to the weight and took a few test steps to ensure she wouldn't fall as she made her way up the small path and to the top of the wall.

The trail started on the ground and led to the base of the wall, then began to ascend quickly. The higher Reina got, the thinner the path became. Eventually, it was only as wide as her shoulders, and she found herself praying she wouldn't lose her balance beneath the large stone and plummet to her untimely death. However, Reina found herself faintly wondering if the fall would be worth it to attain her final goal of freedom.

When she reached the top, she unbuckled the stone from her back and twisted her body so that it wouldn't bump against or crush any part of her when it fell. She then turned and scooped the stone into her arms and carried it over to where she needed to place it. When she was finished, she made her way down the path and back to the pile of stones. That was how her day passed, stone after stone brought to the top of the towering wall. Sometimes she would count the rocks as she carried them to pass the time. Her record was thirty-two stones in one day, but it wasn't a record she wanted to beat.

When it came time for lunch, the Criedans lined up on their knees and waited with their heads down for the guards to give them their water and then their bowl of slop. Reina no longer minded the way the gunk slid down her throat in spongey clumps. She had learned any food that kept her going was a miracle.

Reina ended up knelt next to an elderly woman who was gasping vigorously. Her wrinkled hands shook atop her knees, and she looked as if she were about to collapse from the exertion. Reina tried to ignore the pained noises from the woman's mouth and cast her eyes to the ground in anticipation of the nourishment she was about to receive.

A guard made his way down the line with small bowls of water, and each person took the water in their hands and greedily drank the clear liquid. The air was so hot it was a miracle any of them could have gone the whole morning without water. When the guard made it to the old woman, he paused. He looked to her and then to the admiral in charge of the stone yard. "None for her," the admiral yelled. "She won't survive the day, and with the drought, we hardly have enough to go around. Save it for those who need it." The guard nodded dutifully and moved on to give Reina her bowl.

The sound that escaped the elderly woman's mouth made Reina pause with the edge of the bowl to her lips. The woman shook even more, and the quiet sobs that came from her sounded broken. Reina took a small swallow of water, and even as her body begged her for more, she held the rest out to the woman beside her.

"We can share," Reina whispered to her, and the woman met her eyes in disbelief. "We can make it through this." Reina held her arms closer to the woman in an invitation to take the bowl. The woman quickly reached out with trembling hands and downed the rest of the water from the wooden bowl. Reina gave her a soft smile, and the woman returned a nod of gratitude.

Reina felt a harsh blow to her back, and she fell forward onto her hands. When she turned to see what had caused her fall, she was met with a boot to her face. She found herself looking at the cloudless sky and tasted blood in the bile that ran down the back of her throat. The admiral moved into her view and stared down at her in disgust.

"There is no water for her!" The admiral shouted from above, and Reina squinted up at him.

"A little late for that, isn't it?" She groaned.

The admiral's boot connected with Reina's ribs, and she rolled over to cough out the bloody bile from her mouth. Before she could push herself to her feet, the admiral's hand was in her hair, pulling her up. When she stood upright, he shoved her forward, and she stumbled but managed to keep her feet under her. She turned to look at him.

"Learn your place," he snarled, his lips pulled back to reveal cracked yellow teeth.

Reina felt her lips pull back in a grimace. "Learn yours," she growled and spat scarlet on the admiral's boot.

2

MALYSSANDRA

The hard stone beneath Malyssandra's folded legs made her knees ache as she leaned over to reset yet another trap. She didn't mind the menial task of resetting the rat traps. In fact, she preferred it to other duties within the palace. While most other maids shied away from the encompassing darkness of the basement, Malyssandra found it soothing. She could get away from the expectant eyes of the palace habitants down there. She could breathe.

There were no expectations in the forgotten rooms of Yulsa's heart. She could live in her thoughts as she nimbly worked to pull the many small metal jaws open. Sometimes she would hum a tune she remembered from a lifetime before. A tune she would get lashed for if she were to bring it to life in the busy atmosphere of the palace above.

She often wondered if anyone else remembered the Criedan anthem. If anyone even dared to remember Crieda at all anymore. It seemed unfair that she would be the only one left in the world to bear the memories of her home. Though, she supposed fairness had died long ago.

She had only been ten years old when she had been introduced to her life in Yulsa. Eleven years had passed. Eleven cruel, hopeless years. Her family hadn't made it that day, and for that, they had Malyssandra to blame. If she had kept her mouth shut, her father might have lived that day. He might have saved her mother.

If she had told her brothers not to go, would they have listened? They might have. And for that, she blamed herself. If she had only known what that day would turn into, she could have saved them all. She wouldn't have been the only survivor of her family. She wouldn't have been so alone.

"Oh!" Malyssandra was startled at the loud snap that echoed throughout the abandoned basement and the resulting pain that bloomed in her finger. She yanked her hand back to her chest and inspected it in the dim light of her torch. "That's what you get for not paying attention," she muttered to herself as she flexed her fingers to ensure nothing had been broken by the trap she had managed to set off.

The dark skin of her hand was covered in scars from her years spent working at the traps. Her nails were kept short to avoid any pain that could have come from breaking them. She flipped her wrist to look at her palm and noticed the calloused tips of her fingers. A soft sigh escaped her lips, and she reached out to reset the trap that she had strewn on the floor.

There were no rats to be found in the basement traps, and Malyssandra marveled at how they managed to set almost every single one off without having met their demise. She smiled sadly at the realization that she was jealous of the rodents. They had been able to escape. It was something she couldn't do.

As Malyssandra placed the last trap on the ground, her stomach let out a harsh gargle. It had to be near lunch; her body had been trained well. She climbed to her feet. The soft crack of her knees faded into the background as she grabbed her torch from the sconce and exited the basement.

The palace above was another world entirely. Ambassadors hustled briskly from one room to another, the golden walls complimenting the deep blue of their doublets. Paintings of long-dead royals stared out at the crowds of lords and ladies that had come to meet with the king's cabinet. Malyssandra hated those paintings. She hated how they watched her, daring her to disobey. Reminding her of what would happen if she did.

Her eyelids drooped as she stared intensely at the floor to avoid any contact with the high-born citizens around her. She moved tightly against the walls to stay out of the way, to the second floor toward maid's quarters which sat hidden behind the kitchen.

She made her way past the cooks and through a small door that opened into a small room with thirty cots smooshed tightly together. Her deep brown eyes immediately latched onto a fair-headed woman who sat staring out a large window that looked north to Den Zei.

Ivanka spent most of her time by that dreaded window. It was a reminder to those in the room: obey or be thrown into the pits of hell. Ivanka had always been haunted by the knowledge of what awaited them if they didn't do as they were told.

"No lunch?" Malyssandra stepped up beside her and pulled her from her thoughts. Ivanka flashed a smile in greeting, but it didn't quite meet her pale-blue eyes.

"Not until we finish setting up for the king's party," she responded, waving her hand through the air. "We'll get something after the tables are set, did you forget?"

Malyssandra chewed on her bottom lip in response. She had forgotten, but she didn't want to admit it. Her stomach growled again, and her cheeks grew warm.

"It could be worse," Ivanka muttered, but Malyssandra knew it wasn't meant for her ears. The phrase was one Malyssandra knew well. Ivanka had uttered the words to herself many times since Malyssandra had met the woman.

In the beginning, it had served as a reminder to follow orders. To recognize that they had been the lucky ones. Over time, it had begun to sound different coming from Ivanka's lips. It had become empty, meaningless. As if she only said it out of habit.

Malyssandra sauntered over to the other side of the window and looked out at the encampment to the north. Her gut twisted, and she looked back over to Ivanka, who had retreated into the dark recesses of her mind. There were some things about the beautiful woman that Malyssandra would never understand. She went places Malyssandra could never follow, and although she wanted to help her friend, she never wanted to know the horrors that Ivanka was familiar with.

She gave Ivanka's arm a soft nudge, and the porcelain-skinned woman turned slowly and blinked at her. Malyssandra motioned to the door, an invitation for Ivanka to go down to the ballroom with her. Ivanka gave a slight nod in affirmation.

As they made their way to the ballroom, Malyssandra watched the blue carpet turn to polished wooden floorboards beneath her feet. The rugs customarily kept within the large room had been rolled up and stored elsewhere, tables had been set up to frame the dancefloor in the center. Arms of gold reached out and rained down strings of diamonds from the chandelier above, the size of which rivaled the dancefloor below.

The king's table was already set. A deep blue tablecloth adorned the surface and made the royal table stand out from the others, which were being covered in white cloth. Malyssandra's stomach rolled at the thought of the royals who would be sitting there later in the evening. She never liked being in the same room as the man who could decide her fate in a matter of seconds.

Ivanka moved away from Malyssandra toward a table other maids had prepared with piles of tablecloths and dinnerware. The instinct to do what was expected of her took over, and Malyssandra began dressing the tables around her.

As Malyssandra flattened tablecloths, her eyes trailed back to the king's table. He would be there, looking out at his people, unchecked power in his eyes. He believed himself invincible, and his people had been tricked into believing the same.

The king was a hungry man in more ways than one. Every maid within the palace feared the night they might be called upon to join him in his chambers. Malyssandra knew there was no reason to worry, though, not as long as Ivanka lived within the palace.

She looked to her friend, who seemed dedicated to polishing a glass before she set it onto a table across the room. Ivanka was his favorite. He would send for her many times a month, and Ivanka would go without a single word. They never spoke about what happened with Ivanka and the king on those nights, though Malyssandra knew that was where her mind lived. That was the horror that kept her saying *it could be worse.*

"How beautiful." The voice grated against Malyssandra's ears, and she hunched her back over the table she was working on. She knew the owner of that voice, and the elderly woman terrified her. "Your king will be quite pleased."

The king's priestess made her way across the room, inspecting the tables for any sign of disarray. Two guards trailed behind her, their eyes alert and ready. Malyssandra never believed the armed guards were necessary for the woman. People either respected her or feared her. Nobody would have dared to make an attempt on her life. But the king would not take a chance on it, not when she was so crucial in helping him to keep his people in line.

"My dear," the priestess croaked in her ear, and Malyssandra straightened her back quickly enough to elicit a small crack. Somehow, even with her two guards, the woman had managed to approach her without her noticing. "I believe that tablecloth is flattened quite enough."

Malyssandra's cheeks heated as she realized she had been vigorously pulling at the tablecloth. "I wanted it to be perfect for my king," she replied softly.

The priestess's wrinkled face morphed into a grotesque smile, but her unnaturally green eyes stared at her flatly. "Your king thanks you for your dedication, but perhaps you should move on to another table?"

Malyssandra's head bounced at the recommendation. "May I be excused," she asked, "to tend to the other tables?"

The priestess gave a small nod, and Malyssandra forced herself to stroll away from the strange woman. Her heart pounded in her chest, but she refused to look back to see if the woman had watched her.

As Malyssandra reached to take another tablecloth, Ivanka's hand fell over hers. She gave her a knowing look, and Malyssandra smiled in thanks. Then, Ivanka was off with an armful of dinnerware, and Malyssandra released a shaky breath as she heard the priestess and her guards leave the room.

When the room was set, the maids went back to their quarters to eat before the party started. Malyssandra feared she would see the priestess again on her way up, but as she passed the chapel, the priestess was nowhere to be seen.

The soup was cold and flavorless, but she ate it fast. The party was set to start soon, and she refused to spend the night on an empty stomach. Ivanka had abandoned hers on the windowsill as she stared back out into the world beyond. Malyssandra opted not to say anything. She didn't feel much like speaking anyways.

It wasn't long until the maids were summoned to return to the ballroom and prepare for the guests' arrival. Malyssandra prayed to the gods that the party would be a quick one and downed the rest of her soup.

. . .

Malyssandra clung to the edge of the room as guests were led in to be seated. Music sounded quietly from the harpist who sat to the left of the king's table, and laughter filled the air as lords and ladies flirted shamelessly with each other. The ladies wore jewel-encrusted ball gowns that ranged from all shades of blue to muted shades of yellow. It was known throughout the kingdom that the king enjoyed seeing Yulsan colors plastered on his subjects. It was believed to be patriotism, but Malyssandra thought it nothing more than a show of the king's absurd control over his people.

The lords wore fitted suits with black vests, and their long white sleeves made it easy to see the sweat stains under their arms. Their black pants hung loosely at their ankles, and a few lords were seen with stomachs that jutted out far beyond the tops of their trousers.

When the upper-class commoners were allowed to be seated, it was a clear difference from the people of high lineage. Their dresses were still lovely but looked much scratchier than the dazzling dresses the ladies had floated in wearing. The men entered in suits with wool-woven brown vests and much shorter black knickers. Their stomachs were flat, and Malyssandra could see no bulging waistlines that threatened to expand over the tops of their pants. It was evident that although they were considered wealthy among the commoners, they still had to work to maintain that wealth. The lords and ladies were born into money and had never seen a day of work in their lives.

As the rest of the stragglers began to be seated, Malyssandra saw movement at the far corner of the room and turned her head to see the high priestess make her way to the table nearest the king's. Her guards trailed behind her as Yulsans stared on in adoration. She had promised them all an afterlife in the land of the gods. That's what being Yulsan got them. If they served the king wholeheartedly, they would have eternal life beyond death. Criedan slaved would never be so lucky. After years of serving a king that wasn't theirs, the best the priestess could offer them was an eternity in purgatory. Their only sin was that they were not born Yulsan.

Malyssandra never believed in the tales of the priestess, but what she believed or did not believe had not mattered to the world in eleven years. She kept her thoughts to herself and her eyes downcast to avoid any more attention from the priestess as she blessed the Yulsans she passed, her eyes as emotionless as ever.

A lord who sat at the table in front of Malyssandra looked back in agitation, and she realized his water glass was empty. She shuffled forward from her place against the wall and poured the water from her pitcher into the crystal glass. As she looked around at the other drinks on the table, she opted to fill them in hopes she wouldn't be called back anytime soon. As she finished up, the room fell silent, and everyone climbed to their feet.

The royal family entered from a side door stationed near their table. Guards pooled in behind them, and Malyssandra couldn't help herself as she stared at the spectacle. Long, golden hair flowed down the king's back from beneath his golden crown. Finely groomed facial hair lined his jaw and upper lip while thick eyebrows framed his power-hungry dark gaze. His appearance clashed with his family's in every way.

Dark hair and crystal eyes followed behind him. Prince Ferix resembled his mother with his olive skin and sharp jawline. They both towered over the king, their heads held high, and their shoulders pulled back. If Malyssandra could have seen them through different eyes, she would have thought them beautiful. But all she felt as she watched them stand before their table was disgust. They were the people responsible for so much death.

Malyssandra was startled by the sound of a throat clearing beside her, and she turned to face the lord who had called her over. Her cheeks blazed as she realized she hadn't yet left the table. She mumbled an apology before she excused herself and shuffled back against the wall. The lord's eyes followed her until she was far enough away from the table before he looked back to the royal family.

The king motioned for his guests to be seated, and the sound of chairs scuffing against the floor filled the room while everyone situated themselves at their tables. When the noise quieted, the king began to speak. "Thank you, everyone, for attending tonight's party on such short notice. It wasn't easy to get this place pulled together so quickly, so I hope everyone has a wonderful evening. I sent for you all to join me tonight in celebrating an extraordinary occasion. However, I do not believe business should be spoken of on empty stomachs! So please, I invite you to all dine with me tonight." The king flourished his hand, and maids began walking into the room with silver trays propped on their palms.

The king's table was served first, and the room watched on as the royal tasters brought food to their lips. Malyssandra always found the spectacle to be dramatic, but she knew that was the point. It was a statement to the people. They would be found out if they were ever to make an attempt on the royal family's lives.

When the testers finished, and the food was deemed safe, the maids served the tables throughout the room. Plates of roasted lamb and corn were laid before the guests. Malyssandra's mouth watered at the smell, and she wondered what it would have been like to eat a warm meal again.

Loud conversation filled the room as people conversed over their meals, and Malyssandra watched spittle fly from a lord's mouth as he threw his head back in laughter at something that had been said. Smiles plastered every face in the crowd except for the maids who stood solemnly on the edges. If the guests had spared a moment to acknowledge the broken women who stood among them, maybe they would have felt guilt stir in their guts. Or perhaps they wouldn't have cared at all.

When plates were empty, the maids who had brought in the food scurried forward to clear the tables as efficiently as possible.

They dodged the arms of men as they reached forward to shake hands and avoided the women's elbows as they pulled back napkins to dab at their faces. As quickly as they had leaped to clear the tables, they disappeared. The tables looked as if the food had never sat upon them, and it seemed the guests didn't even notice the absence.

The room quieted once again as the king raised his hand to silence the crowd, and Malyssandra marveled at the sight of what one man could do to a room full of people. "Now that we've all eaten," the king began, "we can discuss the reason why you are all here today. My advisors received word from across the Carnavan Sea that the Kingdom of Pretha has accepted a trade deal we have been discussing for years." The king paused and looked around the room with a hungry stare. "This trade will help Yulsa to expand her borders on this continent and become more economically rich than she has ever been before. This deal does not come without sacrifice, though, and each of you will be asked to give up your household assets to help your kingdom grow. You will each be rewarded generously, however, for the sacrifices you must make. Your kingdom thanks you, your king thanks you, and your pockets thank you." The king laughed loudly, and the crowd clapped in response.

Before the king could finish his speech, a young man stood from the far tables of the upper-middle class. "What you ask for is not ours to give! The king wants your slaves; this is a slave trade!" The man shouted, his face reddened, and his eyes darted around the room. "These are lives you are giving away, lives you never owned. Please, I beg of you. Do not ship off the people who raise your children and harvest your crop. Let them go!"

Guards ran from behind the king, rushing the man who had pulled out a large throwing knife. "They are not dogs. They are *people*. What sort of king abuses his power against the powerless? No king of mine!" The blade's silver reflected off the chandelier as his arm pulled back, aimed at the king.

The guards tackled him before he could finish what he set out to do, and as they dragged him through the doors, Malyssandra's head spun with what she had just heard. If the king meant to trade the slaves, what would become of her?

She felt her hands begin to shake, and she felt moisture at her foot. Her eyes looked down to see she still held the pitcher; her hands clenched tightly around the handle. The water within trembled and splashed to the floor around her. She looked around to ensure nobody noticed and set the pitcher down at an empty table. Goosebumps rose on her skin, and her neck snapped around to find the prince staring right at her.

Storms flashed in his eyes, and his evident anger startled her. She looked to the floor beneath her, covered in water. When she looked back, he had turned his attention elsewhere. Her breathing was fast and panicked, and the sound of the doors slamming shut as the guards led the man away made her jump and feel for the wall at her back.

Disbelieving whispers filled the room as the guests looked at each other in outrage at what the man had just said. The king's hand lifted into the air, but the whispering continued. It spread like wildfire and grew louder within seconds. Malyssandra watched the king's face morph into an expression of rage, and he shouted, "Silence!" The room fell quiet, and the king's voice ricocheted off the walls. His face relaxed into a default expression as he looked out to the concerned crowd.

The king gave a slight chuckle. "I'm unsure if I need better guards or better advisors." The crowd let out nervous laughter, and the king waited for it to settle down before he continued. "I am asking for your slaves, of that the man was correct. However, I am asking you to give up your slaves to pave the way for something *better*. Pretha has offered weapons and soldiers in exchange for our slaves. This deal will allow us to expand our kingdom and acquire more slaves so that even the commoners could acquire these necessities we treasure." Malyssandra realized that was why the wealthier commoners were there. They had never been able to afford slaves for themselves in the past. The king was using them as a way to pressure the lords into agreeing to the deal. "Imagine how much more this kingdom could be if each person within it were able to have something as useful as we do? Imagine how much more we could accomplish." The guests looked to each other in uncertainty, but some heads began to nod as the seconds ticked by. Malyssandra's heart froze in her chest, and horror bubbled under her skin.

As the crowd seemed to reach a consensus, the king clapped his hands together in joy. "Wonderful! The Prethans are set to arrive in two months, and this will be discussed more when they are in our company. Now," the king spoke with a grin on his face, "Who's for dancing?"

Music started before anyone could say otherwise, and the guests seemed to forget about the situation which had unfolded seconds earlier. Women dragged their spouses to the dancefloor and begged to be spun around. Dresses flared up and off the floor, and laughter echoed off the walls.

Malyssandra stood frozen and stared at the man who had taken her life from her once before. His eyes trailed the room, his lips lightly curled in annoyance at the disruption which had occurred. She hated him more at that moment than she had before, and tears threatened behind her eyes.

The crowd thinned as the night grew late, and soon the royal family exited the room. The party was declared over. Maids ran about, folding the table cloths and pushing the tables and chairs against the walls. Malyssandra moved through the motions. Her eyes were glazed over, and her body trembled.

When they were finished, Malyssandra sauntered back into the maids' quarters and stood by the window to look out at Den Zei in the distance. None of those people knew what was to come.

3

REINA

Reina's back felt as though it were on fire, and the flames refused to be put out by the damp air of the cell block. Her teeth clenched tightly around the inside of her cheek, and blood filled her mouth. The coppery taste grounded her and kept her sane. The moisture of her breath ricocheted off the ground inches from her nose and clung to her skin. She was used to the pain and knew that it would disappear with the arrival of the golden circle on her collarbone within the day.

The sound of Keane sliding the bars of their adjacent cells made Reina turn her head. The motion pulled at the skin on her back, and she grunted through her teeth. His shadow hung its head in the darkness, and she watched the shape of his mouth as it fluttered from open to closed in search of words to fill the space between them.

"What did you do?" The shape of his right hand snaked across the floor and absentmindedly grabbed at the bottom of the bars. His ear tilted in Reina's direction, and she closed her eyes to avoid the sight of him in the dim light that filtered down the stairs.

"I helped someone who needed it." Reina opened her eyes to see as Keane's outline shook his head.

"That's not the whole story," he stated, his words flat and careful.

"It's the only part that matters. Someone needed water, and I gave it to them. They would have died without it Keane, what was I supposed to-?" Her vision blurred, and she arched her back in agony as the pain flared, and she gasped to catch her breath against the onslaught.

Keane waited patiently for Reina to regain her ability to respond, then asked, "Why didn't the guards give her water? Couldn't you have waited before acting out?"

Her head shook. "The drought. The guards said there wasn't enough water to waste on her. They expected her to die today. Hell, she might have died anyway, for all I know. But I had to do something, Keane. I couldn't just watch her die."

Keane went quiet. He knew better than to argue the point with her, not when she knew she had done the right thing. His head turned to look at her. The brown of his eyes flared into view as the golden circle on her shoulder lit up. As her back began to knit itself together, she slowly pulled herself upward through the pain and threw her head back to stare up at the stone ceiling above her. She placed her hands over the mark so as not to draw attention to her cell. Keane showed no sign of shock, but he had known her secret for years. He had seen the golden circle time and time again and had shown no fear at the sight of its bright light.

When the light faded and her back was pieced together, Keane let out a soft sigh. "I remember when I first saw you do that."

"I was sure you'd believe me to be a freak."

"You are a freak, but that's not why."

Reina let out a quiet chuckle and scooted closer to where Keane sat at the bars. The moonlight gave just enough light for Reina to see the defeated look in his eyes. "You've always held the weight of the world on your shoulders. Even back then." She reached between the bars to lay a hand on his cheek, but he turned away from her. Her hand dropped to her lap, and she chewed on her bottom lip. "You watched me cry for hours after you saw it the first time, and you didn't say anything," she stated, attempting to reignite the conversation.

He shrugged. "Didn't really seem like you wanted to talk about it."

Reina laughed. "Well, the second time you saw it, you didn't seem to care much at all if I wanted to talk about it or not."

"You needed to know how dangerous it was. If the guards had seen you... I'm not sure what would have happened." Keane had set ground rules for Reina to follow. She wasn't allowed to ever let the light on her shoulder show when she healed, and she wasn't allowed to play with the strange ability. He had told her it was for her own good, and she had believed him. If the guards had found out what she could do as a child, she might have been killed. In a way, Keane had saved her life.

He had always been one to see the whole picture, to plan. Keane played by the rules and tried to always see how one action could affect the future. Even as a child, he had been strict, focused. He held himself differently than the other inhabitants of Den Zei. Reina could never figure out why.

"I thank the gods every day that I have you in my life, Keane. But I'm not your responsibility anymore. You helped me back then, but I can make my own rules now." She watched him tense and immediately knew she had said the wrong thing.

"You could have died today." The words were stiff, anger bubbled beneath the surface.

"But I didn't," she pointed out.

"Maybe not. But that doesn't mean you won't next time. I know you can heal yourself, Reina, and I know you think that makes you invincible. But it doesn't. You could die, and that would be it." He looked down at his calloused hands, then turned back to Reina. "It's been you and me for so long, Rein. I don't know what I'd do if you didn't come back one day. You can't be so careless. Not when we're so close."

Reina's ears perked up, and she cocked her head at Keane. His face grew taught, and his eyes widened as if he had slipped up. "So close? To what?"

"Never mind," he brushed her off as he pulled himself to his feet, "forget I said anything. Just be careful, okay?" He began to walk away from Reina, deeper into his cell where the moonlight couldn't reach him.

She stared after him as the darkness swallowed him whole.

...

Keys rattled against metal and threw her from her sleep as she was welcomed back into the world by a guard's voice. "Line up for your assignments!" She rubbed at her eyes as they adjusted to the sunlight that cascaded into the cellblock. Having been assigned the last cell on the right side of the stairs meant she only had Keane as a neighbor and was granted the ability to utilize whatever light shone down the stairs. Many cells toward the back of the block were pitch black no matter the time of day.

She glanced over at Keane's cell as the guard unlocked her door and pulled it open, but Keane had already been let out and made his way up the stairs without her. Reina pushed herself to her feet, and the guard moved on. She allowed herself a quick stretch and made her way up the stairs and back out into the yard.

The sun seemed almost hotter than the day before, and Reina's mouth felt as if it was stuffed with cotton. She knew that water wouldn't come until later that day, and her head began to pulse in pain at the thought. Her gaze scanned the crowd of Criedans for a place to line up. When she picked a spot, she dragged herself across the yard and stood between a middle-aged man with a scruffy silver beard and a girl who couldn't have been much older than Reina was. They faced forward and looked up to the captain of the guard as he shouted out for the stragglers to get in line.

When the guards were sent out to assign placements, Reina was told to report to beams. She looked for Keane to see if he had been placed with her that day, but she couldn't find him in the crowd. Her feet carried her to the wagon that would take her south toward the outskirts of the city.

She climbed onto the wagon and claimed a spot in the center before the guard at the front signaled for the mules to pull it forward. Her stare clung to her feet the whole ride, callused and brown from the years of dirt that stained them. Faintly, she wished for a puddle to plunge them into so that she could feel the slightest bit cleaner. But with the drought, she knew it would be impossible to find any amount of water that could be spared on her feet.

When the wagon halted, she climbed off and stood to be placed in a team. The beams were made of heavy metal that required a group to pull up together. A rope would be wrapped over the top of a pulley high above their heads and trail down to the ground where they would tie the rope to the metal beams. Then, they would lift it off the ground and to the top of the structure. In terms of placements at Den Zei, it wasn't the worst.

Reina got her team, and they moved in unison to the first beam of the day. A young boy of maybe sixteen stepped forward to tie the rope to the grey metal in front of them, and Reina felt a pang of sadness in her gut at the sight of him. They had been so young when Yulsa had invaded. Den Zei was practically the only life they had ever known.

The team began to pull the heavy beam to the top of the structure. Grunts of effort sounded from their lips as sweat ran down their brows. Their hands held steady to the rope; years of work had made them callused and rough. The beam rocked through the air until it reached the top, where an unlucky Criedan had been assigned to maneuver it into place and untie the rope. Reina watched as the man high in the air shuffled across the thin structure and grabbed the metal. He slowly guided it until it reached its destination, and he signaled for them to lower it. Reina held her breath as they gradually gave more rope, and the beam descended a few feet. When the man had it placed, he squatted beside it and untied the rope before throwing it back down to them, and they proceeded to the next beam.

When lunchtime came, Reina kept her eyes glued to the dried ground and accepted her water without complaint. Her chapped lips moved to the bowl and greedily took in all the liquid. She wished for more but didn't dare ask. The food was the same brown clump it had always been, but she still savored the spongey nourishment as it stuck to the edges of her throat on its way down. She didn't mind swallowing a few times to keep it moving. She was used to it and was starving after not having had food the day before. When lunch was over, she was paired with a different team. They worked until the sun went down.

The moon was bright, and when the guards called for the Criedans to make their way back to the wagon, she could see the path perfectly. She began to do as she was told, but something made her look back over her shoulder to the top of the beams.

A man still stood up there, and he looked down at the world below with unflinching certainty. Reina didn't recognize him, but she knew what he meant to do. Her expression became one of sad understanding, and her eyes stayed glued to the man. Nobody else stopped to look, and it didn't seem like anyone cared. It was something they had seen many times before and would likely see again. For some reason, Reina couldn't bring herself to let that man be alone in his final moments. He needed someone to know when he was gone.

The man shifted his feet closer to the edge, and Reina watched as his chest expanded with his last breath. Then he took a step forward into the open air.

His body fell fast, and it was over in a matter of seconds. Reina exhaled harshly as he made contact with the dirt. The shape of his body on the ground was unnatural, and she wondered who might have missed the man had the world been different. She didn't know if he had a daughter who used to be his world or a son who used to fill him with pride. Or even a wife who he had loved with every piece of his being. She wondered what his life had been like eleven years earlier before it was taken from him.

The guards shouted their final warning to get on the wagon, and Reina tore her eyes away from the broken body. The whole way back to the cellblock, she thought about the stranger who had been both hopeless and brave enough to take that final step toward freedom. It weighed heavily on her chest, and she hoped that wherever he was, he had found peace.

When she made her way back into her cell, she didn't even look to Keane as the guard locked her door. She moved into the deepest corner of her cell and allowed a few tears to fall to the cool dirt beneath her.

4

MALYSSANDRA

Malyssandra watched through the window as the early rays of light began to break over the horizon. Her head felt foggy from lack of sleep, and a dull throb started behind her eyes. Exhaustion beckoned her to stay in her cot and allow herself to rest, but she knew she had to get up. The other maids had already begun to get ready for the day, and if Malyssandra stayed in bed much longer, she would likely be noticed.

She sat up slowly and blinked her swollen eyes at the women who ran about the room donning their aprons and grabbing at supplies for the day. Ivanka was already gone from the area, and Malyssandra wondered when she had left. She hadn't seen her exit the maid's quarters. The more Malyssandra thought about it, she realized she hadn't seen Ivanka come back that night either.

A sickly feeling began to settle in her stomach, and she stared somberly at Ivanka's empty cot. The king must have summoned her after the ball, and it wasn't uncommon for Ivanka to not arrive back to the maid's quarters until later in the morning.

The king and queen slept in separate bedrooms within the palace for as long as Malyssandra had known. It allowed the king to keep his chosen lovers the entirety of the night without the risk of the queen finding out. Although, it was unlikely the queen didn't know about what happened within the confines of his chambers. She simply refused to acknowledge it, as if she didn't care as long as she wasn't forced to witness the king's adultery.

There was something different that day though, Malyssandra could feel it. She couldn't explain where the certainty came from, but she hoped she was wrong and Ivanka would be back by lunch.

Malyssandra stood and pulled on a new apron that hung beside her cot. It was large on her petite frame, but she had grown used to the feeling of the extra fabric over the years. She supposed it was better than the alternative, and she turned to make her bed.

There wasn't much to do there; each maid only had one thin sheet and a pillow. However, they were still required to make the room look tidy before they left to tend to their chores.

The cooks didn't even look in her direction as she walked over to the waste bucket filled with rotting meat. She grabbed handfuls of the browned flesh and shoved them in her apron pockets. For a while, she had tried to carry the bucket with her throughout the palace. Her short stature caused the bottom to bump painfully against her ankles and made her steps choppy as she struggled to the farther ends of the castle. It was much easier for her to simply scoop up the meat in her hands and carry it within her pockets. She didn't mind the deep red stains that appeared on her apron or the smell that followed her throughout the day. Her nose had become used to the stench, and she hardly noticed it anymore. Besides, nobody noticed her presence within the palace either way.

With the meat pocketed, she exited the kitchen and made her way to the eastern sector of the palace. It was her favorite place to go, as it was most often abandoned compared to the newer sectors. The rooms on the eastern side were rarely used, which meant Malyssandra could be alone with her thoughts for the entirety of the morning.

She watched as the golden walls turned to stone, and the paintings of the royal family disappeared. The crowds became thinner until there were no people at all to avoid. Malyssandra allowed herself to walk in the center of the hallway instead of forcing herself to cling to the edges. The light faded significantly as fewer windows lined the sides, and she felt herself breathe freely in the darker atmosphere.

When the maids had been younger, they made up stories about the eastern sector. They spun tales of the ghosts of old royals who haunted the halls searching for their crowns but were doomed to never find them. The spirits would spend eternity trapped within the nearly forgotten stone walls of the old palace. Sometimes, if someone were to listen closely, their cries could be heard echoing faintly through the darkness.

Malyssandra gave a sad smile at the memory. They didn't create stories anymore, and they hadn't in a long time. She guessed that most of the maids had forgotten the tales of the past, but she kept them tucked away in her memories to revisit on her days spent alone.

She frequently wondered why the palace bothered with rat traps in the abandoned parts of the castle, but she had never dared to ask. Malyssandra was too afraid that they would agree it was pointless and her sanctuary would be taken from her. The shadows within the eastern sector were too precious for her to risk losing. It was a place of her own in a world where she was allowed nothing.

She rounded a corner and entered a room on her left where dust-covered maps and old books sat forgotten. Old records were archived back there, outdated by many years. They may have at one point been helpful, but as new maps were drawn up and new books created, they lost their importance.

The meat in her pockets made a wet protest as she crouched and reached for a floorboard in the corner. Her hand lifted the old wood, and a slight creak sounded as it bent slightly before popping out of the ground. She looked to the traps under the floor, and her fingers gave a ghost ache as she saw most of them had been set off. A soft hum began in her throat as she got to work on pulling them out and resetting them with the old meat from her pockets. She had gone through quite a few floorboards and quite a few traps before she found the first victim.

The rat looked small, and she pondered how young it must have been. Its body was stiff, and its tail flopped about as Malyssandra pulled the metal off of the animal's crushed skull. There was hardly any blood beneath the body as she slid it out of the trap, and she watched as its tongue lolled from its small brown mouth. She hated finding successful traps. The sight of the dead animals always made her feel somber and more aware of her own situation. The older rats seemed wiser to the ways of the mechanisms, but the young ones always seemed to be caught within the metal fangs.

Malyssandra set the dead rat on the ground beside her to dispose of later and reset the trap as she had all the others. She began to wonder if she would end up like that rat in a few months. If she would be shipped over the Carnavan Sea only to be ensnared in the fangs of another kingdom far away.

The kingdoms across the sea were a mystery to her, and she didn't know if life over there would be better or worse. She wanted desperately to hope for the former, but she wouldn't allow herself to do so. Hope was deadly in her world; hope could kill someone just as fast as a sword.

The final trap settled between the others, and Malyssandra breathed a sigh of relief when she lifted her hand away. She grabbed the floorboard she had set aside and placed it back in its rightful spot. It gave a satisfying click when it was back where it belonged, and Malyssandra scooped the dead rat beside her back into her hand and rose to her feet. She began walking toward the door when she heard the sound of shuffling feet in the hallway.

She froze, and her heart began to pump blood rapidly through her body. The sound stopped suddenly, and her hand wrapped tightly around the body of the rat in her hand. She didn't know if she should call out or remain silent and carry on with her task. There was one more room on the eastern side she had to go to, and she assumed whoever was out there would overlook a maid doing her job. She wasn't used to having company in the eastern sector. The idea of someone being there felt like an invasion of privacy.

Her feet carried her slowly toward the door, and silence rang unnervingly in her ears. When she looked out into the hallway, it was empty. Nobody stood in the shadows or appeared in either direction. She released the breath she had been holding and told herself she was just paranoid. The eastern side was abandoned, and people rarely appeared down there.

Her legs shook as she took a left down the hallway. The next room appeared on her right, and she entered quickly to put the strange incident behind her. She looked down to her hand where she still held the rat in a clenched fist and loosened her grip.

The room she had entered was more spacious than the last. It looked like an old chapel. A stand was proudly placed in the front of the room atop a few steps. At one point, it must have been a lively space to praise the gods.

Unlit wax candles lined a small table that presented itself behind the stand, and sconces were riddled along the room's walls. Rows of benches filled the space at the base of the stairs where Malyssandra stood, and she imagined people sitting and listening to the inspirational words the priest would yell joyfully into the crowd.

Religion had changed dramatically since the old ways had died out. It was no longer something that people loved but something they feared. The high priestess who stood beside the king had taken something people turned to for hope and morphed it into something people used to justify their actions on the king's behalf.

Malyssandra ran her fingers absentmindedly along the wooden benches and thought back to the chapel she attended as a small child. There had been music and food, and people had been kind and understanding. The priest would talk about gods who created mankind to do the things in which they could not. Malyssandra had wondered as a child what humans could do that gods could not, but she could never bring herself to stand before the crowd of people and ask the priest the question which burned in her mind. She guessed she would never know the answer.

The tops of the stairs came off quickly and without a sound as Malyssandra lifted them to reveal the traps beneath. Many more rats were seen within the traps in the chapel, and she slowly collected a small pile of them beside the one she had found earlier. As she placed the traps back under the stairs with more rotten meat as bait, her stomach began to signal that it was time for lunch. She put the tops of the stairs back and stuffed the collection of dead rats into her pockets where the meat had been diminished.

As she exited the room and turned to head back to the maid's quarters for lunch, she saw a shadow disappear around the corner at the end of the hallway. She froze; her mind ran through everything she had done. If someone had seen her, was there anything they could report to the guards? Her stomach dropped. She had been humming the Criedan anthem in the archives. If someone had heard her, she was dead.

Her feet moved cautiously forward, dread built within her. Someone had been there, but there was no way of telling what they heard. She hadn't noticed someone was down there until after she had finished in the archives. Perhaps they hadn't heard anything.

She rounded the corner and peeked down the hallway, but there was nobody there. Malyssandra shook her head and decided she was just tired. She hadn't slept all night, and so she was seeing things out of pure exhaustion. There was no other explanation that made sense.

She watched as the crowds of people slowly grew thicker, and the walls changed from the shadow-covered stone back to gold adorned with paintings of people the Yulsans treasured. It was always strange, watching life come back to the palace after spending her morning in the past. She walked through the kitchen and grabbed a bowl of cold soup.

As she walked into the maid's quarters, her eyes scanned for Ivanka. She wanted to tell her about her delusional moment in the eastern sector. Ivanka wasn't there. Her absence began to weigh heavily on Malyssandra, and the sickly feeling returned. The king had never kept her that long, and she found herself hoping that Ivanka was just running late from her chores. She opted to wait and sipped absently at the cold broth of her soup.

Maids came and went, grabbing their soup and scarfing it down before they headed back into the palace to finish whatever they had been tasked with that day. Malyssandra grew impatient and knew she had to leave the room soon before someone began to ask her questions.

Her soup no longer seemed appetizing, and she passed it along to another maid who had been looking at it hungrily. The maid grabbed it with a quick thanks and walked to the other side of the room, leaving Malyssandra to her thoughts. Her worry was eating at her insides, but she didn't know what to do to put herself at ease. Ivanka should have been there by then. Lunch was wrapping up, and no more bowls were being passed off to maids. Malyssandra stood from the cot she had sat down on absentmindedly and began to pace the room. When the last maid left, she sighed dejectedly and walked out into the kitchen. When the cooks weren't looking, she grabbed the pile of dead rats from her apron pocket and threw them in the waste bin.

· · ·

She sat back in the basement where she had been the day before, but the darkness didn't seem as welcoming anymore. It made her feel claustrophobic, and the thoughts her mind produced made her solidarity feel endless.

She buried her face in her hands and allowed herself a few seconds to breathe. After she pulled herself back together, she put all of her focus into the work in front of her. She refused to let her mind trail off into the dark places they wished to go, and she pulled dead rats from the traps that had been empty the day before.

There was already so much death in that kingdom, and the king planned to bring more. The idea of Yulsa expanding made Malyssandra outwardly flinch. She placed the final trap back where it belonged and climbed to her feet. The darkness of the basement taunted her, and she spun to escape as fast as she could. She froze when she saw a dark shape in the doorway.

It was a genderless swirl of shadows, shaped like a person, but it held no density, and Malyssandra could faintly see the light from atop the stairs filtering through. There was no way to tell if it was facing her, but she felt eyes boring into her skin. The fear that rose within her kept her quiet, and it felt as if she were choking on terror.

The figure stood there, silent and ominous, in the doorway that led to her escape. Malyssandra tried to force her feet to run, to fling herself through the darkness and onto the stairs that would take her back to the central sector of the palace. Something about the shadow felt dangerous, feral. Seconds ticked by, and Malyssandra couldn't bring herself to take a breath. Her legs shook beneath her, and her heart pounded furiously in her chest. The shadow simply stared back at her, the room stilled.

Then, a peal of soft laughter filled the basement. It grew manic and loud, and Malyssandra stumbled backward. "*Malyssandra,*" It whispered before it disappeared into the darkness of the room.

Malyssandra immediately bolted into action and ran to the doorway and up the stairs. Her breathing was ragged, and sweat pooled under her arms and down her back. She looked crazed as she stood on top of the steps and looked at the groups of people walking through the center sector of the palace. Nobody looked back at her as if she were invisible to the world.

"Are you alright?"

Malyssandra jumped at the voice in her ear and lowered her eyes as she recognized the priestess. She was everywhere, and Malyssandra had a strange feeling the woman had been following her. Guards stared down at her, and her skin crawled under their scrutiny.

"Yes, high priestess. Thank you." Her voice was meek, respectful. Even as her insides churned at the proximity of the woman.

The priestess peaked around Malyssandra to look down the stairs. Her green eyes flashed in amusement. "Not scared of the dark, are we?"

Malyssandra shook her head. "No, high priestess. I finished my work and am headed to the maid's quarters to get some rest so I can better serve my king tomorrow." It had never become easier for Malyssandra to refer to the king as hers. He wasn't. But she knew better than to say otherwise.

"How dutiful of you!" The priestess exclaimed and clapped her hands to gather the attention of those in the central sector. "To serve your king is to have an afterlife of joy," she began, "Although this maid is but a Criedan, she has made it her life's purpose to serve her king. She may only be destined for purgatory, but that is greater than the hell she would have experienced had we not rescued her from that dreaded kingdom." The onlookers nodded their heads in agreement and spared looks of disgust and pity at Malyssandra. "May you all recognize your Yulsan heritage and work to serve our king as she does, and you will be welcomed into paradise with the gods when your lives end." The priestess raised her hands to the sky, and those around her clapped their approval.

Malyssandra's cheeks heated at the attention, and she focused on the ground beneath her feet. As the clapping died down, the onlookers began to move along, and the priestess turned back to her.

"Please, go get your rest so you may serve the king another day."

Malyssandra nodded, "Am I excused, high priestess?"

"You are, my dear." The priestess moved past Malyssandra with her guards in tow, and Malyssandra forced herself to walk calmly back to the maid's quarters.

As she entered, she looked to see the sky outside had darkened and brought the night. Her hands shakily undid her apron and threw it in the hamper. She didn't bother to remove the dead rats from her pockets. On still shaking legs, she walked over to her cot and threw the sheet over her head.

The sound of the other maids as they entered the room caused her to slowly come back to herself, and she peeked over the sheet to see the other women getting ready for bed. Her heart rate began to slow, and she allowed herself to watch for Ivanka to enter the room. She knew it was an unlikely possibility, but when the last maid entered and Ivanka hadn't appeared, her heart still sank.

She looked to her friend's empty cot as the light in the room went out. Her thoughts went back to what she had seen in the basement. She didn't know what it was or how it had known her name. The terror that she had felt still simmered under her skin, and she closed her eyes tight against the darkness in the room. She wondered faintly if she was going crazy, but it had felt so real. Although she supposed that was what someone crazy would say to justify their own delusions.

She thought back to the eastern sector earlier that day and felt a certainty that the sounds she had heard and the shadow she had seen disappear beyond the corner had been the same thing she had seen in the basement.

Whatever it was, it had taken a liking to her. She wasn't sure what that meant for her, but she knew she didn't like it.

5

REINA

A strange sound startled Reina from her sleep. She sat up quickly and peered into the faint blue light of the moon that filtered down the stairway near her cell. She wondered what time it was and how far away the sun was from their sky.

Her alarmed stare dragged across her cell, searching for what had awoken her. The aisle of the cellblock by the stairs was clear. Confusion wrinkled her brow, and she rolled to her side to try and allow sleep to take her back.

Before she could close her eyes, she saw Keane's outline in the moonlight tucked into the corner opposite her cell. His figure was hunched over something, and his long hair blew gently in the wind that funneled down the stairway into the cell block. Something about the way he stood felt secretive to Reina, and she couldn't help but silently place her feet beneath her body and creep over to the bars they shared.

The way his body was angled, the soft light lit up the harsh curve of his jawline. His shoulders rose and fell in even bursts, and Reina was mesmerized by the look of him. He truly was a sight to behold. Her heart fluttered lightly in her chest, and the silence between them felt soft and peaceful. His arms moved slightly, and Reina wondered at what he held in front of him that she couldn't see. She leaned her body against the bars in an attempt to see around him.

A soft squeak emitted from the metal bars in protest, and Keane whipped his head around. When he saw Reina looking on curiously, he spun his body to face her. She looked to his hands which hung at his sides, but nothing was within his open palms. Reina cocked her head to the side in a quiet question. Within moments he had absorbed his shock and gave her a friendly smile.

"What are you doing up?" His whisper crossed the room and barely made it to Reina's ears. She straightened her head as she realized he wasn't going to offer an explanation for his strange behavior.

"I could ask you the same." Their eyes collided across the space between them in the soft light. Reina had known Keane long enough to realize she had caught him off guard. Whatever he had been doing, he hadn't wanted anyone to see. It was unlucky for him that Reina was too curious to let his peculiar actions go unnoticed. His broad shoulders shrugged slightly before they fell back down. "What were you looking at over there?" She casually pushed, her soft whisper glided into his cell.

He glanced at the dark corner in which he had been standing, then back to Reina. "What do you mean?" His thick eyebrows rose to wrinkle his forehead in feigned puzzlement. Reina shifted her eyes between Keane and where he had stood moments earlier. Her eyes narrowed in suspicion, and he stared at her unflinchingly.

"I mean," she started, her voice slightly rising in irritation, "when you were standing in that corner, what were you looking at? What did you have in your hands?" She flexed her fingers around the bars that stood between them as Keane sauntered closer so that they stood only inches apart. His breath warmed her scalp as he looked down, and she realized how much bigger than her he was. She squared her shoulders and lifted her chin as she clenched her jaw and stood her ground.

Keane's brown eyes stared down into her piercing blue ones, with that smile confidently plastered on his face, "There's nothing over there but rocks and mud, Rein. What could I have possibly been looking at?" A soft chuckle escaped his lips, and Reina's heart thundered at their proximity.

She took a deep breath to calm herself and scowled up at him. "I saw you. There was something in your hands, Keane. You were looking at something." She refused to let him keep a secret from her, especially when he knew everything about her.

He looked at her in exasperation and shifted his weight as he leaned against the bars between them. His hair swung softly behind him and brushed against Reina's fingers. She released her grip on the bars and opted to cross her arms. "I was just thinking about something. Is that a crime?" His eyes sparkled in amusement, and Reina's frustration grew.

"You woke up in the middle of the night just to think? Keane, I'm not stupid. I've seen you lost in thought before, and that wasn't it. You had something in your hands." Reina's voice came out louder than she intended, and she flinched as the stone walls echoed it around them. She hoped the guards wouldn't hear, and she swallowed her frustration as Keane shook his head at her.

"I wasn't doing anything, Rein," he answered flatly. "I couldn't sleep. I just got up to walk around my cell and got lost in thought. That's all I was doing, I swear it." He seemed so honest and was giving Reina all the signals that he was done with the conversation. She ground her teeth together to keep from lashing out at him.

"If you don't want to tell me, fine." She turned her back to him and began to walk to the other side of the cell.

"Rein, wait. Don't be like that. I was just thinking." His whisper followed after her, but she ignored it and settled down on the stone floor. His heavy sigh filled the air around them as he lifted his weight off the metal bars. Reina's annoyance stayed with her the rest of the night, and she couldn't sleep as the sun came up and the guards exited their quarters.

She waited for the sound of keys clanging against the cell bars, but it didn't come. She thought it was odd, but then she heard quiet whispers from the guards. She stood and walked to the front of her cell to peer down the aisle beyond. The guards walked in a small group, and she couldn't make out the words they mumbled to each other. They seemed distracted by something, and Reina wondered what news they had received that could have made them so uncharacteristically talkative.

She was released from her cell without a word from the guard who opened her door, and she looked to Keane with an eyebrow raised in confusion as she momentarily forgot her irritation with him. He looked back at her and shook his head in answer before he exited his cell and made his way up the stairs. Reina followed distractedly as she looked over her shoulder at the guard, who seemed lost in thought.

The yard was no different, and the guards who bordered the area leaned over to each other and whispered about whatever had garnered their attention. They looked uncertain about something, and Reina's gut twisted at the idea of whatever made the men who had tormented the Criedans for years uncomfortable. She lined up and noticed the guard's strange behavior had captured the attention of most of the others in the yard. They looked around with concern evident on their faces, and the unrest made Reina feel jittery.

She shifted her weight back and forth between her feet and looked up to the commander, who had his back turned to them and seemed to be in a heated discussion with someone just beyond her line of sight. Her head turned to the woman who stood beside her, and the woman looked back in confusion.

Before Reina could whisper anything, the commander turned back to the people below him and silenced the yard with a loud shout, "*Enough!*" The guards snapped to attention and looked up at the man above. "Give them their placements and send them on their way." He flicked his wrist at the crowd and spun back around to continue whatever discussion he had been having.

The guards dispersed into the gathering of Criedans and began to assign their placements for the day. Reina was told to go to sewage control, and she walked dazedly to the wagon that would take her outside the kingdom's walls.

Sewage drains were scattered throughout the kingdom, and many tunnels ran underneath the ground. The place where it all ended up was just beyond the kingdom walls in a sewage dump. Their job was to ensure the sewage didn't overflow, and they would spend the day clearing the ditch that led to the dump and expanding the cesspool itself so it was prepared to hold more human excrement. The smell of the landfill was pungent. It was why the kingdom had opted to place it outside of the walls where the scent wouldn't be noticeable to those within the area.

As Reina climbed onto the wagon, she noticed Keane had been placed on sewage control that day as well. Her spirits lifted slightly before she remembered her annoyance at him from the night before. When he offered her a small smile, she looked away and ignored him during the ride outside of the kingdom.

Their wagon passed through the exit on the western wall, which the Criedans had finished building years earlier. Reina watched as the scenery became wilder and forests came into view. The trees stood tall and proud, although she noted that the drought had taken a toll on them. Their leaves sagged slightly, and she felt a pang of sorrow for the struggling trees. The wagon rolled to a stop, and Reina shouldered past Keane to climb off and grab a shovel.

She moved down a small hill and to the wide ditch that had been maintained over the years. The odor hit her almost immediately, and her nose scrunched up in disgust. Her breathing naturally switched to come through her mouth, avoiding the stench as she plunged her shovel into the small stream of human waste that trickled down the hill and into the dump at the base. She felt around with her shovel for any rocks, or large clumps of things she didn't wish to think about that could have been blocking the sewage path. When her shovel would find something, she would scoop it up as gently as she could to avoid splashing the vile substances back onto herself. She moved slowly down the ditch with the other Criedans that worked alongside her. The trench itself had to of been half a mile long, and on occasion, she would find herself pulling out the bodies of dead rodents that had met their unfortunate demise within the waste.

The sun traveled slowly across the sky and baked the Criedans who stood underneath it. Reina's skin itched under the rays, and she wiped at her brow to keep the sweat from burning her eyes. She looked down the ditch to the dump where Keane dug the edges to make it wider. His muscles tensed as he plunged his shovel into the hard ground and threw chunks of dirt over his shoulder into the forest behind him. Reina faintly pondered what they would do when the dump reached the forest line and there was no more room to expand. She guessed that they would then be forced to pull the trees down or possibly create a new sewage dump somewhere else.

Her train of thought halted as she spotted movement in the forest. Her muscles froze as she squinted her eyes to see what it had been but failed to see anything. She scanned the tree line, but whatever had caused the disturbance within the thicket had disappeared.

The knowledge that it was likely an animal of some sort curbed Reina's curiosity, and she went back to digging around in the ditch. Water and lunch came and went, and she continued her way down the path to the dump.

When she stood to wipe her hands on her shirt, she looked to Keane once again. Instead of working at the hard dirt around the dump, he stared out into the forest. Her eyes darted off in the direction Keane was staring, and she dropped her shovel in surprise. There was a person within the trees, and they were facing Keane.

Reina gasped as her shovel plunged into the ditch and splashed the disgusting stream up at her, causing her attention to dart away from the forest. A greenish-brown stain appeared on her shirt, and she felt droplets of moisture on her face. Her hand reached up slowly and wiped off the human waste from her cheek. She looked down to where her shovel had disappeared and knew she was going to have to reach into the ditch to pull it back out.

She looked back to the forest, but the person was gone, and Keane had gone back to digging. Her head shook from side to side in exasperation, but she could not ponder the moment as a guard walked behind her to see why she wasn't working.

"I dropped my shovel," she explained dumbly, and the guard smirked at her.

"Then you better retrieve it." Was his only answer as he stood there with his arms crossed to watch her. She nodded in affirmation and lowered herself to the ground to lay alongside the ditch. Her body gave a slight pause before she reached into the sewage and felt around for the wooden handle of her shovel. The texture was thick, and the warmth of it made her stomach churn as her arm sloshed about. When she found the wooden handle, she pulled it out victoriously and looked over her shoulder to see the guard walk past her and down the line of slaves who dutifully plunged their shovels into the ditch.

She rubbed her soiled arm against the grass on the ground to try and get the gunk off and then rolled the shovel around in the same manner so she wouldn't be forced to hold onto the disgusting sewage all day. When it was as clean as it was going to get, she stood back up and continued digging. Her eyes trailed up to the forest often, but she never saw the person within the foliage again that day.

When they were back on the wagon, she spared Keane a few odd glances, but the only thing he wanted to acknowledge about her was the awful stench that emitted from her arm. A wide smile was planted across his face, and although no sound came from his mouth, Reina knew he was laughing at her. She scowled at him.

Reina made sure to beat Keane to the cells when they dismounted the wagon, and her hurried steps almost caused her to fall down the steep stairs that led to the third level. She slowed slightly until she reached the bottom and darted into her cell to sit at their shared bars. A guard locked her door behind her with a glazed expression over his face and wandered off to close the other cells. As Keane entered his own, Reina's eyes trailed after him, and he looked at her in confusion. Reina glanced between the guard and Keane to signify they needed to talk when the guards left and Keane's shoulders drooped slightly as the guard locked his door.

Reina made a show of looking around the space distractedly as the guards finished up, and Keane settled down in the center of his cell to look as if he were about to fall asleep. Impatience rose within Reina as the guards took longer to lock the doors than usual, and she began to tap her cracked fingernails on the ground.

When the guards finally disappeared into their quarters to prepare for bed, Reina spun on Keane and gave him an accusatory glare. "See anything unusual today?"

Keane rolled over to face her from the middle of his cell. His right eyebrow cocked at her, and his eyes looked tired. "You mean besides you playing in a river of shit?" His body rose to sit, and his legs crossed as he settled.

"It's not a river. It's a ditch. And I dropped my shovel," she explained, and Keane let out a laugh. Her jaw clenched in response, and he shook his head.

"Unfortunate," he mused.

"That's not the point, Keane. There was someone in the woods today. Who were they?" She left no room for argument in her words, but Keane looked unimpressed as he pushed his hair out of his face.

"I didn't see anyone."

"Yes, you did."

"No, I didn't."

Reina let out a grunt of annoyance. "Stop playing with me, Keane. I saw someone in the woods, and you were looking right at them. Just tell me the truth."

"I'm not playing, Reina; I genuinely don't know what you're talking about. You're making up stories in your head. It was likely just a deer you saw, and I turned around when I heard a noise in the woods." His explanation would have seemed logical to Reina if she hadn't *seen* the person. She knew what a deer looked like, and what she had seen hadn't been an animal.

She gave him a steely stare and spoke dangerously low. "You've been acting strange." His silence echoed back at her, and she continued, "Last night I found you standing in that corner," she jutted her chin out to point to where she was speaking of, "holding something in your hands, and you denied it when I had caught you." He shook his head, about to speak up to argue the fact once again, but Reina pushed onward. "*Then* I see you staring into the forest earlier and sharing a moment with some strange person. I saw you, yet you still refuse to acknowledge that it happened? You're telling me that an obvious *person* was a *deer*?"

Then, he pulled himself together, and his face snapped back to being confused and slightly concerned. "There was no person in the forest, Reina." He sounded defeated and small.

"You're hiding something from me. I know you. And I will find out what's going on, Keane. You know I will. So why don't you just tell me?" Reina didn't want to let him know how alone she felt. He was all she had in the world, and there was a secret between them. In a prison with no hope of escape, her only bright spot was coming back to him at night. It was all she wanted, to not be alone. Den Zei could do its worst, but as long as she had him, she could endure.

He took a deep inhale and closed his eyes as he released it. As he rose to his feet, he extended his arms to signify he didn't know what Reina wanted from him. "Nothing is going on Reina, I wish there was more to say, but there isn't. I can't give you whatever answers your looking for."

With that, Reina spun away from him and walked to the far side of her cell. When she turned back around to face Keane, he had already disappeared into the dark corner of his own. She was left standing in the faint light of the stairs. Her throat tightened at the feeling of loneliness that pulsed from her chest.

6

MALYSSANDRA

Malyssandra woke with a start, and her hands flew to cover her face. Her breathing was labored, the sheet around her was soaked with sweat. Her hands shook, and tears stained her dark cheeks. When she finally pulled her hands away, she noticed the other maids in the room staring at her. She shakily took a breath before giving the other maids a sheepish smile. They quickly lost interest and turned away while Malyssandra pulled the wet sheet aside and threw her legs off the edge of the bed.

As she stood, she allowed herself to look at Ivanka's cot one last time in the hope her friend had come back in the dead of night. Malyssandra noted that the bed looked unslept in, and Ivanka was nowhere to be seen around the room. She thought back to the dream she had woken from mere moments earlier. The image of her friend's lifeless body, suspended in the air as shadows escaped her unhinged jaw, made a shiver run down Malyssandra's spine as, once again, her terror began to take space inside her.

She grabbed a new apron and began to pull it around her slim shoulders. Memories from the night before made her stop. The shadow had seemed so real, and Malyssandra dreaded another day spent alone resetting the rat traps. She didn't wish to go to the eastern sector and reside in the dark rooms, and she lightly played with the idea of volunteering for a different chore. She didn't know how the other maids would take it, but she couldn't stand the idea of the shadow coming back to taunt her.

She had frozen the night before. The shadow had appeared, and she had only stood there in fear. If the shadow had charged at her, she wasn't sure she would have been able to move. There was no way to explain that to the other maids without sounding crazy, so she tried desperately to think of another excuse in her head as to why she would wish for a different chore that day. She couldn't simply tell them she was disgusted by the meat, as she had been handling it for years. Every excuse that came to her mind fell short, and she huffed in resignation that she would simply have to state she didn't wish to reset the traps and hope the other maids wouldn't ask questions.

As she walked to the group of maids at the front of the room, a guard entered their quarters, and everyone stopped. Guards rarely entered their room, and when they did, it was only to tell a maid they had been summoned by the king. Everyone held their breath as the guard scanned them over, and Malyssandra waited expectantly for the guard to tell someone the king requested them so he could leave.

When the guard's eyes fell on Malyssandra, he stopped looking about and approached her. Malyssandra's heart stopped, and her stomach rolled. The king had never called upon her before, and she had thought herself safe from him. She pulled her hands behind her back to hide their shaking, and the guard stopped in front of her. The words that came from his mouth were unheard of.

"The prince requests your company." The guard's face remained stoic as he delivered the message he had been sent to give. Malyssandra was certain that the maids would have gasped if they hadn't been afraid to draw the guard's attention.

The prince had never summoned anyone before, and Malyssandra felt her eyes widen as she clenched her jaw in surprise. She gave the guard a slight nod and followed him as he left the maid's quarters to lead her to the prince. The other maids stared after her in confusion as she disappeared from view.

Malyssandra's mind ran wild while she followed calmly behind the guard. She wondered at what she could have done to garner to prince's attention. Desperately she hoped she wasn't meant to service him in the way Ivanka serviced the king. She had never done such a thing, and she hadn't thought she would ever have to. The king had never shown her any interest, and as far as she was concerned, the prince hadn't either.

The only time she had seen the prince look at her was when she had splashed water on the floor at the party. He had been so angry; she had seen his eyes bore into her with a look of pure hatred. Her heart faltered. She wondered if he had summoned her to punish her for what had happened at the party. That didn't make any sense to her, though, as the party had been days before. If he had wished to punish her, wouldn't he have done so before then?

Her thoughts refused to settle down as the guard led her through the halls and to the large oak door that would enter the prince's chambers. The guard didn't bother to look back at her as he raised a fist to knock on the door. Malyssandra's heart thundered, and her breath hitched in her throat. She felt as though she couldn't breathe, and she barely heard the prince's voice beckon them into his bedroom.

The guard opened the door slowly, and Malyssandra followed him into the magnificent chamber. It was more spacious than the maid's quarters and the kitchen combined. Tapestries and weapons decorated the walls. A large blue rug covered the porcelain floor, and yellow tassels adorned the edges of the carpet. A door led to another room, and Malyssandra assumed it was the prince's washroom.

The thing that grabbed her attention the most was the large canopy bed that stood proudly in the center of the chamber. Blue and yellow silken sheets were laid flat atop it as if it had been freshly made, and the golden curtains were pulled back. It stood high off the ground, and Malyssandra imagined it would come up to her navel if she stood beside it. She wondered horrifically if that was where she would be forced to spend her day. Malyssandra thought back to the dark halls of the eastern sector and decided she would have much preferably braved the shadows than brave the prince's private quarters.

Her eyes trailed to the prince as he signaled for the guard to leave the room. He stood tall and proud, his shoulders pulled back, and his chin held high. The short crop of his black hair made his eyes stand out bright blue from his face. His jaw was set firmly and cast a sharp shadow across his neck. There was something very appealing about the prince who stood before her, although Malyssandra's terror overshadowed any sort of attraction her body could feel toward the man.

The door clicked shut behind the guard, and Malyssandra fell into a deep curtsey. "What would you like me to do, your majes-?"

"Stand up." His voice was sincere, but Malyssandra was afraid he meant to trick her.

"Your majesty, it is customary that I curtsey in your presence."

"Please, stand up," he repeated.

"Yes, your majesty." She slowly straightened her knees but kept her eyes downcast.

"You don't need to call me that."

"Then what shall I call you, your majesty?" Confusion muddled Malyssandra's brain. He didn't seem angry, but the royals were unpredictable. Malyssandra had heard the rumors of their temper. She feared offending the prince.

He let out a deep sigh, and Malyssandra heard the bed creak as he sat on its edge. "I know where Ivanka is."

Malyssandra's head snapped, shock evident in her stare. Her face heated as their gazes met, and she forced herself to look back at the ground. The prince knew Ivanka? That wasn't possible. But he had just spoken her name. How did he know her name?

"Your majesty, with all due respect, how is it you know of Ivanka?"

"My father is a cruel man, of that I'm sure you are well aware."

"I wouldn't say that, your-."

"You don't have to say it; I've already done so." His words left no room for Malyssandra to protest, and she swallowed in response. "My father called on Ivanka quite often to join him in his chambers. When I was able, I would sometimes intercept Ivanka on her way to his room. My father is frequently too incapacitated with the finer things in life to even remember that he called for her. I would give her refuge on those nights until my father was fast asleep."

Malyssandra deflated. "She never told me." The words were a pained whisper in the large room.

"No, I didn't suppose she would have. If my father were to find out, I wouldn't have been able to help her anymore. Ivanka knew this."

"I wouldn't have told anyone," Malyssandra stated.

"Perhaps not, but it wasn't worth the risk. It no longer matters anymore. Ivanka has been sent to Den Zei."

"What? Why?" Malyssandra momentarily forgot who she was speaking to, and she stared in mortification at the prince as she realized she had demanded answers from him. "Please, forgive me, your highness. I didn't mean to disrespect you so brazenly."

Prince Ferix waved off the apology. "My father had called upon her to service him in his bedroom the night before last. I wasn't able to intercept her as my father hadn't drunk that night. He has been sober since the trade deal he recently made. Basking in his power, I assume." The prince's tone turned sharp, and his eyes darkened. "My mother has been aware of his... antics for quite some time now. She usually chooses to ignore it, but my father had become overly confident in his ability to bed other women without my mother confronting him. He kept Ivanka in his bedroom long past sun-up, and my mother walked in on them." He paused for a second to allow Malyssandra to register what he had just said. She didn't like where the story was going, but she nodded for him to continue. "My mother was furious that my father would be so bold as to keep a maid in his bed so late into the day where everyone would see her exit his quarters. She felt she had been made a fool of and demanded Ivanka be punished for assisting my father in his adultery. She had the guards take their whips to her face and body. There was a moment where I thought my mother would have her killed, and I offered up a different option." Malyssandra felt tears well up in her eyes and break over her eyelids to fall down her face. Her breathing became hitched, and the knot in her throat was uncomfortable to swallow. "Den Zei was the only thing I could offer to save her life. Ivanka was taken there yesterday." He looked at Malyssandra, and she felt hopelessness rise in her gut.

"Why would you offer up such an option?" Malyssandra asked quietly.

"It saved her life," he stated.

"She would have rather died." Malyssandra's shoulders drooped forward, and she lifted her hand to wipe at the wetness on her face. The prince watched on in silence, and Malyssandra stared back with sorrow in her eyes. "I'm sorry, your majesty. But why are you telling me this?"

"Because," He stated quietly. "I am not a monster like those who raised me. Believe it or not, our world has not always been this unjust. She is your friend, and she always spoke highly of you. I thought you should know what has become of her." His voice was laced with a sadness Malyssandra didn't understand.

He was one of them. When the king entered a crowded room, the prince stood beside him and stared down at the same people. The prince had stared at her during the party, disgust, and anger in his eyes. She had assumed the emotions had been pointed at her.

She looked at him quietly, and tears continued to flow freely down her face. Malyssandra took a shaky breath. "Am I excused?" She sounded defeated, and there was a small plea in her voice. The idea of spending more time in the room with the prince made her uneasy. He hadn't seemed like he meant her any harm, but years of fear still simmered under the surface of her thoughts.

The prince shook his head slightly. "You must stay in here for a little while longer; the palace has to believe we laid with each other, or else they'll ask questions neither one of us would like to answer." Malyssandra's heart dropped, and she looked longingly at the door. The prince gazed at her in understanding. "I'll go to the washroom for the remainder of the time. You won't even have to see me. Feel free to make yourself at home. You only need to be in here for an hour, then you can leave." The prince left the room without another word and closed the washroom's door behind his tall figure.

Malyssandra allowed herself to look around the room. Ivanka had been in there countless times. She had spent nights with the prince, speaking of Malyssandra. Yet, she had never uttered a word about it. She had kept that secret as close to her chest as she could, and Malyssandra hadn't suspected a thing.

Malyssandra didn't wish to sit upon the prince's bed, so she found a spot on the floor where she curled up against the wall and allowed herself to silently sob into her hands. Her friend was in Den Zei, the one place she had never wished to go.

Their hopes of waiting to be rescued were gone. Malyssandra couldn't do it without Ivanka at her side. She was stuck in the palace with a shadow and a priestess that couldn't seem to leave her be. And she didn't have her friend to help her through it.

It could be worse, Mallie. The words echoed in her mind. She had never thought Ivanka would end up in the very place she feared. She had played the game so carefully. But there was no way to win, and that thought caused another sob to tear through Malyssandra's body.

When the hour had passed, Malyssandra crawled to her feet and wiped the tears from her face. She forced herself to swallow the knot in her throat and made her way to the large oak door. The guard stood outside, ready to escort her back to the maid's quarters.

When she arrived to grab her lunch, the other maids looked at her unabashedly. Malyssandra's cheeks flared, and she stumbled to her cot to try and eat her cold bowl of soup away from the prying stares. She felt their eyes follow her, and she sat quietly to stare out the window at Den Zei as the whispers of the other maids surrounded her. She needed to see Ivanka again.

7

REINA

Reina found herself wanting to speak to Keane all night but was unable to bring herself to do so. She was hurt by the secrets he kept, and she couldn't understand why he didn't trust her. They had told each other everything since the day he had discovered her secret, or at least she thought they had. She wasn't sure anymore, and she didn't know what to do with the feelings of betrayal that bubbled up from within her. She missed talking with him already but refused to apologize.

She missed the days where they would lay beside each other with just the bars to separate them, and they would talk about Crieda. The magic of the kingdom and the happiness of their people. They never spoke about the day Yulsa invaded and tore their lives from them. There was no room for that darkness in their mystical thoughts.

As they laid down in their cells to fall asleep at night, Reina had talked about how her father had been a hero. How he had been recognized by the king himself. They made up stories as if they still lived within the walls of Crieda, and Keane would ask

Reina what she had done that day in town. It had been their own way of escaping the world they had been painfully dragged into. They hadn't spoken that way in years.

The sound of guards making their way down the aisle outside her cell pulled her from her thoughts. She watched as a guard unlocked her door. It was quiet. The guards weren't whispering to one another as they had the day before or taunting the Criedans as they released them from their cells. Reina observed the guard as he walked away to unlock the cells on the opposite side of the aisle.

She quickly made her way up the stairs to avoid Keane but froze. Her breath caught in her throat, and her eyebrows lifted as she looked at the crowd within the yard. It wasn't just Criedans anymore. There were more people lined up, chains shackled around their hands. Reina thought back with a chill to the day Yulsa had invaded.

A harsh voice sounded at her back to keep moving, and Reina turned her head slightly to see a guard behind her with anger evident on his face. Her eyes stayed glued to the chains as she made her way across the yard. As she went, she saw a familiar young boy. His tawny hair dully absorbed the sun, and his speckled green eyes looked up at her in sadness. She noted that he looked different up close and that he had been given clothes to wear. The image of him running from his grandmother, laughing into the wind, nude as could be, floated into Reina's mind. She stared in disbelief at the somber boy that stood before her. She wondered faintly where his grandmother was but halted her thought process before it could go too far. It was likely the woman had been killed due to her age. The Yulsans had no need for a slave who couldn't handle the work of Den Zei.

They were enslaving their own people. Reina's eyes scanned painfully over the bound individuals. They had rounded up the Yulsans who lived in poverty, the ones that couldn't help their economy to thrive, and they had thrown them in chains. The guards who stood around the chained Yulsans looked unsure of themselves. They rocked back and forth between their feet and looked at each other guiltily. Reina found herself hoping that their consciences would weigh heavily at what they had done, and somehow she knew that they already did.

She realized that must have been why the guards had been distracted the day before and quiet that morning. They knew what they were doing to their own people was wrong, but they had followed the orders anyway. It made Reina sick to her stomach, and she spat bile onto the ground.

Reina made her way into the line of Criedans and watched as the Yulsans were led back into Den Zei to get their assigned cells. They would be locked in there all day, as the Criedans had been when they first arrived. As they received their cell assignments, they would enter the metal cages and watch the doors close. They would start working the next day and would continue doing so for the rest of their lives.

The king had done the unthinkable, although Reina wasn't entirely surprised. The Criedans were diminishing every day. He needed slaves to keep everything running. That was the world he had created.

As a guard approached Reina and stated that she was to make her way to beams, she looked at him for a second. For once, the guard had nothing to say. He turned away from her and moved on, assigning the other Criedans in line to their positions.

She shook her head. The king was in dangerous territory, having turned his own people against each other. Her feet led her to the wagon, and she settled down into the center while she watched the young boy disappear into the cell blocks.

...

When Reina arrived back at Den Zei that night, she felt exhaustion nip at her heels. She wanted to make her way quickly down to her cell and allow herself to fall into a deep sleep. The thought of the enslaved boy had bounced around her head all day, and she desperately wanted a break from those sad green eyes.

As she entered the cell blocks, a strange feeling tugged at her gut. She tried to ignore it, but it became restless. It intensified the more she fought it, and confusion riddled her features as she remained on the first level instead of going down the stairs to her cell.

Something wanted her to go down the first level. She thought about it for a moment but decided to follow the sensation. As she moved past the cells, the feeling slowly receded until she stood at a locked enclosure that held a woman within.

Her pale-blonde hair reflected the moonlight from the opening to the cell blocks, and Reina crouched down beside the woman. At the sound of Reina's feet, the woman looked up, and Reina flinched. Her face was gruesomely marked with lashes, and Reina could only see slight signs of blue as the woman's swollen eyes tried to peek at her. She looked flayed. Blood gushed from open wounds, and Reina wondered how the woman was still alive. Her bloodied arms shook aggressively at her sides, and a soft moan sounded from her abused lips.

The woman scurried from Reina as quickly as she could, and Reina knew that her expression would have been fearful if not for the wounds on her face. She wondered what the woman had done to deserve such a beating. She knew the amount of pain the woman had to be in was excruciating, as Reina had received many lashes throughout her life. Though, none had been quite as bad. Reina had only ever received lashes on her back and legs. Her face had never been touched by the end of a whip.

Reina felt another aggressive tug in her core, and she rose from her crouch to look around for any sign of guards. When she saw none, she crouched back down beside the woman and reached carefully into the bars. The woman watched Reina cautiously through the slits of her eyes, and Reina looked to her empathetically. "Let me help you," she whispered and hoped the woman could hear her. "I won't hurt you, I promise."

The woman seemed to pause but slowly dragged herself to where Reina stood. The sound that emitted from the woman's lips was otherworldly. A dying animal, trapped in a cage. Reina didn't know what she was going to do to help, but she felt the need in her gut to do something.

When the woman got close enough, Reina lightly placed her palm on the woman's shoulder. She grunted in pain, and Reina's head snapped around to ensure nobody was coming.

Reina's shoulder began to burn slightly, and she whipped her head back to face the woman as she began to heal. Amazement lit up Reina's face in the soft golden light as she watched the other woman's skin knit back together, the same way hers had hundreds of times before. Reina was speechless, and her breathing slowed at the sight of what she was doing.

She had never healed anyone else before. She had never even attempted to do so. Keane hadn't wanted her to experiment with her ability, and she hadn't. It had never even occurred to her that she could heal anyone other than herself, and as the woman's final lash mended back together, Reina felt a tear fall from her cheek and land on her outstretched arm.

The woman looked to her body which held no scars, and a sob tore from her lips loud and pained. Reina jolted to her feet at the sound of guards entering the cell blocks and spun to take off toward the stairs.

She took the steps quickly and prayed she wouldn't trip over her own feet and hit the hard ground below. Reina shrugged the worry off with the knowledge that she would be fine in a few hours even if she did fall and smiled wide at the new certainty that anyone would be fine if they fell. Reina could heal them; she could help them.

She hit the ground of level three running, and she dodged into her cell before the guards showed up to lock her in. Keane looked at her curiously, but she shrugged him off. He had his secrets. She could have hers.

8

MALYSSANDRA

Malyssandra's attention stayed glued to Den Zei all night. She tried to force herself to sleep, but all she saw behind closed eyes was Ivanka's hopeless stare. The urge to see her friend ate at her, and she felt restless.

The maids had left her alone for the second part of the day, but Malyssandra still felt their penetrating stares under her skin. She knew what they thought had happened between her and the prince, and she knew it had to stay that way.

Ivanka had kept her secret from Malyssandra for years. She was hurt that her friend hadn't trusted her, but a small part of her understood. Still, it stung. Were Ivanka and the prince... friends? Or was there something more to it? After years spent fearing the royals, it didn't seem possible that one of them could have been anything but cruel and cold.

Malyssandra pondered if Prince Ferix could have been lying. It hadn't seemed like it. There was nothing he could have gained by telling her what had become of Ivanka. She needed to see for herself.

Den Zei stood solemnly in the distance, a scar on the otherwise pristine kingdom of Yulsa. Within sat hundreds of Criedans in cells. Hundreds of Criedans who led lives much more horrific than her own.

Malyssandra had never been to the northern structure. She had always been too afraid to see the life she could have had if things had been different for her. Malyssandra felt she had to go. She had no choice if Ivanka was inside. Malyssandra wondered how her friend would look. If she would even recognize her when she got there.

As the maids dragged themselves from their cots to start their day, Malyssandra meekly stated, "I'll take the laundry to Den Zei today." She flinched as she waited for the other maids to question why she didn't wish to handle the rat traps as she usually did. Nobody said anything, though. They only stared at her with the same disapproving stares they had given her the day before.

A blush heated up Malyssandra's dark cheeks, and she stared back at the maids sheepishly. She knew what they thought when they looked at her, and she could almost hear the word *whore* echo across the room. Ivanka had dealt with those stares most of her life, the judgment palpable in the air. If the other maids had been in the same position Ivanka had been, they would have made their way to the king's quarters without question. They were lucky to have never been called upon. So they dealt with that luck by pretending they were better than those who had been summoned. It didn't matter that Malyssandra hadn't actually slept with the prince. The other maids believed she had. To them, she was nothing more than a royal's whore.

Ivanka had ignored the scrutiny much better than Malyssandra could. Her shoulders had stayed tall, and her eyes focused ahead on the day that stretched out before her. Malyssandra couldn't handle herself in the same manner. The hostility of the room made her slim shoulders hunch forward and her eyes glued to the floor. She shuffled to the doorway as the maids watched her go.

Malyssandra made her way to the undercroft, a storage room that held clean clothes for the guards. Guards in Den Zei were not allowed to leave their station, and the maids had been tasked with bringing clean clothes down to them once a week. None of the maids enjoyed the job, and quite often, Malyssandra had heard them fight over who was to make the delivery. Nobody had ever asked Malyssandra to take the chore, though. They hated resetting the rat traps even more than they hated spending a day in Den Zei.

The small storage room was filled with yellow and blue shirts and black trousers for the guards to wear underneath their armor. Malyssandra ran her fingers over the fabric and noted that it felt scratchy within her hands. She supposed it made sense, as there were too many guards within the kingdom to grant each one fine clothing.

Her arms made quick work of grabbing at piles of shirts and pants before she exited the room and made her way to the front of the palace, where a wagon sat waiting to be loaded. She placed the first pile within the wooden wagon, and the mule attached to the front looked at her disinterestedly before it went back to its attempt to find fresh grass on the dried ground.

"You're new," the guard at the head of the wagon observed.

Malyssandra gave a sheepish nod. "I am here to serve my king."

The guard grunted. "Get on with it then." He looked at her expectantly, and she turned back into the castle. It took three trips through the palace to get all the clothes gathered.

She climbed aboard the back of the wagon and leaned her weight against the railing on the edge as it hitched forward. The sound of the mule's hooves on the brick roads of the kingdom calmed Malyssandra's nerves, and she watched as the stone buildings that lined the streets passed by.

As much as she hated to admit it, Yulsa was beautiful. Malyssandra was awestruck by how lively it was. Children ran in front of the mule laughing as the guard shouted at them to move, and women made their way into the market to buy food. Bells rang as people entered shops, and girls gossiped happily as they linked arms.

Malyssandra smiled somberly at the noise of the kingdom, and a pang of sadness filled her. She was a stranger to the world that surrounded her, and she found herself wishing she could join the Yulsans that happily moved through their lives unaffected by the king's cruelty.

As the wagon passed the busy atmosphere of the kingdom, Malyssandra watched the buildings grow darker. Some were near the point of crumbling, and the unkempt grass was dead from the impossible heat that filled the air. She looked to the cloudless sky and pondered when it had rained last. She hadn't been outside since she had been brought to the kingdom and hadn't noticed the dry atmosphere that plagued Yulsa. The palace had devoured her whole. It had been as if the outside world hadn't existed.

No people stood outside of the hollow buildings, and Malyssandra wondered where they could be. Clothing hung on lines as they passed through the area, indicating that people lived there. However, no sounds of life came from the buildings, and she watched as the clothes hung still from the lack of a breeze.

The sun slowly moved across the sky, and Malyssandra wondered how long it would be until they reached Den Zei. She had known the encampment was far to the north, but she hadn't realized how long it would take to arrive. As the thought crossed her mind, the mule pulled the wagon by a tall structure made of metal beams, and Malyssandra stared up at it in astonishment. A shudder made its way up her spine at the way the moon cast long shadows beneath it. The image of the creature in the basement flashed through her mind. For once, she was happy to be in the presence of a guard.

Gradually, Den Zei came into view. Air left Malyssandra's lungs as she watched as it grew closer, and her jaw hung slack at the sight. A large fence surrounded a yard of dry earth, and a strange grey building stood deep within the fenced area. Guards stood stationed outside the camp to keep watch, and their interest piqued at the wagon as it rolled closer.

The sound of the mule's hooves slowed down and stopped as they came to a metal gate that reached dauntingly into the night sky. "Delivery," the guard at the head of the wagon stated down to the man who stood at the gate. The man nodded and held his hand up into the air. For a second, nothing happened. Malyssandra's racing heart filled the silence in her head. Then, the gate began to creak open, and the mule continued.

Malyssandra's hands flexed in front of her, and she reminded herself she was there for Ivanka. As the wagon halted, she took a deep breath and climbed off the back. The sun beat down, hot on Malyssandra's skin, and she began to sweat as she hefted the first pile of clothes into her arms. The guard climbed from the wagon and gave her a stern stare before walking off to speak with the other guards in the yard.

Uncertainty riddled Malyssandra's features as she sauntered toward the opening of Den Zei's cell blocks. She stepped into the doorway, and her heavy breathing mixed with the sounds of soft moans from those locked within metal cages. She spared a dread-filled glance at the steep steps that led down into the earth. The idea of going deep into the ground scared her, but she kept her eyes forward and walked by the ominous stone steps.

She scanned the cells for any sign of Ivanka. People stared back at her, pleas for mercy evident upon their faces. Some looked frail and sickly, while others looked resigned and broken. She felt their eyes as she made her way toward the door at the end of the aisle. Her steps began to quicken under the uncomfortable scrutiny, and she almost missed the flash of pale-blonde hair that caught the distant light of the sun.

The pile of clothes fell from Malyssandra's hands as she recognized the shape of the woman to whom the hair belonged, and she dodged to the side to bring herself closer. The woman's eyes slowly trailed up until a hopeless blue met Malyssandra's gaze. Recognition startled her face, and Malyssandra became speechless.

Ivanka bore no sign of having been lashed, and Malyssandra wondered if the prince had lied to her about the beating Ivanka had received. Confusion wrinkled her brow as she looked down at Ivanka's unscarred body. Ivanka offered a soft smile, but Malyssandra saw the ghosts in her eyes. She wanted desperately to throw the cage door open and escape with her friend, but Malyssandra knew it was an impossible dream.

"Hey." Ivanka's gravelly voice scratched at the air, and Malyssandra brought herself to crouch beside her friend, "What're you doing here?"

Malyssandra's mouth opened and closed multiple times before she could find the words to reply. She pointed to the clothes she had dropped and gave her friend a sad smile. "Delivery." Ivanka nodded and gave Malyssandra a stare that meant she knew there was more to it than that. "The prince told me you were here. I needed to know it was true."

"You spoke to Ferix?" Ivanka's eyebrow arched. "What did he tell you?"

"That he's been helping you. He summoned me to his chambers. He said you spoke of me often, and he thought I needed to know what happened. Why didn't you tell me?"

"I meant to. Many times I wanted to. But I was scared, Mallie. I suppose it doesn't matter now, though." A lifeless laugh escaped Ivanka's mouth, and she leaned her forehead against the metal bars.

Malyssandra dropped her gaze to the hard ground. "No, I suppose it doesn't." Silence radiated between them, and Malyssandra reached her hand through the bars to place over Ivanka's. "The prince told me you had been lashed, but there are no marks on your skin. You look okay."

"I'm the farthest thing from okay, Mallie. You should know that." Her eyes seemed duller than they had been within the palace, and her chest rose and fell slowly.

"I thought they had taken the whip to you. I was made to think you were practically dead within this cell." Malyssandra further explained, and Ivanka's head whipped up.

"They did. They lashed my face, my hands. They mutilated anywhere there was skin to slice through. I thought myself dead. They brought me here, and I lay in pain so great that I begged death to take me. I begged to be accepted into darkness and freed from this damned world." Her voice mounted in the darkness, and Malyssandra flinched at that version of her friend she had never seen before. Ivanka had never raised her voice. Malyssandra had never even seen her angry. The girl who sat before her wasn't one she recognized as she stared out into the world with violence in her eyes. Then, she softened. Her face relaxed, and her eyes became shells of confusion. "A woman came to my cell last night."

"A woman?" Malyssandra's voice echoed back carefully, and Ivanka blinked slowly in the dim light.

"A woman," she repeated, "or a goddess, of which I am not certain. She was beautiful. She came to my cell and looked at me with kindness in her eyes. She told me she would help, and when she touched me, my body healed." Malyssandra looked on with doubt in her eyes, and tears fell freely down Ivanka's cheeks. "I know I sound crazed, but I swear it. She healed me, and the world turned golden for just long enough for me to really see her. I don't know what happened or how, but it did. You have to believe me." The plea in Ivanka's voice tugged at Malyssandra's chest, and although she believed her friend had lost her mind, she gave her a small smile and a nod.

"I believe you," Malyssandra murmured into the space between them, and Ivanka nodded to herself before her expression crumpled. Malyssandra stood there for a few more seconds and stared somberly at her friend. "The other maids believe me to be a whore. After I came back from the prince's chambers, they looked at me as if I had just sold my soul."

Ivanka scoffed, a small smile tugged at her pale lips. "Nosey wenches. They're always waiting for the next big gossip."

Relief filled Malyssandra at the sight of Ivanka's smile. She hadn't lost her friend completely. "Speaking of gossip. Did you and the prince ever…?"

"Gods, no!" Ivanka's eyes widened. "He was only ever just kind to me."

Malyssandra nodded in understanding, and silence settled upon them once again. She didn't wish to leave her friend locked within a cell. But the sun at the end of the cellblock was starting to disappear from the sky. She chewed on the inside of her cheek. "I'll come back for you, Ivanka. Just please don't give up."

Ivanka dipped her head in acknowledgment. "You neither."

She quickly collected the clothing back into her arms and shot one last look at her friend before she scurried down the rest of the aisle. The guard's door stood tall before her, and she brought her fist up to give a knock.

The face of a man popped up in the small window that peered into the room. He opened the door cautiously to see what Malyssandra wanted. She held the clothes up to show him she had a delivery, and he opened the door the rest of the way before he made his way back to the other guards, who sat around a small table with cards splayed in front of them.

Malyssandra marveled at how normal the men looked as they sat with cigars on their lips and yelled across the table at each other as someone won the hand and gathered whatever money they had bet. They paid her no mind as she shuffled through the room to lay the clothes flat on their beds, and she listened faintly to their laughter and shouts as the game they played continued.

She walked briskly to exit their quarters and marched down the cellblock when she was done. Malyssandra walked back to the wagon and grabbed the next pile of clothing. Her stare darted to the horizon as she heard the rattling of wheels.

Wagons filled with people made their way back to the encampment. Slaves were being transported to their cells after a long day of work. Malyssandra quickly spun back to the cell blocks to make her next delivery.

As the stairs came back into view, she forced herself to swallow the uncomfortable feeling that rose within her. She took the steps slowly, one at a time, and stared at the stone with deep concentration. When she made it to the second level, she began to make the trek to the end of the cellblock.

The level was empty except for a few stragglers left within their cages. They paid her no mind, and she forced herself to stay focused. She knocked on the metal door and was let in to lay the clothes on the soldiers' beds yet again. They didn't play cards at a table. Instead, they watched after her as she made her way around the room. She tripped over a pair of boots on the floor and mumbled an apology. The men watched on in silence, and their stares crawled along her skin.

The guards followed her out, and she froze when she saw Criedans making their way into their cells. She held her breath as the guards moved around her and began locking the metal doors. Strange looks were thrown her way, but she cast her eyes down to avoid them. When the last cell was locked, Malyssandra moved forward again on unsteady legs.

As she went to grab the last pile of clothes, she scanned the area for the guard that was supposed to take her back. Logically she knew he wasn't going to leave her, but the idea of having to spend the night in Den Zei terrified her. She spotted him off on the far side of the yard, still talking with another guard, and she let out a sigh of relief.

It felt as if she were being buried alive as she sunk down into the third level. Her eyes struggled to adjust to the darkness that filled the cellblock around her. A faint sliver of moonlight made its way down with her, but only the first few cells were light enough to see the outlines of those within.

The air was damp that deep into the earth, and the cool air brought goosebumps to her arms. She hustled past the dark cells and toward the faint light that shone from the small window at the aisle's end. Her fist banged against the door harder than she had intended, and it flew open for Malyssandra to be met with the face of an irritated guard. She smiled timidly, and he flung the door open when he noted the clothes in her hands.

There weren't as many men in the guards' quarters on the third level, and Malyssandra only had a few beds to place clothes on. The men sat in silence but didn't watch her as she moved about. They seemed to be lost in their own thoughts, and Malyssandra was able to sneak out of the room and slowly close the door without any of them deigning to notice her presence. Her breathing began to slow as she recognized that she was done, and all she needed to do was make her way back to the wagon. She neared the base of the stairs, escape so close she could touch it.

"You're new," the voice came from the darkness, and Malyssandra turned her head slightly to see a young woman who stood against the bars of her cell. Malyssandra looked down and turned back to the stairs. "You live in the palace?" The woman's voice persisted, and Malyssandra took a shaky breath.

"I do," she stated quietly. She peeked up through her lashes, and Malyssandra could make out the blonde of the woman's hair, and her blue eyes reflected the dim moonlight. She was effortlessly beautiful. Her skin was bare of blemishes, although dirt and dried blood speckled her face and body.

"Must be nice," the woman mused. "You must get fed the good stuff." The woman's eyes looked at Malyssandra's frame, and although Malyssandra was thin, she looked plump compared to the emaciated girl before her.

"Cold soup, actually." Malyssandra's voice was uncertain, and the woman looked on curiously.

"How'd you draw the short straw to come up to Den Zei?" She shifted her weight, and Malyssandra watched as her knotted hair bobbed around at the movement.

Malyssandra chewed on her words and debated walking away from the conversation before the guard that had brought her started wondering where she was.

A male voice sounded from the cell beside the woman, "Leave her be, Reina." His voice was deep, although it was but a whisper in the blackness. Malyssandra squinted her eyes as he walked to the front corner of his cell so she could faintly see him.

His dark hair hung to his waist, and his broad shoulders filled her view. Dark eyes stared into her soul as he scanned her up and down before she turned to look at the woman beside him through the bars.

Reina rolled her eyes before focusing back on Malyssandra. "Ignore him. He has an awful habit of inserting himself in conversations that do not concern him."

Keane sighed in exasperation and met Malyssandra's stare. "You should go." Malyssandra paused. She thought back to Ivanka upstairs, curled up in her cell. She had spoken of a woman who had appeared before her the night before, and although Malyssandra believed it couldn't have been real, she felt a strange pull to ask.

"Do either of you know of a woman who visits other cells at night?" The question sounded ludicrous to her own ears, and she shook her head. "I'm sorry, I-."

"Why do you ask?" Reina's voice was soft.

Malyssandra sighed. "You asked how I drew the short straw to come here; I didn't. My friend was sent here yesterday. I was told she had been lashed nearly to death, but she was completely healthy within her cell when I arrived. She said a woman came by her cell last night and healed her." Keane gave Reina a strange look, but Reina's attention was on Malyssandra. "I'm sorry, I shouldn't have said anything. I should really go."

"Could you come here?" Reina asked.

"I-I really should get going."

"Come here." Reina's voice was forceful, and years of being taught to obey commands had Malyssandra moving in her direction before she could stop to think.

Reina's hand darted between the bars and grabbed onto Malyssandra's wrist as she approached the cell. Their eyes met for a split second before Malyssandra felt a surge of energy, and the world around her changed.

Complete silence filled Malyssandra's head. She watched people gathered around a bed; their mouths moved, but no sound came out. Recognition filled Malyssandra as she looked closer.

Reina stared down at the king. He was sickly, his skin pale and his breathing ragged. The queen stood on the opposite side of the extravagant bed, a plea in her eyes. Reina shook her head, disagreeing with whatever had been said. The king pulled his chapped lips into a cruel smile as he began to speak.

Reina's eyes flashed in anger, and she opened her mouth to say something. The king cut her off, and Reina looked around in disgust. A guard stood behind her, his arms crossed in front of his chest, blocking her way to the door.

She steeled her jaw and turned back to the king, hatred evident on her face. Reina nodded, and the king smiled victoriously. Moments passed where Reina simply continued to stare down at the man before she lifted her hand and placed it on his own.

The world flashed back into view, and Malyssandra yanked her arm from Reina's hand. "What was that?" She sputtered, and Reina looked at her in confusion.

"What was what?" Reina raised an eyebrow, and Malyssandra looked back at Keane, who watched on in silence.

"You didn't just see that? You were with the king in his chambers." Malyssandra's voice was breathy and exasperated, and Reina's brow dropped at the words.

"I have never met the king in my life. What are you talking about?" Reina looked unsettled, and Malyssandra shifted her gaze between Keane and Reina. Before anything else could be said between them, Malyssandra spun and sprinted up the stairs. Neither of them called after her as she ran out of the cell blocks and into the moonlit yard. She looked out to see the guard was sitting in wait at the head of the wagon.

She swiftly made her way to the back, and the guard shot her an annoyed glare at having been made to wait so long. Malyssandra gave him a mumbled apology and looked back at the Den Zei cell block as the gate to the yard closed behind them and faded from view. When Reina had grabbed her arm, she had seen something. The memory rattled through her mind as the wagon pulled her through the moonlit kingdom back to the palace.

9

REINA

Reina watched as the small woman disappeared up the stairway, and her hand flexed absentmindedly in front of her. She hadn't meant to grab the girl's arm; it had just happened. Something had roared inside her and had practically forced her to touch the woman. It had been a feeling akin to what had happened the day before with the woman in the cell. A gut instinct that had pushed her into action. *What is happening to me?* She thought to herself.

When she had grabbed her arm, she had felt a strange surge between them. Her shoulder hadn't burned, though, and there was nothing that had visibly healed on either of them. The moment replayed itself in her mind, and she failed to wrap her head around the other girl's reaction. Her dark eyes had slackened for a moment and seemed to stare off into a void. She had been unfocused as if her mind hadn't been in the moment with Reina at all. Then she had snapped back. She had looked fearful and confused and had rambled something about Reina being in the king's chambers. Reina shook her head as she tried to piece together the puzzle of what had just occurred, but there were no answers ready to spring to the surface of her thoughts.

"What was that about?" Keane's voice came from the darkness, and Reina was startled. She had forgotten his presence.

"I don't know," Reina replied, and her eyes looked up at him in hopes of finding comfort, "I just needed to touch her."

Keane's eyebrow darted up at her in silent judgment, "Touch her?"

Reina let loose a breath. She had to tell him. "You know that woman she was talking about? The one that was visiting cells?"

"It was you."

Reina was taken aback by the statement. "How do you know?"

"I wasn't born yesterday, Rein. Her friend shows up covered in lashes but is magically healed? I don't know about you, but I don't know many people with healing capabilities." He crossed his arms.

"You don't know many people at all," Reina grumbled, but Keane's eyes darkened. He wasn't in the mood for bantering. She threw her hands up, irritated. "I couldn't help it, okay? Something inside me made me help her. I had no choice. And the same thing happened again just now. I don't know why I needed to touch her, but I had no choice. Something inside me made me do it."

"You always have a choice, Reina. We agreed that you'd never play with your ability. That you'd never practice it. It's too dangerous. You could have been caught, and you still might be.

If the girl you healed can't keep her mouth shut, people will start asking questions. You never think anything through. Just charge in without a second thought." He raised his voice as he spoke, and Reina glanced back at the guard's chambers in fear they would emerge.

"I'm not a child, Keane," she stated.

"Then stop acting like one."

"I helped someone. That's all I did. She would have died if I hadn't done something, and I don't regret it. If you think that's me acting like a child, then so be it." Her skin was vibrating in anger. "But that's not the point. That woman," she pointed at the stairs the woman had just escaped up, "when we touched, something happened. There was some sort of energy that flew out of me and into her. You saw her face. You heard her. *Something happened.*"

Keane shook his head. "It doesn't matter. You need to stop this now before you get yourself killed."

There was a movement from within the darkness, and she jerked her head to see what it was. But she was greeted with nothing but blackness. Keane started to say something, but she lifted her hand into the air to signal him to be quiet. She could hear a soft shuffling sound from just outside her cell. She crept forward slowly, but she couldn't see anything that could be the cause of the noise.

"What are you doing?" He asked, and Reina shushed him again. She could feel eyes on her, but she couldn't pinpoint where they were coming from. The weight of the gaze felt awful on her skin, and goosebumps began to appear on her arms.

"Do you hear that?" She whispered, and the sound stopped suddenly. The feeling of being watched slowly dissipated, and Reina looked around in confusion. Her head pressed against the bars to peer down the aisle of the cell block. She still couldn't see what had caused the sound.

"Hear what?" Keane replied, and Reina heard the sound of his bars creaking as he leaned his weight against them. She sighed and shook her head. She could have sworn something was there.

"Nothing," she started as she began to turn back to Keane, "It must have been a-." Her voice halted immediately, and her eyes grew in surprise as a large shadow stood between her and Keane. The ground rushed up to meet her as she tripped over her feet. She pushed herself across the cell and further away from the thing that stood before her. "What is that?" She whispered into the air.

"What is what? There's nothing there Reina, what are you doing?" His question passed through the shadow, and Reina felt goosebumps reappear on her skin under the scrutiny of its gaze. It had no eyes, but she knew she was being watched closely. The shadows swirled around formed in the shape of a human, and its head slowly cocked to the side.

"It's right there. How can you not see it?" The question squeaked out of her, and her hands trembled against the ground beneath her. It slowly moved closer to where she sat, and she pushed herself farther back until she felt the stone wall behind her refuse any more movement.

"Reina, I swear to you there's nothing there. What are you seeing?" As the shadow drew itself tall and halted at her outstretched feet, Keane's words faded into the background. Her heart thundered wildly in her chest, and her breathing became shallow. She felt her fear coil itself around her neck, and it felt as though she were suffocating. The shadow stood quietly. It towered over her, the height of two grown men. Keane still spoke in the distance, but she couldn't hear him anymore over the sound of her blood as it rushed through her body.

Slowly, she clenched her jaw and allowed herself to stand on shaky legs. As she grew, her eyes stayed latched to the head of the creature and refused to look away. When she was at full height, she stilled. The shadow and Reina stared directly at each other in the silence of the cell block. There was nothing there but the two of them, and Reina steeled her eyes and squared her shoulders. As the seconds ticked by, the shadow began to laugh.

The sound was feminine and manic. Reina felt as if she were drowning in the noise as it filled her head, but still, she stood tall. The laughter grew louder, and Reina brought her hands up to cover her ears. However, it was no use as the laughter was not in the air around her but within her own head.

When Reina thought she couldn't take it anymore, the shadow dissipated into the darkness. She looked around, afraid the shadow would reappear before her or stand in the dark just out of sight. But she couldn't feel its piercing gaze anymore, and the laughter was only an echo in her mind.

When she was confident that the shadow had left, she turned back to Keane, who stared in concern. "What was that about?" He breathed, and Reina opened her mouth to reply.

Before she could say anything, her mind flashed back to the secrets he kept from her. She gave him a shrug, "I don't know what you're talking about. There was nothing there." Keane scowled and opened his mouth to chastise her.

Reina turned away from him before anything more could be said. The lack of trust on his part had made Reina hesitant to share any more about herself than she had to. As she walked away from Keane and deeper into her cell, she tried to hide the trembling of her legs.

10

MALYSSANDRA

Malyssandra slurped at her cold soup absentmindedly. It had been two days since she had been to Den Zei, but the thoughts that had taken up space within her head had shown no signs of leaving. Her arm tingled in remembrance of Reina's hand on her skin. The strange vision weighed heavily on her mind, and her eyes gazed out distractedly at the encampment through the window.

I have never met the king in my life, Reina's words echoed loudly in her head. It made no sense to Malyssandra. She had seen Reina clear as could be, standing over the king. It was almost as if she had been there with them. She shook her head, baffled by the experience. She believed Reina though, the look on her face hadn't been once of secrecy. The woman meant it when she said she had never been to the palace. *But I saw it,* the thought refused to be tucked away.

A frustrated sigh sounded from Malyssandra's lips, and as she jolted her attention to the room around her, she noticed it had been quiet for quite some time. The other maids had left to continue their chores for the day, and Malyssandra felt panic rise within her as she realized that she had been looking out the window during lunch for way longer than she should have allowed. She hastily made her way back to the kitchen to drop off her half-eaten bowl of soup and scooped more rotted meat into her apron.

Her nerves got the best of her as she headed toward the eastern sector. Her eyes darted through the darkness in search of anything that could have been hidden within. It didn't matter how many times she looked to the same darkened area; she remained just as flighty as she had been when looking at it seconds before. She hadn't seen the shadow figure since that night in the basement, but it still haunted her as she moved into the darker sector of the palace.

In an attempt to distract herself from her growing fear, she forced herself to think of the kingdom as she had been taken through it. She longed to be outside again under the blistering sun. Years in the palace had made her forget what it was like to be out in the open. It had been magical, even if it hadn't been her own kingdom. The people had seemed happy, truly happy. It was an emotion that Malyssandra missed, and she couldn't remember the last time real happiness had graced her. The world outside had been so busy, but not in the mundane way Malyssandra had grown accustomed to. It was chaotically busy. As if the people within the kingdom had so much to do but didn't know where to start. As she sat down to begin her work on the rat traps, she found herself wishing her life was less repetitive and more unpredictable.

The idea of never knowing where to start her morning appealed greatly to her. She loved the idea of all the wild possibilities that filled the air out in the kingdom. The randomness of the world seemed like a blessing to Malyssandra, a blessing that was not hers to have. As the traps stared back at her, taunting her with eternity, she exhaled in defeat. She tilted her head back to combat the knots in her neck, and the world faded away.

She was in the cellblock. An intense quiet filled her head as she looked around in confusion. Keane stood by the bars of his cell, a smile on his face. He was speaking with someone, having what looked to be a pleasant conversation.

Malyssandra felt as if she were intruding on something private. The bars he leaned against were shared with Reina's, but Malyssandra couldn't see Reina from where she stood. She slowly began to move across Keane's cell, her curiosity beating out her feeling of eavesdropping.

As she made it to the bars, she peaked inside. Her throat closed up in disbelief as her stomach clenched. It wasn't Reina inside the cell. The woman was small, the dark skin of her cheeks flushed as she laughed at whatever Keane had just said.

Malyssandra shook her head as she realized she was staring at herself. Locked in a cage at Den Zei.

Malyssandra gasped as she was brought back to herself, and she dropped the rat trap from her grip. She looked around the archive room in shock at what she had just seen in hopes of finding an answer that wasn't there. It had happened again. She had been in Den Zei.

Her hand hurriedly reset the other traps, attempting to distract herself from the image of her within a cell. She moved into the chapel and lifted up the stairs without a thought spared to her actions.

No matter how hard she tried, she couldn't shake the vision that had flashed through her mind. It had seemed so real. With trembling hands, she finished resetting the rat traps and briskly walked out of the chapel.

As she gained distance from the eastern sector, the noise of conversation slowly settled around her. Her nervousness still trailed closely behind her, and she watched all who passed with suspicion. She wondered if she looked as fanatical as she felt.

Nobody spared her a glance, and she slowly made herself push the paranoia that had ascended within her to the back of her mind. In the palace, she was invisible. Nobody cared to look closely enough to see the frantic look in her eyes.

She followed the halls to the kitchen and ducked back into the maid's quarters, where the other maids were settling in for the night. Her ability to go unseen quickly vanished, and she felt all of the maids' eyes on her as she threw her apron into the bin and headed toward her cot. Clouds filled the sky beyond the window, and as she laid down in bed to ponder what had happened within the archives, she realized she could not see Den Zei in the distance.

. . .

Malyssandra woke to the sound of whispered gossip in the air, and her eyes peaked open into the faint light of early morning. The sky outside was young, and only the faintest rays of the sun peaked through the horizon to tinge the room a soft blue. The maids stood about in a small gathering, and Malyssandra rubbed sleepily at her eyes as she stood to make her way over to them.

"Yeah, but how ill *is* he?" A red-haired maid whispered quietly into the group, and an older maid looked at her incredulously.

"I don't know, I wasn't allowed *in* the room," she answered and rolled her eyes at having been asked the question in the first place. Malyssandra's stomach churned, and her sleep-fogged brain quickly became alert as she neared the conversation. "All I saw were nurses coming in and out. I didn't stick around and ask any questions. I just finished the floors and left. There were a lot of nurses, though. It has to be pretty bad."

The vision of Reina as she stood over the king replayed in her head, and as Malyssandra came to a halt by the group, her voice came out dazed, "Has the king fallen sick?" All heads turned to her in unison, and she shifted uncomfortably between her feet. They had been so caught up in their whispers that they hadn't even noticed Malyssandra as she walked nearer to them. When the shock fell from their faces, they went back to their whispers without answering Malyssandra's question. She looked on at them uncertainly but inhaled deeply before she pushed farther, "Is he bedridden?"

The heads snapped back at her, but that time they seemed annoyed by the disturbance. The red-headed maid sneered at Malyssandra in response as the older woman looked at her and flippantly said, "Why don't you ask your prince? I'm sure he knows more than us anyway."

Malyssandra felt her face heat up at the comment, and she pinched her lips together to draw them in a straight line. Her eyes sparkled in embarrassment, and some of the maids chuckled at what the older woman had said. She lowered her eyes to the floor, and the maids continued their conversation.

"The prince requests your company." Malyssandra looked up sharply at the words, and the maids stopped speaking. A guard stood in the doorway, his eyes locked on her. She nodded and moved to follow.

When they arrived at the prince's chambers, Prince Ferix pulled the door open before the guard could even knock. He gave the guard a sharp nod of dismissal and motioned for Malyssandra to enter.

Once the door was shut, he turned back to say something, but Malyssandra cut in, "Is your father ill?" His eyes lit up in shock, and Malyssandra's cheeks grew hot as she realized what she had just done. "I'm sorry, your majesty. I don't know what went through me right then. It won't happen again." She lowered herself into a deep curtsey, and the prince approached.

"It's quite alright. I just wasn't expecting it. Please, stand. There's truly no need for that." Malyssandra slowly stood up and kept her eyes glued to the floor. "Yes, my father is sick. How did you hear that?"

She pondered if she should say anything about the other maids' gossip but decided she didn't much care to keep it a secret. "The maids knew about it. I heard them speaking this morning."

The prince nodded thoughtfully. "Would you like any tea?" He turned and walked to a small table he had set in the corner, a tea kettle placed in the middle.

"No, thank you, your majesty."

"I really do wish you'd stop calling me that." He poured himself a cup of tea. "You went to Den Zei yesterday?"

"How did you-?"

"I pay attention. Did you see Ivanka?"

Malyssandra gave a polite nod. The prince lifted a spoon from the sugar jar and stirred some into his tea before he took a tentative sip.

"How is she?" His voice seemed genuinely worried, and Malyssandra furrowed her brows.

"She looked okay. There were no lash marks on her body, your majesty. I thought you said they had taken the whip to her."

Prince Ferix froze with the cup to his mouth. He looked up at her in confusion. The storms in his eyes began to wake up. "They did; I saw it with my own eyes. That's impossible." Malyssandra looked back to the ground.

"She told me she was healed by a woman. That the world turned golden, and that when the woman touched her, she had been healed. It doesn't make any sense. I believe she's gone mad, your majesty." It was all she could do to stand still. She felt fidgety. The king was ill, and Malyssandra had seen it before it happened. But she had seen Reina with him, and Reina was in Den Zei. It had to of been a coincidence. Malyssandra couldn't see the future. That was impossible.

The prince set down his cup. "Perhaps, or maybe, she's telling the truth." Malyssandra's head snapped up, and she looked at him in disbelief, but he wasn't paying her any attention. He was lost in deep thought.

"Your majesty, all due respect, I really don't think-."

"I have something I need to do. You are excused." He stood up and walked over to the door.

"I don't need to stay?"

"Not this time. If anyone asks, just say something urgent came up I needed to take care of." He opened the door and looked at the guard beyond. "Can you escort her back to the maids' quarters?"

"Of course, my prince." The guard bowed, and Malyssandra moved through the open door with her head buzzing. She didn't understand what had just happened. Had she said something wrong? She turned back to apologize to the prince, but he had already closed the door.

The entire walk back to the maids' quarters, Malyssandra felt locked in a dangerous game she didn't know how to play.

11

REINA

Days had passed since Reina had seen the shadow, and exhaustion had taken up residence within her. Sleep had not been easy within the darkness of her cell. She was ready for the creature to rear itself in front of her again, and she was afraid of what would happen if she weren't prepared. Small sounds would startle her to her feet, and she would look about frantically before she would realize it had simply been a rat or another person within their cell. The darkness had never been something Reina had feared before. It seemed strange to Reina to fear something so natural, something nobody could escape from. It hadn't even occurred to her to be afraid of the dark until she had stared into it and found that it could stare back.

Occasionally she would find Keane's dark eyes on her in the dim light, and she noted the concern etched into his brow. She longed to speak with him, but her anger still sat fresh on the surface of her mind, and she refused to let it go.

He knew better than to reach out to her, so instead, he stood protectively within his cell. There was a sort of comfort that came with the knowledge that he watched over her, although she would never admit it out loud.

The blistering heat took the breath from her lungs as she stepped into the yard, and she wiped her arm across her forehead at the sweat that appeared within seconds. She hauled herself over to the lineup and yearned for the dampness of her cell.

"Sewage control," The guard mumbled as he walked by, and she wondered how hot he was under his armor. The metal had to be hot to the touch under the persistent sunlight, and she didn't know how the guards kept from being baked alive within. She imagined they would have blisters along their arms when they took the metal plates off at night, and she looked curiously at other guards for any signs of pain as she made her way to the wagon.

She settled within the center of the old wood and closed her eyes against the light of the day. For a split second, she thought she would doze off right there, where she felt safe from the shadow that had haunted her thoughts over the past few days. However, as the wagon lurched forward, she felt eyes on her. A quiver ran down her spine as she slowly turned her head in fear of seeing darkness beside her. What she saw was entirely different.

A woman with deep blue eyes and pale blonde hair stared at her in a look of amazement. Recognition ignited in Reina's brain, and her eyes flew open. Immediately, she felt awake in the sunlight as the girl she had healed looked on at her in wonder. Reina gave her head a sharp shake in fear the woman would say something that could draw the guard's attention. She simply stared back in silence.

Reina blinked slowly as she inspected the woman's youthful face. Her skin was smooth along her cheekbones which elegantly protruded from her face, but redness burned deep from the few days she had spent in the sun. Reina imagined those raised in the palace didn't get outside much, and she felt poorly for the girl as splotches of burns riddled her skin. Her hair was long, although knots had begun to tangle it upwards toward her scalp. It was so blonde it looked much like what Reina imagined snow did. Nearly white, it reflected the sun. Her eyes were sapphire and held a deep sadness.

The wagon came to a halt, and Reina looked around in surprise at having already arrived at the dump. She hadn't noticed the time that passed as the wagon meandered beyond the wall to the outskirts of the forest. She shook her head to get a grip on her thoughts and threw her legs over the edge of the wagon before she launched herself off.

She grabbed a shovel and made her way past the ditch and to the dump itself. The trees on the outskirts of the forest provided shade, and the heat of the day was sure to drive her crazy if she didn't have some form of relief. Her eyes skidded over the ditch and noted that the stream of liquefied waste had dried into the ground. There was no movement to push the excrement into the dump, and Reina wondered what they were supposed to do if there was nothing to maintain. As the other slaves made their way to the ditch, their expressions echoed the same thought. Everyone looked to the guards.

The admiral made his way through the crowd of people in annoyance and looked down at the dried-up ditch. He stared in silence for a moment, and Reina could see the gears that turned in his head. Suddenly, he looked up at the people around him and shouted, "Get to work. There's still digging to be done!" The slaves quickly complied and took to burrowing the ditch deeper into the ground. Reina shook her head at the knowledge that it would be harder to manage if they dug it deeper. Their shovels wouldn't be able to reach the bottom of the ditch anymore.

As Reina began to dig at the rugged ground, she felt a presence beside her. She looked over to once again see the woman from the wagon. When they locked eyes, the woman whispered, "Thank you." Reina gave a slight nod and turned back to the ground. The feeling of the woman's gaze still clung to her, and Reina's attention flitted back up.

"Don't stand too close. They'll see," Reina muttered and nodded in the direction of the guards. The woman's face darkened with fear, and she moved away from Reina's side without another word. The dirt in front of Reina refused to give. She put all of her weight into the shovel as she brought the spade down harshly.

The day wore on slowly, and they were called in for water and bowls of brown gunk. As Reina was handed her water bowl, she noticed the pathetic amount of liquid that sloshed around within. Her eyes skimmed the ground back to the ditch, and she wondered how many more days of water the kingdom had to spare for the people of Den Zei. As the clear warm fluid hit the back of her throat, she sighed in relief and wished for more. Instead, she was handed a bowl of spongey brown food and forced herself to swallow it.

She went back to work and allowed herself to check on the woman from the wagon. Her stomach knotted at the sight of the woman's hands. The shovel's wooden handle had torn blisters open on her skin, and fresh blood appeared on the shaft before it dried up in the heat of the day. Reina supposed being a slave within the palace didn't require people to have calluses on their palms. It was likely softer work, and as Reina looked up at the other new faces that had joined Den Zei over the past week, she noticed their hands hadn't fared too well either. Her jaw clenched.

A noise sounded from the forest behind her, and she jerked around. She wasn't sure if she was afraid to see a shadow loom over her or if she was excited at the possibility of seeing the person that had appeared within the thicket before. It didn't matter, as nothing stood hidden in the trees. A grunt of disappointment emitted from her as she jammed the shovel back into the ground.

The sun went down as the day progressed, and soon they were loaded back onto the wagon. Reina regarded the woman as she came to sit in front of her and spared a sidelong glance. "Ivanka." The name floated from the woman's mouth, and Reina looked around before she dared to speak.

"Reina," she responded. Ivanka's eyes sparkled in the fading light of the day as the wagon moved forward and left the stench of the sewage dump behind.

No more words were said between them as they traveled away from the forests and back through the kingdom's wall. Reina appreciated the silence, and she felt a familiar fear creep up inside her as they neared the cell blocks of Den Zei.

Keane stood near the bars they shared and gave her a soft look as she walked by him into the center of her small space. The door shut her in moments later as the guards closed them in for the night. She felt Keane's unspoken words float through the air as he watched her settle down into the spot they both knew she wouldn't be able to fall asleep in that night.

A small part of her wished he would say something, even if that something was the start of an argument. But his voice never scraped across the stone around them, and she knew as the sound of his weight settled against the bars that nothing would be said between them that night. He would sit in silence and watch over her as she tried to force sleep to take her. It never did, though, and they both sat awake in the deafening stillness as they waited for daylight to break.

. . .

The following day Reina was placed on beams with Keane. She avoided his eyes as the wagon rumbled over potholes and watched as the distant city grew a little closer on the horizon. She pondered what it was like within the kingdom's streets. If the people of Yulsa believed it to be as magical as she used to think Crieda was. If they knew how lucky they were to still have a home. The thought brought sadness to Reina's heart, and she looked away from the far-off buildings.

When she slid off the wagon, she heard the soft crunch of dead grass beneath her feet. The cloudless sky taunted her as she looked up at it and yearned for pregnant clouds to rain down on her scorched skin. She felt as though the gods were laughing at her misfortune and gave a foul glare into the sun before she made her way to line up for her team assignment.

Her eyes scanned the area as she got paired with a group of Criedans she faintly recognized from her years at Den Zei. She spotted Keane as he walked off toward a beam with slaves she hadn't seen before, and she hoped he could help them through the day. A soft grunt sounded from behind her, and she turned to see an older man assigned to her team motion for her to hurry up. She nodded and followed after him as they made their way over to the beams.

The man grabbed the rope that hung down and tied it to the metal in front of them, and when he was done, they began to heft it up. The closeness of the woman who stood behind Reina made the world feel hotter, more suffocating.

She became light-headed as the day rolled on, and she felt as though she were going to vomit onto the scorched earth beneath her feet. With shaking limbs, she pulled at another rope and then another. There was no end in sight, and she was afraid she would pass out from exhaustion when a loud shout startled her, and she spun around. Her team grunted in protest as more weight fell on them, but Reina paid them no mind.

She watched as a beam that had become untied in midair fell rapidly toward the earth. It was likely someone hadn't tied it right, and the loose knot had slipped under the weight of the heavy metal. There was a hollow thud as it connected with the ground, and Reina flinched as she noticed a body had been crushed beneath it.

One of the team members looked as if they were going to be sick, and Reina's eyes squinted at the individual for a moment before her heart sank in her chest. She frantically scanned the faces of the people in the team in search of one person but failed to find him. In horror, she watched as the beam was lifted from the body, and Keane lay motionless in the dirt.

Air ceased to fill her lungs, and a feeling of panic rose within her chest and built slowly. She felt as if she were about to explode as guards moved forward to grab Keane's body and drag him out of the way. Reina's head swiveled back and forth at the people who didn't seem to care that a man had been injured, and as the guards put their hands under Keane's arms to pull him away, Reina felt a scream burst from her chest.

"*No!*"

Heads snapped to watch her as her feet carried her swiftly over to the men who held Keane, and the world blurred past Reina's eyes as she focused on his body. Guards moved from their places to interfere with her path, but she dodged around them and slid across the dry grass as she came to Keane's side and grabbed his arm.

Please, she begged. Nothing happened as she stared in horror at Keane's limp arm. She didn't know who she was pleading with, but she didn't know what else to do. When she had grabbed Ivanka's shoulder in the cell that night, she immediately healed her. There hadn't been a stalling period. It had just simply happened.

Her hand shook vigorously at Keane's arm as a guard came up behind her and pulled his whip out from his belt. Distantly she felt the burn as it lashed against her back, but it was barely noticeable amidst her panic. *Please*, she thought again and her vision blurred as tears filled her eyes. A lump formed in her throat, and her breathing became uneven around it. She felt as though her airway was closing up, and she couldn't breathe. Still, nothing happened.

She felt a guard grab her by her arm, and she gave an animalistic snarl in response. The guard tugged at her, but as she was lifted away, she refused to let up on her death grip around Keane's arm. His body was already bruised a deep purple, and she couldn't tell if he was breathing or not. She wondered if he was dead. If that was why she wasn't able to heal him.

No, she thought harshly to herself, *look, right there. His eyes fluttered. He's alive.* Reina's heart sped up, and it felt as though it were going to rip free from her chest. The guard gave another tug, and she felt her hand slipping as the guards that held Keane began to try and pull him away from her. She closed her eyes against the hectic world around her and focused on the burning in her back. The pain flared up as she became hyper-focused on it, and a scream tore from her throat.

It was a scream that held all of the torment she had endured over the past eleven years. It echoed the lives she had seen lost within the walls of Den Zei and the walls that had crumbled around her kingdom. The screams of thousands filled the air around her as she pushed their pain through her lungs and into the world. Pain had been all she had known since her life had been taken from her. It had followed her to the kingdom of Yulsa as she walked days in chains to get there.

She had seen the worst of the world and held out hope that things could change throughout her life. The belief that she could help change it had sat within her for so long that the realization she might have been wrong tore open her heart as her voice gave life to the tragedy that had befallen her people. She was the embodiment of agony, and she knew if she couldn't save the only friend she had in that gods forsaken place, she would let the pain win. She would succumb to the harsh truth that the world couldn't change, and she would watch herself wither away into nothingness within a dark cell under the earth.

The guards lightened their grip on her arm in shock at the noise that sounded from her mouth, and her hands tightened back around Keane's skin as she felt herself drop closer to the ground. The scream turned into a heart-wrenching sob, and the guards moved back to grab her. Before they could do so, Reina felt something break open within her.

Her body jerked back as energy flooded within. The world around her began to glow bright gold as the circle on her shoulder illuminated the space in which Reina kneeled. Her eyes widened in wonder at how vibrant the light was. Even in the darkness of the cell, it had never been so bright. The skin of her back mended itself as the energy within her caused her body to hum with power. It sped down her arm and through her hand to Keane's bruised body. He jolted once as energy filled him and his bruises began to disappear. His natural color slowly returned, and his chest expanded as his ribcage fused itself back together. His shoulders grew broad once again as the bones snapped back into place, and his head rocked to the side to show his eyes were slowly opening.

Another sob escaped Reina's lips as his confused brown eyes met hers, and she smiled in relief as the light around them began to dim. He opened his mouth to say something, but nothing came out. His speechlessness caused Reina to let out a sudden laugh through her tears, and a soft smile spread across Keane's face.

The world around them stood still in stunned silence. The guards looked unsure of themselves, and the slaves watched on in wonder. Reina couldn't imagine what they made of what they had seen, and her stomach dropped at the knowledge of what she had just done. Her face morphed into one of fear as she looked deep into Keane's eyes, and understanding dawned on his face.

"No," he rasped out in a panicked whisper and broke the silence that had settled around them. The guards who had stood stunned seconds earlier quickly took action and moved forward to seize Reina by the arms again. Her eyes looked into the crowd of slaves, begging them to do something. But they shrunk away from her as the guards dragged her past.

"No!" Keane's voice grew louder as he tried to climb to his feet, but the guards who stood behind him tackled him to the ground.

Reina watched helplessly as she was roughly pulled away from the beams, and Keane's body grew smaller as he thrashed beneath the guards. "Reina!" He shouted after her, and as she struggled against the men who held her. She felt like the same little girl who had tried to fight the grip of a conqueror eleven years ago.

As she was chained to the wagon that had brought her there that morning, she watched as the beams faded in the distance and swore she could still hear Keane's faint voice echoing after her.

12

REINA

The chains around Reina's wrists cut deep and rattled aggressively as the guards pushed her through the palace entrance. The journey through the kingdom had been filled with terrifying thoughts and strange looks from the armored men. Everything had happened so quickly that Reina felt as though she wasn't able to fully comprehend the severity of what had occurred.

It had been a long ride as the wagon bumped repetitively over the brick streets, and the sun had slowly made its way across the sky. Reina realized as her feet stumbled through the palace doors that Keane would likely have made his way back to his cell by then. She wondered what he was doing. If he stared emptily into her uninhabited cell while she was forced into the lair of the man who had caused their lives to collapse.

As the entrance passed overhead, she was presented with the prestigious existence inside the palace walls. A large golden hallway welcomed them in as a tiled walkway directed them deeper into the castle. Paintings of people who must have been held in high regard stared at her in judgment as she shuffled past. Torches lit the way as the light disappeared outside and caused the windows to be of no use. Casual conversations stopped as the people who lived within the palace gawked at the thin, dirt-stained woman that looked around with terror-crazed eyes. It was an entirely different world than Reina was used to, and she had never seen anything so overly dramatic in her life.

The guards led her into a large open area that broke off in many directions. Reina felt small within the overwhelming space, and the guards said nothing as they took a sharp right turn and tugged at the excess chain that hung from her hands.

She watched as the walls closed in and the hallway became thinner. The number of people slowly lessened until it was just her and three guards. The sound of their footsteps mixed with the jingle of her chains, and as they came to the top of a dark stairwell, Reina felt a chill at the base of her neck.

One of the guards took a torch from the sconce on the wall and motioned for the others to follow. Reina tried to put up some resistance as they yanked on her chain to drag her into the darkness, but she was tired, and all she could give was a pathetic tug. The guard who held her chains looked back at her in annoyance and gave the metal line an overpowered jerk. Reina's feet barely caught her as she started to fall down the steep steps before her.

With trembling legs, she gave in and slowly descended the steps with the light of the torch to guide her. The air became cooler the further they went, and as Reina's arm brushed against the wall, she noted the moisture that covered her skin. It reminded her slightly of the third level of Den Zei, and she felt strangely homesick for her cell.

As they reached the bottom, they came upon a small gate in the stone wall, and the leading guard pulled out a key. A loud creak resounded as it swung open, which caused Reina to flinch. Her nerves were on edge, and the epic blackness that creeped just out of reach of the light scared her. The sound of moans filled the air, and Reina looked about rapidly. A rat ran across her toes, and she jumped into the air with a slight squeak that made the guards look back at her in irritation.

They continued deeper into the darkness. When they halted, the guard held his torch up and illuminated a set of bars. Reina's stomach sank as she realized she was in the castle prison. She didn't know where she had expected to be taken, but the prison hadn't even crossed her mind. She had done nothing wrong.

Keys jingled loudly as the guard brought a ring full of them toward the door, and the sound of the cell as it unlocked echoed down the corridor they had come through. The man pushed the door open, and Reina felt hands at her back throw her forward and into the darkness. She scrambled to get up and run back to the door as she heard it slam shut.

"Please don't leave me here," she begged them, but they paid her no mind. They turned to walk away, and as the light grew smaller in the distance, Reina screamed, *"Please!"* The gate at the base of the stairs creaked again, then crashed closed. The distant light faded completely from Reina's view, and she was left staring into a void.

She thought she had known of the dark her whole life, but she had been wrong. Within Den Zei, she could see shapes and outlines, and sometimes, if the moon hit something just right, she could see it all. She and Keane had harnessed the light of the moon throughout their time in Den Zei, and they had used it to see each other when the sun went down. There was no faint moonlight within the prison. It was just blackness that threatened to swallow her whole.

She couldn't catch her breath, and she stumbled around with her hands outstretched in front of her. The need for a wall to lay against rose within her. She needed something solid and steady to ground her. Without it, she felt as though she would be lost wandering in the darkness forever.

When her trembling hand jammed into the moist rock, her palms flattened against it in relief. She slowly spun her body around to place her back against it, and she felt the fabric of her shirt dampen. Bile rose in her throat, and she hunched over to the side as she expelled whatever contents she had in her stomach. She didn't have much within her to give up, and soon she was dry heaving into the nothingness around her.

When she was done, she shakily righted herself against the wall and stared into the void. Goosebumps rose on her arms, and the hair on the nape of her neck rose as she felt the void stare back. Eyes she couldn't see tore through her, and she closed her eyes tight as she pushed herself hard against the wall.

"Go away," she pleaded, "I don't know what you are or why you're here but please, just leave me alone." The shadow was back. She couldn't see it, but she knew the feeling. It had haunted her mind for days, and she had dreaded the idea of its return.

She felt a soft caress at her leg, and she jerked it closer to her body. There was nowhere to go. The idea of moving through the darkness to escape the creature scared her more than sitting with her back to the wall. So she stayed and felt as the shadow grew closer to her. A soft breeze caressed her cheek, and her head lurched away from it. Then, it was gone.

She tightened her arms around her knees. There had been no laughter from the being like there had been before. It had simply watched her, and for some reason, that knowledge unsettled her more.

She didn't know how much time had passed when she heard the creak of the door at the end of the hall. A small light bobbed through the air until it illuminated the front of her cell. She scurried forward as a guard threw her door open. He grabbed her chains, and she righted herself quickly before he could give them a tug. Nothing was said between them as they walked together through the gate.

. . .

The palace was quieter than it had been when Reina entered it. Most people were likely asleep at that hour of the night, and Reina caught glimpses of the moon as she passed by the large windows which adorned the castle. The torches on the walls flickered as she followed the guard. She watched as the scenery around her became more elegant, and she wondered where she was being taken. The doors along the walls stretched taller, and more space slowly grew between them.

They stopped at a large wooden door at the end of a hall-way, and Reina stood muted as the guard raised his fist to knock. The thick wood absorbed the hollow thud, and the guard stood straight as he waited for an answer.

Slowly, the door was pulled open by a plump woman in white. When she looked to Reina, her eyes opened wide, and she quickly ushered them into a room more significant than any Reina ever could have imagined. The ceiling was a blue that re-minded Reina of the sky, and the walls held paintings of more people. A golden rug sat beneath a sizeable oaken bed, and atop that bed laid a man.

Multiple women in white shuffled around the room and stopped at the sight of Reina as she was dragged toward the bed. Confusion wrinkled her brow as her eyes connected with an el-egant woman who stood on the opposite side. Her dark hair cascaded over her shoulders, and her bright blue eyes glinted at Reina as if she had cried recently. Reina followed the line of the woman's arm to see it rested on the shoulder of the man who lay within the sheets of the bed.

His breathing was ragged, and sweat soaked the blanket he was tucked beneath. As Reina came to stand over the man, she opened her mouth to speak. "Who are you?"

The man's eyes flashed with anger. "How is it you don't know who I am?" His voice was weak. The scent of death caught a ride on his breath, and Reina scrunched her nose at the stench.

"I guess I don't get around much." She clasped her hands behind her back so the man wouldn't see them shake. Reina was out of her element, and she knew she had no control of the situation. She feared she had been brought there to die. But the scene she was presented with wasn't her death bed. It was a stranger in his.

Something hard collided with the back of her knees, and she fell to the ground. She turned to see the guard's face inches from her own, rage in his stare. "You will treat your king with respect!"

Reina's eyes bulged as she looked between the guard and the man on the bed. The king? That was who laid before her? She let out a harsh laugh. "He is not my king."

The guard lifted his hand, and Reina closed her eyes in anticipation of the blow. But it never came.

"*Stop.*" It was a demand, and as Reina peaked through her eyelids, she watched the guard lower his hand and straighten up. "Nurses, you are excused." The women in white curtseyed and scurried from the room. Reina shook her head and pulled herself upright.

She looked to the woman on the opposite side of the bed. The pieces clicked into place. If the king was on the bed, she had to be the queen. Reina recoiled in disgust. The queen stared on sympathetically, but Reina refused to meet her gaze. The people in that room were the cause of her kingdom's destruction. They had so much blood on their hands that they could never even imagine, yet they lived in such extravagance. It made her sick.

A faint croak rose from the bed as the king spoke into the unsettled air around them, "The guards told me of what you did for that man in Den Zei." Reina swung her head around to look at the king in horror. The sound as she swallowed the dryness in her throat was her only response. The king shifted himself slightly and tried to tilt his head up to better see her. "Is this true?"

Reina stood there in silence as the seconds ticked by, and she looked into the king's dull eyes. Whatever ailment he had was something the nurses couldn't heal, and his days were numbered. "Well?" His strained voice rose slightly; she gave a slight nod. "How?" He asked, and Reina looked down at his pale face. Her shoulders went up in response, and his eyes closed in exhaustion.

The room fell silent yet again, and Reina wondered if the king had fallen asleep. She looked up across the room at two large glass doors that led onto a balcony, and she yearned to be back within Den Zei. A strange hysteria rose inside her, and she fought to keep a smile from forming on her lips. She had never thought she would miss such a place. The strangeness of it was not lost on her. A hand bolted out from underneath the covers and grabbed Reina's arm right above her chained wrists. She yelped in surprise and looked down to see the king's frail hand on her skin. "Can you heal me?"

Reina was taken aback by the question, and she jerked her arm from the king's grip. "No."

The king's eyes narrowed. "Try."

"And why would I?" Reina's voice was defiant, and the queen's eyebrows darted up. Her gaze softened, and she looked down to the king's pathetic form in the bed.

The king sighed as if he were a disappointed father. "You must care for that boy quite a lot," he mused. The passive threat caused Reina's heart to thunder in her chest, and she squared her shoulders.

"I've cared for a lot of people," Reina growled, "Most are dead now."

The king's eyes sparkled in the light of the torches, and his chapped lips pulled into a smirk. "Wouldn't it be a shame if he joined them?"

Reina opened her mouth to reply, but the king cut her off.

"I think we've met an agreement." His voice became steely, and Reina flexed her fingers at her sides.

She looked around for an escape, but the guard stood behind her, blocking her exit. The queen looked up at her hopefully, and goosebumps rose on Reina's flesh at what she was about to do. She gave the king a curt nod. "Wonderful."

Reina reached out to place her hand upon the king's own. Her heart twisted at the thought of what she was about to do. The man who had enslaved her people was beneath her touch, and she was attempting to save his life. She wondered if she was making a mistake, if she would even be able to do what was asked of her. She hoped she wouldn't be. She hoped that she would fail and simply be executed at the hands of the guard behind her.

Almost immediately, though, she felt the power within her. Something that had been hard to grasp mere hours earlier was suddenly at her disposal. She remembered back to the feeling of something tearing open inside her as she desperately pleaded for the ability to save Keane's life. Whatever she had broken through was no longer a barrier. She had unlocked something deep inside her that controlled what she was able to do.

She gently tugged at the power within her core, and she felt as it slowly snaked down her arm and into the king's frail body. His skin began to darken into a healthier shade of peach, and his breathing slowly relaxed as if it were no longer difficult for him to draw air into his lungs. The body beneath the sheets began to fill out slightly, and his dark eyes became more lively. Reina watched on in horror as she healed the man who had caused her father's death. She loathed the moment, and she tore her hand from his as her power retreated back into the depths of her body.

The king sat up before her and looked around as if he had just woken up from a rejuvenating nap. He stared in awe and threw the sweat-stained covers to the side to stand in front of her. She took a few steps back and glared at him. The queen smiled softly in the background, and the king scanned Reina over in wonder.

"Have her taken to the finest guest room in the palace, and make sure she wants for nothing," he spoke to the guard without taking his gaze from Reina, "Ensure she's comfortable. She will be staying with us for quite some time." Reina's eyes flashed at him as the guard tugged once again at the chains around her wrists. She was pulled back to the door, but before they could exit, the king's voice sounded from behind them once again, "Lock the door, though. It'd be a shame if we lost such a valuable... resource."

The guard nodded and dragged Reina into the hallway beyond. She began to struggle against him, but he continued firmly down the maze of halls to another wooden door which he threw open and pulled her into. He quickly undid her chains, and before she could lunge at him, he slammed the wood shut in her face. The sound of the lock clicking filled the room, and she slammed her hands loudly against the door.

Her defeated sigh echoed in her ears as she spun around to face her new prison. It wasn't as large as the king's chamber had been, but it was still more space than Reina knew what to do with. The bed stood proudly beside a window that peered out high above the ground outside, and the golden-trimmed walls lay bare around her. An open door on her right led to a washroom, and the porcelain tub inside taunted her.

She brought shaking hands to her face and slid her back down the door. Within a few hours, her life had significantly changed, and she wondered again what Keane was doing within his small cell on the third level of Den Zei. The last time they had spoken, they had fought, and she yearned to tell him she was sorry. The argument seemed so small to her then. She questioned if he worried for her and hoped he didn't think her dead. Her head knocked quietly against the wooden door at her back, and silence filled the decadent room as Reina realized she had traded in one cell for another.

13

MALYSSANDRA

A Criedan from Den Zei had been brought to the castle. The news was everywhere. It had started as a whisper from the people who muddled the hallways, and by the time it had reached Malyssandra's ears, it had grown exponentially. Rumors were hard to stop within the palace once they started moving. There were many different versions of why the woman had been brought there. Some said that she was the Yulsan king's long-lost daughter from a past affair, while others stated that she had been a spy within Den Zei all along and had never truly been Criedan. One, in particular, had piqued Malyssandra's interest, though. She heard a maid within their quarters declare that the woman had healed a man with nothing more than a touch.

Malyssandra couldn't shake the memory from her head of Ivanka on the floor of her cell as she made the same statement. She wondered if it was just a coincidence, but a strange feeling within her wouldn't allow her to let it go. An inexplicable need to see the woman who had been brought to the palace fluttered within her, and she offered to bring dinner to her chamber that night. The other maids didn't argue, as they simply wanted to slide within their cots and go to sleep. Malyssandra didn't mind the late chore as she hadn't had a good night's sleep in over a week and figured she would rather go on a late jaunt through the palace than toss and turn within the suffocating darkness of the maid's quarters.

She arrived outside of the wooden door with a tray of roasted duck, and Malyssandra's mouth watered at the decadent smell as it entered her nostrils. A guard stood beside the door, and when he saw her arrive, he spun over his shoulder to quickly unlock it. He moved to the side and allowed Malyssandra to enter, slamming the door behind her as if he were afraid the woman inside would lunge at the opportunity to escape the divine room Malyssandra was faced with.

She scanned the area and was startled by the figure of the woman on the ground. Malyssandra's brow furrowed as she looked between the bed that looked unslept in and the body on the floor. She made her way across the room to set the tray upon the dresser beside the bed and crept slowly toward the woman.

Blonde hair was knotted about her head, and Malyssandra noted that she was still wearing the clothes given to slaves in Den Zei. Malyssandra's eyes trailed to the open door in the wall that led to a fully stocked closet that hadn't been utilized. Her feet stopped before the woman, and Malyssandra watched as the crumpled form slowly rolled over to look up at her. Shock registered on both of their expressions, and the woman sat up suddenly.

"You?" Malyssandra asked incredulously as she stared into Reina's eyes. She took an involuntary step back, and Reina brutishly pushed herself to her feet. Silence stretched between them and pulled tight as the seconds passed. Reina said nothing, and Malyssandra didn't know what to say other than, "You didn't sleep in your bed." The words sounded dumb out in the open, and Malyssandra's cheeks heated.

The skin on Reina's forehead wrinkled at the oddness of the question, and her mouth slowly opened to give birth to words. "I've slept on the ground for so many years. I guess it just didn't occur to me." She looked disdainfully at the soft bed. "Besides, it just seems wrong."

Malyssandra nodded in understanding, and the same uncomfortable silence filled the room. She looked around at anything other than the filthy woman and the air built with unspoken words that yearned to be given life.

"I healed Ivanka," Reina blurted out, and Malyssandra's head snapped back around to look at her with wide eyes. Her mouth fell open to interject, but Reina kept speaking, "I guess it doesn't matter if you know or not anymore. She wasn't crazy when she told you about the woman who had healed her. It was me. I did it. I don't know how I can do it, but I can. I've always been able to heal myself, and I didn't know I could heal others until I saw Ivanka flayed within her cell. That's why I'm here. They know what I can do."

"No, Ivanka wouldn't have told-?" Malyssandra started but was cut off by Reina's rushed voice.

"Ivanka didn't tell. I made a mistake, my friend was dying, and I had no choice. I had to heal him or let him die, and I healed him. The guards saw me do it, and they brought me here. They wanted me to heal the king." Reina's blue eyes flashed in exhausted rage and darted to the porcelain tiles beneath her callused feet.

"You saw the king," Malyssandra's breathed. She had seen it happen. Before Reina had even stepped foot in the palace, Malyssandra had seen her standing over the king's bed. She fidgeted. The realization weighed heavily on her mind. "Well," she cleared her throat, "Did you help him?" The question seemed pointless as Malyssandra felt she already knew the answer, and Reina nodded in confirmation. "Why?" She whispered.

Reina raised her chin to better show Malyssandra the regret that lived in her eyes as she stated, "They were going to kill him if I didn't." There was no need to ask Reina who they meant to kill as Malyssandra recalled the man who had stood in the cell beside Reina's. She gave a nod of understanding and knew she would have done the same if they had threatened Ivanka's life.

"What else are you able to do?" Malyssandra asked.

Reina stared at her in confusion. "What do you mean?"

"I've been seeing things," Malyssandra started, "Ever since you touched me, I've been seeing impossible things. I saw you with the king before it ever happened." She paused and decided not to offer up the vision she had of herself within Den Zei. "Did you do this to me?" She brought her arm in front of her face, so Reina was looking at the smooth dark skin she had touched. Reina shook her head in exasperation.

"I don't know," she explained, "I felt some sort of energy between when I grabbed you, but I've never felt that before. If I did do something, I don't know what it was. I just knew I needed to touch you. Something within me forced me to do so. It seemed important." Her eyes grew distant.

Goosebumps began to rise along Malyssandra's arms, and a sinister feeling settled in the air. Reina's eyes snapped back into the present. Fear transformed Reina's body as she hunched forward and looked around the room in a panic. Her eyes widened when they settled on something. Malyssandra knew what she would see when she followed Reina's gaze, and she felt her insides tremble as she turned her head to look.

The shadow sat in the corner of the room as torches flickered lazily around it. Darkness swirled, lively and unpredictable within the human shape it held. Malyssandra's hands grew slick with sweat, and she watched Reina's head snap around to look at her out of the periphery of her vision. "You can see it too." It was a statement, not a question. Malyssandra's stance had already shown Reina that it was true. "What is it?" Reina threw her voice at Malyssandra, and Malyssandra felt the familiar ball of terror rise within her throat.

She couldn't bring herself to speak in its presence. All she could do was raise her shaking shoulders in response to Reina's question as she stared in horror at the shadow as it moved toward them. Reina's form grew taller in the side of Malyssandra's sight. She stood before the darkness as it rose in front of them, and as Malyssandra cast her gaze to the floor, she could see Reina's rise to stare back into the eyeless creature.

A tendril of the living shadow shot out at Malyssandra's foot. She stumbled backward and tripped in surprise. Her eyes flew up to look directly at Reina, but she seemed to be locked in a battle of wills with the shaded mass. Malyssandra was paralyzed in place, and she held her breath. A soft tether of shadow reached out and ran itself along the side of Reina's face, and Reina stood frozen with steely eyes focused on the being. When it retracted itself from her skin, a breathy sigh filled the room, and it disappeared back to wherever it had come from.

Malyssandra laid on the ground, aghast at what had just played out in front of her. Reina's chest deflated, and she stared off into the distance in a look of petrification. Stillness hung heavy around them, and neither of them moved.

The sound of a knock on the door startled them, and Malyssandra jumped to her feet as the guard opened it and looked to Malyssandra expectantly, "Out," he declared, and Malyssandra began to stumble toward the door.

"Wait." Reina's voice filled the air, and the guard's attention snapped to her, "I need help in brushing these knots out of my hair." The man's eyes looked at Reina in annoyance and motioned for Malyssandra to continue out the door. "The king stated I was to want for nothing. Are you about to disobey his command?" Her voice was confident and filled the impressive space with her certainty. The guard's eyes flashed at her, but he gave a stiff nod before he closed the door. Malyssandra turned her shoulders to face Reina directly and stared in shock. Reina didn't skip a beat as she hurried into the washroom and motioned for Malyssandra to follow.

Malyssandra moved shakily after Reina's fleeting form and watched as Reina dug around within the cupboards to find a brush. Her hand went up victoriously when she discovered one, and she began to brush the knots painfully out of her blonde locks. Malyssandra lifted a confused eyebrow at the woman, and Reina scowled, "If my hair isn't brushed out by the time you leave, the guard will be suspicious," she paused, "And I can manage to brush it myself." Malyssandra nodded and sat on the edge of the tub as Reina's eyes locked on hers. "You saw it too, the shadow. Have you seen it before?" Malyssandra nodded in response. "Where?"

The lump in Malyssandra's throat slowly began to shrink, and she managed to squeeze a few words out around it. "The basement."

Reina bobbed her head, "I saw it once in Den Zei and then again in the prison. Do you know what it is?" Malyssandra shook her head, and Reina's jaw tightened, "So you don't know what it could want." She trailed off in disappointment.

"I didn't say that," she squeaked out, and Reina's eyes lightened as they looked to her in curiosity.

"What does it want?" Her words came out hopeful and fast, and she flinched as the brush tore at her hair painfully.

Malyssandra shrugged, "I don't know. I was just pointing out that I hadn't yet said that I didn't know." Reina's eyes darkened at her response, and Malyssandra stared back apologetically. A strange feeling of relief began to flood Malyssandra as she realized she hadn't been crazy. The shadow actually existed. Reina had seen it too. A part of her wondered if it was worse she had been proven sane, as that meant something had truly cornered her in the basement that night. Something she couldn't begin to understand.

The sound of the brush as it raked through Reina's hair fell over them as they both became lost in thought. Malyssandra watched distractedly as small golden strands that had been pulled from Reina's scalp rocked slowly through the air and settled on the ground at her feet. Unrest tugged at Malyssandra's insides as she sat there quietly and fiddled with the worn fabric of her apron.

She wondered faintly how many more days she had left to wear the article of clothing before she was whisked away to another kingdom. The trade had been pushed to the back of her mind with everything else that had happened, but she realized she had less than two months until she would be taken away from the palace.

Her head snapped up, and words burst from her mouth. "I have to tell you something." Reina's eyes focused on her, and Malyssandra drew a deep breath into her lungs. "The king made a deal with another kingdom across the Carnavan Sea, a trade. He gives them slaves, and they give him soldiers. He plans to conquer more kingdoms and enslave more people. It was announced at a party he held a little over a week ago. Representatives of that kingdom are set to arrive in a little over a month. He's going to send us away." The words blurted out of her in one breath, and Reina's eyes grew in horror.

"Keane," Reina whispered into the air, and her attention focused sharply on Malyssandra, "They deserve to know."

Malyssandra knew she spoke of the people within Den Zei, and she nodded in agreement. "It makes sense," Reina continued. "The king enslaved his own people. He must not have thought the number of Criedans left was enough to garner the number of soldiers he wants. He took his own people captive. He forced them into Den Zei a few days ago. They're a part of his trade."

Malyssandra gave a sad nod in response. Nobody was safe from the king, not even his own people.

Reina was lost in her own world. She furiously tugged at the knots in her hair, but it looked as if it was barely making a dent on the clumps in her head. She growled in frustration and stormed into her bedroom. Malyssandra rose to her feet and trailed after. She watched as Reina sat the brush on the tray of food that had likely grown cold, and she paced the floor.

"The king knows what I can do, so no matter what hell I raise in this castle, he won't send me back there." Her words were quick in the air, and Malyssandra didn't know if she was supposed to respond. "I can try to escape, but even if I succeed, there's no guarantee I will make it all the way to Den Zei. Someone needs to tell them. There might be time for them to fight back. Maybe if they knew what was coming, they'd be scared enough to do something, angry enough to rise up. If they all wake up, there's a small chance they could take the guards. A small chance is better than nothing. How can we-?" She stopped mid-sentence, and she turned to face Malyssandra. "I might not be able to get sent back there, but you can."

Malyssandra's heart stopped as she thought of herself in the dark cells of Den Zei, and she swallowed hard as she shook her head. "I don't know," she drawled out, and Reina's eyes hardened.

"More innocent people are going to die if nothing is done, do you understand that? Do you remember how many people died when we were transported here? Going over the seas will be even worse. Imagine how many people are going to be shoved into small boats. There are children in Den Zei; their lives will be forfeit. We have more people than ever now that the king has added his people to the cell blocks. It is the only time this can work. Please." Reina's eyes pleaded with her, and Malyssandra felt her heart sink, "If not for me, then do it for Ivanka."

Malyssandra knew Reina was right, and she felt the words come up from her chest before she even knew she was going to say them. "I'll do it." The quiver in her voice was prominent, but Malyssandra nodded her head in a promise to herself. She would get sent to Den Zei, and she would tell them of what awaited them. Malyssandra understood what she had to do and prayed she could bring herself to go through with it.

Reina's mouth stretched into a relieved smile, and she nodded her thanks at Malyssandra. "I will try to get out and help as soon as I can, but it's not going to be easy. Thank you for doing this." Malyssandra looked to the ground and turned to leave but stopped as Reina whispered, "Wait."

Malyssandra watched as Reina ran back to the washroom and walked out with scissors in her hands. Shock registered on her face as Reina took the scissors to her hair and aggressively chopped it. The knotted locks fell to the floor, and Reina didn't stop until hardly any hair remained on her head. Her eyes flashed at Malyssandra, and Malyssandra gave her a soft smile. She set the scissors down within the drawer of the dresser beside her bed and stood tall.

The lack of hair made Reina look strong in the flickering lights of the torches, and her sharp cheekbones stood proudly from her dirt-stained face. Shadows cut along her neck from her sharp jawline and made her look made from stone. Her collarbones jutted out against her taut skin, and she brought her hand up to feel the lack of hair at the head.

"What's your name?" Reina asked into the space between them.

"Malyssandra," she replied and knocked on the door for the guard to let her out of the chamber.

14

MALYSSANDRA

Malyssandra had gone to see the prince. She didn't know what else to do. If she needed to go to Den Zei, then she needed his help to not get herself killed in the process. Ivanka had trusted him, so she supposed she could as well.

As she neared his door, the guard outside grabbed for the sword's hilt at his waist. "Turn back," he warned.

"The prince requested my company?" Malyssandra attempted to sound meek and confused, her eyes glued to the ground at the guard's feet.

"The prince did no such thing. Turn back now." His voice boomed across the space between them, and Malyssandra's heart raced in her chest. She looked to the sheathed sword, then back to the ground.

"Of course, my apologies." She cursed herself for being so cowardly as she turned away from the guard. There was nothing that could be done, though. If the guard wouldn't allow her through, then she needed another plan.

When Malyssandra was halfway down the hall, she heard the door creak open. "Are you sending away my maid?" The prince chastised the armed guard, and a smile tugged at Malyssandra's lips. "Maid, didn't I summon you? Come back here this instant!"

As Malyssandra walked back to the prince's chambers, she heard the hurried apologies of the guard. The prince waved him off and slammed the door behind her as she entered. "Poor man is probably so confused," he mused.

Malyssandra looked at him hesitantly. She was in his room, but she didn't know how to explain what she needed him to do.

He looked at her expectantly. "To what do I owe this pleasure?"

"I need you to send me to Den Zei," she blurted, and his eyes widened.

"You need me to *what*? Why?" He moved over to the table in his room and leaned on the edge.

She chewed on her cheek, unsure how much she wanted to say. She settled with, "Ivanka is there. I need to make sure she's okay." She blinked. "Your majesty," she added.

He rolled his eyes at the title. "Absolutely not. I'm not putting another person in that damned prison. Besides, you already saw her. Or did you forget?"

"Ivanka is all I have," she expanded, "I can't stay here while she's in there. It doesn't feel right. Please."

Prince Ferix stared at her, his gaze hard. "You'll die in there."

She loosed a breath. "Maybe, but nonetheless, it's where I need to be right now." Malyssandra diverted her gaze to the floor, afraid of where her next words might take her. "If you don't send me there, I'll do it myself."

Silence. She looked up to see familiar storm clouds in the prince's eyes. They both knew if she took matters into her own hands, she would end up far worse than if the prince were in control of her exile.

"I don't like being lied to," he growled and walked toward Malyssandra. She took a step back. "Nor do I like being thought a fool. There's more to this than what you're telling me." The man that stood in front of her was the one she had seen that night at the party. She wondered if she had made a mistake in trusting him.

"Ivanka needs me," she whimpered, and the prince reined in his anger.

"Fine," he agreed, "but this isn't going to be fun for either of us. I can't just politely ask the guard outside my door to escort you to Den Zei. You're going to be lashed. It's going to hurt more than you can imagine. Then, you'll be transported to the cellblock where you'll lay on the cold, dirt-ridden ground and wish you had never asked me to do this." Malyssandra felt her stomach clench. "And you'll be put to work, no matter your injuries. Out in the sun all day with little to eat or drink. Is that what you want?"

He was trying to scare her. It was working.

But she needed to do it. She needed to go to Den Zei and warn the others. Reina was right: they needed to know. "I'm stronger than you think, your majesty."

He scoffed. "Let's hope so."

Then he began to shout.

"Guards! Guards!" The guard outside the door bolted into the room, followed by two more. "Seize her!" Immediately, rough hands were wrapped around her arms, and she was forced into an uncomfortable position on the ground. "Try to steal from me, and I'll show you what happens," the prince continued, and Malyssandra peered up at him from the floor. A shiver ran down her spine at his stare. He looked irate. "Guards, three lashes for her dishonesty."

Malyssandra's mouth went dry. He had truly meant it when he said she'd be lashed. She had never had the whip taken to her flesh before. The whites of her eyes were exposed as she watched a guard lift the whip into the air.

She cried out in agony as leather crashed against her skin. Her back was on fire. Tears ran freely from her eyes, and her body became soaked in sweat. Her breathing became shallow and uneven, and she felt as though she would never catch her breath again. And that was only the first lash.

As the whip came down again, her body spasmed. Her throat constricted and suffocated her scream. It was pain like she had never felt it. Like her skin had turned inside out, and molten gold had been poured onto her flesh.

When the final lash tore at her back, she vomited onto the floor. The guards pulled her up, and she heaved in protest as her skin pulled taught around the wounds. Her head spun, and her vision blurred as she tried to look up at the prince one last time.

All she saw was his form as he walked away.

"Take her to Den Zei. I don't want her to set foot in this palace ever again." That was it. There was no going back. The prince had just done what she had asked, but she didn't have it in her to feel grateful. Her head lolled to the side as the guards hefted her to her feet.

"Right away, your majesty," a guard said from somewhere far away.

She went in and out of consciousness as she was dragged through the palace. Faintly, she recognized the feeling of wood underneath her cheek as a wagon was pulled away from the castle. She wondered madly when the pain would disappear.

. . .

The entrance to Den Zei was a blur for Malyssandra. Shivers racked her body, and the guards pulled her from the wagon and through the doorway.

Her feet lightly grazed the stone steps as the guards descended into the earth with her in tow. The air grew colder, and she felt claustrophobic as she realized the reality of where she was. She moaned, and the guards ignored her as they continued down the stairs.

When there were no more steps to take, the guards unceremoniously dropped her into an empty cell, and the solid thud of her body as it hit the rocks echoed in the darkness around her. A soft hiss emanated from her mouth. Seconds later, the sound of the cell door clicked shut behind her.

She carefully lowered herself onto her stomach with trembling arms. It felt as if her back was eating itself. Everything she did pulled at the flayed skin, and she wondered how Ivanka could have survived after her entire body had been flayed. She imagined if Reina hadn't gotten to her when she did, her friend wouldn't have made it. Not when the pain was that raw.

A shuffle came from the cell beside her. She turned her head and saw the figure of a man approaching the bars that connected their cells. As she gasped for breath amidst her pain, she noted the sharp line of his jaw in the faint moonlight and the darkness of his eyes as they looked to her in guarded concern. She knew him. Not well, not by any stretch. But he was the man she had seen with Reina the night Malyssandra had been down there. He was the man Reina had traded her life in for.

She knew he recognized her by the way his eyes widened when they made contact with hers, and her ragged breathing scraped across the stones. He peered at her, and sweat ran off of her in rivulets as pain barreled through her. Her fingernails cut small half-moons into the flesh of her palms, and she attempted to use the distant pain as a way to ground herself.

"You'll need to keep your back from touching the ground." Keane's rumbling voice filled the space. "Or else infection could set in." It seemed like he was trying to help, but the kind gesture didn't reach his eyes. He appeared broken and lost in the darkness. It wasn't how Malyssandra remembered him from the week prior, and through her pain, she felt astonishment that his demeanor had changed so quickly over the course of a week. He settled his weight against the barrier between them and rested his head on a bar. "You're the maid that brought the guards' clothes down last week." The words were flat, and Malyssandra managed to dip her chin in response. "What happened?"

"Reina," she grunted.

His eyes lit up. A look of disbelief filled every corner of his face as if he hadn't believed what he had heard. "Reina," he repeated.

"She," Malyssandra shivered, "she sent me."

"Reina's alive?" Malyssandra gave a quick nod of her head, and Keane let loose a long breath as if he had held it in for days. He looked relieved, and Malyssandra feared he would ask more questions. She wasn't prepared to tell anyone about the Prethans. Not yet.

Darkness played at the edges of her vision, and she didn't know how much longer she would be able to stay awake. "Thank you." Was all Keane whispered to her, though, before he walked away from their shared bars and left her alone.

She felt as the darkness gently pulled her deep within her mind. The pain in her back began to ebb slightly but wouldn't vacate her skin altogether. Her eyes fluttered shut as her back became nothing more than a distant throb in time to her heartbeat, and she fell asleep within the confines of Den Zei.

15

REINA

It had been days since Reina had seen Malyssandra, and the woman hadn't visited her since. The fear in the woman's eyes as Reina had asked her to get herself sent to Den Zei made Reina nervous. There was a very real possibility the girl wasn't willing to be sent to the darkened cell blocks, and the reality was that Reina wasn't entirely sure Malyssandra was capable of starting a revolution. Reina needed to get out of the palace.

The maids that brought her food seemed nervous to be around her, and Reina couldn't help but realize the differences between those maids and the people within Den Zei. The women who came and went from her room throughout the day seemed lighter, and Reina supposed their upbringing was much different from hers. To them, Den Zei was simply a horror story. They hadn't lived within the darkness and been lashed by guards for speaking out of turn. That much was evident as their bright eyes looked to her with hesitant curiosity before they scurried from the room.

She still hadn't slept on the bed. The idea of accepting such a luxury disgusted Reina, and she couldn't bring herself to so much as sit upon the plump mattress. Her eyes had trailed off to the bathtub throughout the days, and she was losing the battle within herself not to take a bath. The dirt that clung to her skin was years old and tinted red from blood that had dried from long ago healed wounds. Her clothes hung stiffly from her body, and she imagined that she smelled rancid to those who entered her magnificent prison.

A maid brought her lunch, and she picked at it absentmind-edly as the woman looked on at her. After having only been allowed small amounts of food throughout the years at Den Zei, her appetite was small, and she could never finish the dishes the maids brought in for her to eat. She sighed as her stomach quickly became full, and she looked up at the maid. "Would you like some?" The girl's eyes lit up and fell within an instant.

"I shouldn't," she mumbled, but Reina pushed the plate to-ward her and looked at her expectantly. The girl stood still for a moment and looked over her shoulder to ensure the guard hadn't peered in to see what was going on. When she was confi-dent that nobody was around to see, she reached forward and grabbed a piece of venison from the plate. "It's warm," she breathed, and Reina gave her a smile.

"Have the rest. I'm not hungry." Reina wandered across the space and into the washroom as she left the maid behind to finish her meal. She looked curiously at the porcelain tub within the center of the room and tried to see how it worked. There was no water around to fill it, and she wondered how she was to take a bath in a room with no water. She supposed with the drought that nobody might have been able to bathe. Water was too scarce.

As the silence stretched on, she found herself thinking back to the shadow that had appeared the night Malyssandra had been in the chamber. She found her mind went back to that event often over the days that had passed, and she had come no closer to puzzling out what the creature could want from her. There had been no sign of it since that night, and she didn't know if that should have made her more or less anxious.

"Do you wish for me to draw you a bath?" The maid appeared at the door, and Reina jumped as the silence around her was disrupted. She looked at the girl in confusion before realization dawned on her face as she looked back to the tub she stood in front of.

"Could you?" She queried, and the girl nodded enthusiastically before she exited the room with quick steps. Reina stared after her, unsure of why the girl had asked if she wanted a bath if she only planned to leave after. It seemed slightly off-putting to her, but she assumed the girl must have had other places to be. She made her way back into the main room and sat against the side of the bed.

A few minutes later, the door flew open, and four maids wandered in. Each with a bucket of steaming water. Reina was startled at the intrusion and watched the women as they turned into her washroom. As they filled the tub, the sound of water reached Reina's ears, and she scurried to her feet. She watched as they each dumped their buckets into the porcelain bowl and stared at the girl from earlier as the other three maids exited briskly.

"We have to get the water from elsewhere in the castle and bring it to the tub," she explained to Reina's exasperated stare, "Would you like me to help?"

"Help?" Reina repeated dumbly.

The girl chuckled quietly. "Bathe you," she stated, and Reina's cheeks heated.

"No, I should be all set. Thank you," Reina replied, and the girl's eyes sparkled in amusement at Reina's blatant display of discomfort.

"Well, if you need anything, please let me know." The girl began to walk away but spun her head around before she exited the washroom. "Thank you for the food," she spoke quietly so as not to let the guard outside the bedroom hear. "I haven't had a warm meal since before I can remember." Sadness spun in her eyes, and Reina nodded in understanding.

The girl left, and when Reina heard the wooden door to her chamber close, she peeled the stiff clothes from her body and discarded them onto the floor. She looked into the water in amazement and marveled as she stuck her hand within the warm liquid. The last time she had taken a bath, her mother had forcibly held her in the water as she struggled to free herself. She smiled at the memory and slowly placed her leg into the tub.

She watched the clear water turn brown as the dried dirt on her skin melted off, and she pulled the rest of herself over the lip of porcelain and sunk into aquatic bliss. Her hands rubbed at the earth that had made her skin its home and dunked her head underwater to scrub at her butchered hair. The world became muted as her ears submerged, and she wished she could have lived within the bathwater forever.

When she finally pulled herself from the tub, the skin on her hands and feet were shriveled. She pressed her fingers together absentmindedly and looked to her dirty clothes, which lay crumpled on the floor. The idea of putting them back on did not appeal to Reina, but she didn't wish to discard them either. So after she wrapped a soft towel around her bare body, she reached down and balled the disgusting fabric in her hands. She moved into the main room and placed them underneath her pillow before turning to the closet beside her dresser.

As she walked through the door for the first time, her jaw gaped, and she stared at the overwhelming amount of clothing she had to choose from. New dresses hung from silver hangers, and skirts were folded neatly along the shelves within. Blouses were paired with trousers in the far end, and she grabbed a grey top and black pants. She pondered the shoes that bordered the ground but decided she didn't wish to put anything on her feet. After having been barefoot so long, her feet had callused over, and she didn't think shoes would bring her anything other than discomfort.

She closed the door to the closet as she made her way back into the room and pulled on the clothes she had chosen. The fabric was soft against her freshly cleaned skin, and guilt tugged at her heart as she looked to the areas of her body that had been caked with dirt only hours before. She felt that she had just washed away memories of years spent within Den Zei, and her thoughts went out to Keane.

The door flew open beside her, and she jumped sideways to avoid being hit. The guard stationed outside popped his head in, "The king will see you," he stated.

"Busy," she called out. The guard stepped through the door. "And you know, you should really knock. I was stark naked mere seconds ago, and I wasn't brought here to give free shows." She crossed her arms over her chest, but the guard was unamused. Reina didn't even have a second to compose herself as he grabbed her elbow and dragged her out of the room.

It felt weird being led through the palace without chains on her wrists, and she wondered if the guard had forgotten to put them on or if he just didn't believe her to be a threat. She bristled at the thought, and her face scowled at him as they descended a set of steps into the busy atmosphere of the palace.

Nicely dressed men bustled about without sparing her a second glance, and the faint sound of women's laughter echoed across the high ceiling. The guard took a sharp left and led her through a small corridor to a pair of doors. He pushed them open at the same time and swung them inwards to reveal a simple space.

It wasn't the largest room within the castle, and there wasn't much in it at first glance, but when Reina looked up, she noticed a tall golden throne that stood atop a stairway. There sat the king, and his dark eyes darted to the entrance as Reina entered the room.

An elderly woman stood to the right of him, and her eyes looked to Reina with interest. She was led to the base of the stairs, and she stared up at the king's gaze.

"Bow," the guard commanded behind her, and she set her jaw against the demand. She would not bow to the man who had massacred her people and taken the survivors for his own pleasure. Instead, she squared her shoulders and held her head higher in the air. The guard's boot struck the backs of her legs, and the floor collided with her knees in a resounding crack. She pulled her lips back in a grimace as she watched the guard pull a whip from his side and raise it into the air.

"Leave her be!" The king's voice filled the space, and the guard quickly disengaged and backed away as he lowered the whip. Reina looked back up to the man on the throne and pulled herself to her feet. He smirked. "I apologize for my guard's behavior. Sometimes they can be a little... brash."

"You're telling me," she scoffed. The king looked different than how she had left him last. His skin had grown paler again, and his eyes looked tired while his breathing seemed shallow. The illness had come back, and Reina realized that's why she was there. He motioned for Reina to make her way up the stairs, and she stood in place for a moment before she complied. She felt the old woman's unnaturally green gaze on her as she ascended and stood before the throne.

"I'm afraid that whatever you did for me a few days ago has begun to wear off," the king stated passively, "Although it hasn't reached the point it had grown to before, I'm afraid it will soon. I believe it's for the best that it was caught early this time. That way, I don't lose days of my life confined to a bed. Don't you agree?" His voice was casual as if he were talking with an acquaintance and not a woman he had enslaved for nearly the entirety of her life. When his question was met with silence, he continued. "Anyhow." He shrugged, "I need you to do it again." There was no room for argument within his words, and his eyes stared a warning at Reina.

She gave a curt nod as she realized she had no other option but to comply. He knew she wouldn't risk Keane's life. He thought he had beaten her. *Then let him think that,* she thought, and reached out to place her hand on top of his.

She felt the power bloom within her core as her shoulder burned hot, and she reached for the energy and pushed it out of her and into him. His skin darkened once again before her eyes, and his gaunt face became fuller. He smiled pleasantly at her, but she saw the danger that lurked within his eyes.

"Have you ever seen anything like it?" He asked, and confusion registered on Reina's face before realizing he spoke to the elderly woman beside him. "Can you do anything nearly as powerful?"

"No." The woman's voice grated against Reina's skin. "That is beyond magic. The most I could do for you is take the pain away, your majesty. I would not be able to heal your illness; witches can only do petty magic." Reina's head whipped over to the woman, unsure she had heard her correctly.

The shocked expression on her face caused the king to let out an exaggerated sigh. "My sincerest apologies. You have not met my high priestess yet. She's a very useful woman and has been by my side for years now." He extended his hand in the woman's direction, and her eyes gave a crazed sparkle as her gaze clashed against Reina's.

"What I just saw you do for the king is unlike anything I have ever seen before. I dabble in magic from time to time and do fancy myself a witch. However, pure magic is such a minute thing in the human world. It was a gift from the gods long ago to make things a little more interesting down here." Her eyes flashed, and Reina's brow furrowed. "What you can do surpasses anything I have ever known to be possible. The gods must have really wanted to wreak havoc down here when they sent you."

Reina's mouth opened and closed, but she was speechless. Magic existed. She wasn't the only one in the world that could do otherworldly things. It was a lot to take in, and her wide eyes looked to the priestess. She was overwhelmed by the sudden onslaught of information, and the woman gave her a wide smile.

"Witches?" She finally got out around her shock, and the king bellowed loudly to fill the room with his overdramatic laughter. Her eyes darted to him as he settled down and looked on at her.

"Yes, my dear. Witches." The priestess looked wild as she pulled something from the pocket of her robe. She extended a closed fist into the air. Reina couldn't help herself as she leaned forward, intrigue winning out over caution.

Her hand opened suddenly, and Reina stepped back in fear something would launch from her palm. But there was nothing there. Reina looked between the empty palm and the woman's stare. "There's nothing there," she pointed out. The priestess smiled.

"Give it a moment. Normal magic isn't quite as instantaneous as yours." The priestess allowed her arm to fall to her side as they stood in silence.

Reina wondered what they were waiting for when something heavy appeared in her hand. She jolted and dropped the object. A solid thud sounded from Reina's feet, and she looked down to see she had just dropped a rock. "What?"

"Petty magic," the priestess explained. "All witches are capable of transporting small items into the possession of anyone in the world. If you watch closely, I can pull it back to me."

Reina's eyes locked on the rock, and moments later, it was gone. Her head jolted up to look at the old woman's outstretched palm. Seconds ticked by. Then, it reappeared. Reina stared in amazement. "How did you do that?"

"We don't wish to bore you with the details," the king cut in and spared a meaningful look at the priestess. "We have much to do today, and you have already served your purpose." He looked to the guard at the base of the stairs. "Please escort this girl back to her room. I will need her again in a few days." The guard gave a firm nod and walked up the stairs to grab Reina's elbow once again.

She looked over her shoulder at the priestess, and questions echoed in the depths of her eyes. If there was more magic in the world, then it was possible more people could have been like her.

Her mind went back to what Malyssandra had said to her within her chambers. She had a vision of the future. Perhaps Malyssandra was like her, just with a different ability. Reina hoped for that to be true because otherwise, it felt as though she was alone in the world.

The guard left Reina in her room and locked the door. Her thoughts were already spiraling at the possibilities that had risen within her head. Maybe she was simply a powerful witch. The priestess had stated she could relieve pain but couldn't heal its cause like Reina could. It seemed possible to Reina that she could have been like the priestess, just more powerful.

Frustration grew inside her at all the unanswered questions. She didn't know what she was or why she was able to do the things she did. The truth was, she was grasping at straws. Her hand grabbed at the brush which still sat upon her dresser, and she pulled her arm back in frustration to throw it across the room. Before she could do so, the light on her shoulder began to glow, and she looked down in confusion. She hadn't been injured, so why was her shoulder burning?

As the light began to fade, she became aware of the weight in her hand. It was odd. She didn't remember the brush being that heavy. She turned her head and froze as light glinted off of a golden brush. Her hand released it in shock, and it fell heavily to the floor. She stared at it in confusion. The knowledge that it hadn't been gold before muddled her brain, and she couldn't wrap her mind around what had just occurred.

What is happening to me? She thought and crouched beside the golden brush on the floor. She inspected it closely and reached forward to pick it back up. Wonder sparkled in her eyes.

The sound of the door unlocking clicked behind her and filled her with alarm. She looked around in panic for a place to hide the brush. Her eyes locked on the piece of dirt-stained clothing that stuck out from under her pillow. As the door swung open, she wrapped the brush within the fabric and stuck it back underneath the pillowcase.

The door closed, and she took a second to slow her breathing. As she turned slowly to face the person who had entered her room, she met the gaze of a man with arctic blue eyes.

16

MALYSSANDRA

Malyssandra was jarred awake by the sound of keys as they clanged along cell bars. For a moment, she forgot where she was and jumped back into her cell. However, the quick movement tugged at the skin on her back, and she fell to the stone floor in pain. She felt eyes on her and turned to see Keane as he looked on in pity. Her cheeks flared up, and she reached her hand to her back to try and inspect the damage.

It felt as though the wounds hadn't even begun to close, and her skin was slick and warm with blood. Her head was light, and she felt as though if she stood up, she would faint. She wondered if she would continue to bleed until she died on the floor of her cell.

Malyssandra laid flat onto the moisture of the ground and stared into Keane's cell as he left. She waited to hear her own cell unlock, but it never did. Her shock must have been evident in how she swiveled her head to look because she heard Keane speak up before he made his way up the steps.

"They don't let new arrivals out their first full day. Just stay in there and rest. The pain will subside soon." Then, he was gone, and she was alone on the third level.

She wondered how long it would be until Keane's words were proven true and her pain was gone. It seemed nearly impossible that something so vibrantly painful could ever go away. Her forehead rested against the stone as she tried to focus on something other than the aching of her back.

She needed to talk with Keane when he came back that night, but she didn't know how to approach the subject with him. The night before, she had allowed herself to rest. She couldn't do that again. If she didn't tell anyone of the king's plan to trade the slaves, then she had gotten herself sent to Den Zei for nothing.

The day dragged by exceptionally slow, and the guards came by to give her a laughably small bowl of water beside a bowl of brown sludge. Her appetite was already nearly nonexistent due to the pain that tormented her nerves, but the look of the brown food made it go extinct.

She tried to position herself in a way to comfortably dump the water into her mouth but ended up jerking in pain and spilled the bowl all over her. With shaking hands, she pushed the bowl of slop beside her and tried to throw the empty bowl that the water used to be in toward the bars. She missed, and it rolled lazily around the front of the cell until it came to a halt.

Sunlight faded into moonlight at the top of the stairs. At some point throughout the day, Malyssandra had brought herself into a sitting position. She leaned against the bars that connected her cell with Keane's and waited patiently for the man to return for the night. Exhaustion pulled at her eyelids, and she fought to keep them open as she heard feet thunder against the stone steps beside her cell.

Her head jerked up, and she winced in pain. The third level slaves walked from the stairs and into the aisle beyond, which would lead them to their cells. When Keane appeared, her eyes locked on his form as he entered the cell beside her and gave her a suspicious glance. She couldn't imagine she looked entirely sane with her wide eyes pulled even wider in pain, and her hair frizzed around her head uncontrollably. It was likely the back of her top was shredded and made red from the blood leaking from her wounds.

She watched as guards locked the cell doors, and her heart thundered in her chest as the reality of where she was sunk in yet again. Her hand turned sweaty around the metal bar she clasped between her fingers, and she swallowed loudly as she tried to get control of her emotions. When the guards had passed, she turned to Keane and flinched as she felt fresh blood trickle down her back.

Before she could say anything, Keane burst in with the first round of questions. "Where was Reina taken? What are they doing to her? Why did she send you?" Malyssandra felt overwhelmed by the onslaught and looked at him with uncertain eyes.

"I, um," she started, and Keane's stare tore through her as he awaited an answer. She released the bar and wiped the sweat off her hands as she looked down to regain her confidence. She exhaled loudly and returned her gaze to Keane's. "Reina is in the palace. She is fine." Keane nodded thoughtfully. "She is worried about you."

"Me?" He asked incredulously.

Malyssandra nodded. "She sent me here to deliver a message, Keane." His eyes widened at the use of his name, and she realized it was highly likely that he didn't recall Reina having said it in front of her when she had been down in Den Zei a week prior. She froze, uncertain of how to continue.

"A message," he goaded.

She pushed the rest of the words out. "The king made a trade deal with a kingdom across the Carnavan Sea. He is going to trade slaves for soldiers. Reina wanted you to know, so maybe you can fight back. So maybe you can do something before it's too late." Her voice was breathless by the end, and the pain in her back was building again. That had been all she was sent there to do, and it felt very pointless as Keane stared back at her dumbly. He blinked a few times and shook his head.

"I know," he whispered into the dark, and Malyssandra looked to him in startled confusion.

"What? You know? Did Ivanka tell you?" Malyssandra's voice was outraged. She had gotten herself sent to Den Zei to tell the people something that was already known. The knowledge gave fuel to the panic that rose up inside her.

She had been whipped, dragged down to the third level of Den Zei, and spent the day in pain. And it had all been for nothing. Her back throbbed in time with her rapid heartbeat, and her eyes pleaded for answers from Keane.

He avoided her stare. "I don't even know who Ivanka is," he breathed. "I've known for a while now that this trade was coming. I should have told Reina, but I just couldn't bring myself to do it." He turned his head back to face Malyssandra. "I didn't know how Reina would react. Eventually, I was going to say something, but she was taken away before I could." His excuse sounded more like rambling to Malyssandra, and the back of her neck burned as panic turned into anger.

"How did you know?" She enunciated each word into the space between them, and Keane opened and closed his mouth as if he were gasping for air. Malyssandra clenched her jaw. "I deserve an answer. Reina sent me here, we thought nobody knew, and now you're telling me that you *did*. I didn't have to get myself sent here." The strong words felt strange on her lips. She hadn't spoken that way to anyone in the palace. Even before Yulsa, she had never spoken out against her parents. She jerked at the thought.

Keane rubbed his temples and seemed to deflate, defeated. "There's a rebellion out there, Criedans who had survived the attack on our kingdom and managed to escape. They've been keeping in touch for years, but this year they have been reaching out to me more than usual."

"Reaching out to you?" Malyssandra looked at him in confusion, and he hung his head.

"Have you ever heard of witches?" He asked her.

"The priestess is a witch," she stated, and Keane looked at her as if she had sprouted another head.

"I don't know who that is either. But at least you have a basic understanding. So you know witches can harness small amounts of magic?" Malyssandra nodded. "And that they can transport small objects to and from anyone in the world?" Malyssandra gave another nod. "Objects like... letters?" Understanding dawned in Malyssandra's eyes. "They told me of the trade deal months ago, and they've been trying to organize an attack. It's highly likely if this deal goes through and we are taken to Pretha, they won't be able to get us back from over there. They don't have a lot of resources, but they've been there all along." His words echoed fuzzily around Malyssandra's mind, and she looked at him dazed.

He waited patiently for her to say something, and her words came out breathy. "There's a rebellion."

His mouth stretched into a smile. "There's a rebellion," he repeated.

She sat in silence, a wistful look in her eyes. Then it fell as she noticed the darkness which pooled around her. Reina had seen the shadow in that same cell. Malyssandra wondered if it sat beyond her line of sight, lying in wait of the perfect moment to strike.

"How much do you know about witches?" Malyssandra asked.

"Why?"

She sighed and looked to the dark corner of her cell. "I've been seeing a shadow lately. Reina has as well. Could that be a witch from the rebellion? Could someone be trying to reach out to us?" Her hand ran across the bumps of the stone floor, and she continued to stare off into the darkness. She hoped his answer would be simple and that he would confirm that she and Reina had simply misunderstood a message from the rebellion as something sinister, but he paused.

"*That's* what Reina saw in her cell, a shadow?" Keane ran a hand along his jaw, exasperated. "I've never heard of anything like that before. It's doubtful the rebellion has been trying to get ahold of either of you. They would have mentioned it to me first." His eyes grew concerned, and he turned them on Malyssandra.

"So, what does it mean?" Her voice shook as it pushed its way through the bars and into his cell. Keane shook his head, dumbfounded by what she had just said.

"I have no idea, but it doesn't sound good." He stated flatly and faded back into the dark corner of his own cell.

17

REINA

"So you're the famed healer the palace rumor mill has been going on about." The cool voice glided to where Reina stood, frazzled. She looked at him and tried to force her expression into one of disinterest. He stood tall in the front of her room, and the way he held himself made him seem even larger than he was.

As she focused on regaining her composure, she looked him up and down slowly. She was attempting to draw out the moment so she could prepare herself to speak. Her muscles were tense, and she was afraid her voice would come out nothing more than a small squeak if she opened her mouth without first putting in the effort to relax. As her mind became accustomed to the situation that stood before her, she exhaled and asked, "And you are?" She sounded more confident than she felt, and the thought of the golden brush beneath her pillow tugged at her thoughts. It was all she could do not to glance back at it.

A smile tugged at his lips, and his dark eyebrows lowered in amusement as he looked at her through thick lashes. He was watching her, but not in a predatory manner. He seemed sincerely interested in how she would react to what he said next. "The prince."

She took a moment to decide on her next course of action. If she showed too much surprise at his words, she was afraid she would lose whatever game they were playing. It was better if she came off as if she had expected the absurdity of the answer.

"Of course," Reina blurted out. "And what do you need for me to do, *your majesty*?" She mocked a bow and flicked her head to the side as if to swing her newly nonexistent hair over her shoulder.

His tall form sauntered to the corner of her room and settled into a wooden chair beside a small table. He motioned to the space across from him, but Reina crossed her arms and stared back at him unflinchingly. His head shook from side to side, but he waited patiently.

There was something about the way he looked at her. As if he didn't wish to force her to do anything. He wanted her to choose to sit across from him, not lord his power over her and shove her into the chair. His expectant eyes looked to her and sparkled at her refusal to join him. A soft breath was let loose from his amused smirk, and he sat back against the chair.

"I'm not here to ask for anything," he stated as he crossed his arms across his chest to mimic her. "Just color me intrigued. It's not often we get someone new within the palace, much less someone who can do what you're able to." Reina flexed her toes against the porcelain beneath her feet in discomfort and looked about the room in uncertainty. She had been prepared for the man to ask her for something. She hadn't been ready for someone who simply wished to interrogate her. Casual conversation was not something she knew much about. "Could I ask your name?"

Her attention focused on the prince's casual smile, and suspicion lit up her features. "You likely could," Reina mused. A soft chuckle filled the air, and Reina cocked her head.

"Well then," he breathed, "What would your name be?"

"Why does that matter?" She quickly retorted and uncrossed her arms to allow them to loosely hang by her sides. He leaned forward and placed his elbows upon his knees over the grey trousers he wore.

His shoulders shrugged, and he brought his knuckles up to his lips as he continued to look up at her through his dark lashes. "It's impolite to not know someone's name before holding a conversation with them." The words came out genuine as if he couldn't imagine having a conversation with her without first knowing her name.

She blinked at him. "What's your name?"

"Ferix," he stated without having missed a beat. "Pleased to meet you...?" He left the question open in an invitation for her to divulge her name. She huffed and moved to take the seat across from him.

"Are you toying with me?" She asked.

"Might be." He chewed on the words, but his smile grew as she sat down, "Or I might just genuinely wish to know your name."

She puzzled at him, her brow furrowed and her eyes skeptical. It was obvious he was his mother's son in the way he looked. His hair, although cropped close to his head, was dark and neat. The skin evident on his arms was tanned and toned, and his blue eyes stood proudly from his face. While he held no resemblance whatsoever to his father. He did not seem power-hungry or cruel. He was simply curious as to who the woman was who had wandered into his palace.

She placed her forearms on the table and allowed herself to relax a little bit. There was no evident danger from the man. If anything, the banter would at least keep her sane from her own worries for the moment. Her eyes skirted the room and quickly glanced at the pillow upon her undisturbed bed before they dragged themselves back to the prince's gaze. "Reina," she mumbled into the few feet between them.

"Well, Reina," he spoke smoothly and stood from his seat, "it has been a pleasure to meet you. I thought perhaps you could tell me what happened between you and that maid you had in here the other day?"

Reina froze. She had let her guard down too soon. She scanned him over for a moment before she replied, "I've had many maids in here over the past week. They bring me food."

"But this wasn't just a normal food run. She was in here for quite some time. The guard outside said you had wanted her to help you brush out your hair." Reina tensed up at the word brush and again fought the urge to look back over at her bed. "It appears that went over well," he stated with a pointed look at her scalp. Reina scowled.

"It was knotted from years spent in a cell, nothing to detangle hair with in Den Zei." She shrugged.

"I'm sorry to hear that."

"I'll get over it," she spat out.

He placed his palms flat on the table, and she refused to move back as his face came down in front of hers. "You see, the weird thing about your meeting with *Malyssandra*," his eyes searched hers for any sign of recognition before he continued, "is that she arrived at my chambers not too long after, asking me to send her to Den Zei."

"Why would anyone ever want to go there?" She asked innocently.

"I wondered the same thing." He pushed himself off of the table and walked toward the door. Reina let out the breath she had been holding. "Reina," he said softly, and she turned at the sincerity in his voice. "I am not your enemy. Although, I might be able to give you some answers. At midnight your door will be left unlocked, and there will be no guard outside. If you want, meet me in the far eastern sector of the palace. There's an archive room there." He paused for a moment as he pondered something. "Bring a torch," he added.

His long legs carried him the rest of the way toward the door, and she watched on speechless. He turned to give her one last smile, then he threw the door open and exited her room.

She sat in the chair, dazed by what had just occurred. The interaction had been bizarre. Malyssandra had gone to him. Had asked him to have her sent to Den Zei. Why would she include him in her plans? He was a royal, and as far as Reina was concerned, he was just as bad as his father. Even if he had seemed kind.

Her eyes trailed back to the door which the prince had left out of mere moments earlier, then back to the chair he had sat in. If the prince had answers, why couldn't he have given them within the confines of her chamber? Why would he risk her escape?

Her head spun, and she wandered back to sit on the ground beside her bed. She locked her hands beneath her legs and rested her chin upon her knees. The worst possibilities rose in her mind, and she wondered if she should even consider meeting with the prince. She didn't trust him. He could have been a phenomenal liar, and her meeting him that night could have been a trap.

Her head perked up. On the off chance he was telling the truth, her door would be unlocked at midnight. There would be no guard to keep her within her chamber. What were the chances she could escape the palace?

18

MALYSSANDRA

The day that lay ahead of Malyssandra was daunting as the guards made their way down the cellblock to unlock the doors. She struggled up onto shaking legs and looked around the space in poorly concealed terror. There were no expectations in her mind, as she didn't know what was to happen next. All she knew was that she was ill-prepared for the day that stretched before her. After a life spent in the palace, she lacked the physical strength needed for the labor Den Zei was rumored to force upon people.

She swallowed the tendril of fear that attempted to force its way up her throat as her door swung open and a guard sneered at her. "Let's go, new girl, line up in the yard and prepare for placement." Malyssandra squinted at the faint sunlight that filtered down the stone steps, and panic must have been evident in the rigidity of her shoulders.

Keane came into view ahead of her and peered gently through the bars. His eyes looked kind, and he beckoned her out of her cell. She hunched as she walked to avoid pulling at the wounds that still ached upon her back. Something trickled down her skin, and she wondered if it was more blood, sweat, or moisture from the ground she had laid upon.

"When you get up the stairs, and outside, you'll see a bunch of people lined up. Find a spot in the crowd and stand there. Guards will come up and tell you where to proceed, and you do as you're told. Alright?" Keane whispered from behind her as they ascended the stairs, and she nodded in confirmation that she understood what he was saying.

Nothing could have prepared her for the way the yard looked as it was brimming with people. Malyssandra looked aghast as she became overwhelmed by the heat, which collided aggressively with her skin, and she tried to take in the lines of people who stood before her. She hadn't realized how many people Den Zei held within its cells. There had to be thousands of slaves stretched out in front of her, their faces hopeless as if life had simply left their bodies. Malyssandra's mouth hung open and gaped at the world she had seen from a window most of her life.

The smell of unbathed flesh reached her nose, and she held back a gag as the lashes on her back burned intensely in the harsh sunlight. Her eyes squinted, unused to the onslaught they were experiencing from the brightness all around her. It looked how she imagined the underworld would, with lost souls who stood under the eternal torture of unspeakable heat. Nobody else seemed to mind the aggressive temperature as they continued to pull themselves into tight lines.

Malyssandra felt a nudge at her back, and she hissed in pain as it tugged at her skin. Her head whipped around to see Keane as he sauntered away from her and into the hoard of people. She snapped out of her daze and stumbled into the crowd as blood roared through her ears. Her body was instantly sweaty, and it stung at her wounds painfully as she found a place to stand.

A man stood above them on some sort of balcony, and he shouted out the last call to get in line. Malyssandra watched as the man stared intensely into the somber crowd, and her eyes fell to the dried earth beneath her feet.

After she had arrived, nobody had given her new clothes. She still wore the basic undergarments maids were told to wear beneath their aprons. She picked at the fabric and wondered how long it would hold up in Den Zei and if they would end up giving her the same clothes the others wore.

As the man on the balcony shouted out for the guards to give placements, Malyssandra's head snapped up, and she watched nervously as the guards made their way through the crowd. People broke off without saying a word and headed toward wagons that stood near the yard's fence. She wondered where each wagon went, and her hands trembled at her sides.

"Stone yards," A guard spoke from beside her, and she jumped. Her eyes looked to him desperately, and his face crumpled in annoyance as he faced her. "Do I need to repeat myself?" He growled, and Malyssandra clumsily shook her head. She quickly shuffled toward a wagon and looked helplessly at it before she started to climb on.

"What placement did you get?" She heard the rough voice beside her, and she jerked to see Keane as he climbed onto the wagon. He looked away from where she stood as if he hadn't even spoken to her, but she could see by the way his head was tilted he was awaiting her response.

"Stone yards?" She mumbled quietly, and her voice rose at the end of the words as if it were a question. Keane shook his head softly and turned to look at a wagon halted three to the left of where she stood. She backed away slowly from the wagon she had been about to climb upon and walked over to the one he had hinted her toward.

Her body struggled to pull itself onto the wooden boards, and her arms shook from the pain that flared up across her back. She gasped loudly, and a few people hunched within the back of the wagon turned to look at her. Their interest dropped within seconds, and soon they were simply staring at the dust-covered wood of the wagon.

She scrambled to the side, away from the huddle of people who sat within the center. They looked strange there, especially when there was so much room for them to spread out into. It was almost as if they didn't realize they had more space. They were so lost within their own worlds.

Malyssandra settled on the edge of the area. There were no rails, so she supposed she would be able to better see the world as it passed by. The world she had never believed she would have had to see.

The wagon lurched into motion, and she felt her weight tumble over the edge of the wood. She watched in horror as the wheel beneath the wagon spun close to her face. A hand grabbed at her arm and pulled her back up before she could fall beneath the wheel, and she turned to give the person her thanks.

Before she could say anything, the person had turned back to the group of people within the center of the rumbling wagon. Malyssandra looked at them hesitantly, then back to the open space on the edge of the wagon. She ultimately decided to squeeze into the center with the others and copied them, looking to the wood beneath her.

She did not raise her head again until the wagon stopped. A large wall stood half-finished some little ways in the distance, and she marveled at how high in the air it stood. The people around her began to dismount from the wagon, and she trailed after.

The grass beneath her feet crackled as she stepped on it; the lack of water had caused the blades to wilt. She followed the group of slaves to a small area where a guard was stationed hooking something around their torsos. Malyssandra wiggled her back, unsure how the device would feel upon her raw skin.

When it was her turn to be strapped in, her muscles twitched as the man's hands roughly turned her around so he could buckle the strips of leather in the back. Her breath caught in her throat as he brushed up against her skin, and she clenched her jaw to keep from shouting out. He nudged her forward when he was done, and she tripped over her feet as she tried to find where she was to go next.

Her blood ran cold when she spotted what the slaves were doing. Large stones were strapped onto their backs, and they carried the heavy items up a small path toward the wall. As Malyssandra slowly forced herself to approach the pile of stones, her back began to prematurely protest. Her knees weakened at the thought of the cruel weight of the rock upon her still freshly opened flesh.

A guard grabbed her by her elbow and spun her around impatiently. She clenched her eyes shut against the world as excruciating pain fired up and down the nerves in her back. Her breathing halted in her chest, and she saw colors explode behind her clenched eyelids. It seemed impossible for her to take a step forward, but she knew she couldn't stand there with her eyes closed forever. She was in a different world than she was used to, and if she wanted to survive, she had to push through the torture.

So she placed one heavy foot in front of the other as tears ran freely down her face. Her dark eyes burned in the hot rays of the sun. Sweat pooled at her collarbones, and she watched as people quickly passed her with their own rocks strapped upon their backs. Their legs pumped ferociously up the steep incline of the wall, while hers shook with the effort to stay upright. Onward she pushed, closer to the sun. Soon, the pain in her back became distant as the path thinned out to the width of her shoulders. She looked down to the ground far beneath her and quickly jerked her head back to look straight ahead as she walked.

When she reached the peak of the wall, she watched as other people unbuckled the harness from around them and dropped the stones to the ground. She copied their movements, and as the rock rolled from her body, she stood up in relief. The weight that had been lifted from her made her feel like she could fly. An exhausted smile tugged at her lips.

She quickly realized she wasn't done. The others had picked up their dropped rocks and were moving them along to the side of the wall before they set them down. A defeated sigh sounded from Malyssandra's lips as she spun around to scoop the heavy stone into her arms, and her back convulsed in protest.

She grunted, lifting with her legs to get the stone as high off the ground as she could. Haltingly she shuffled to the edge of the wall, where she dropped the rock with a heavy thud to where she believed it belonged. Sweat trickled down her forehead into her eyes as she turned to look beyond the other side of the wall. Her breath was taken away. It stretched on for miles, and the horizon taunted her in the distance.

The rebellion is out there somewhere, she thought to herself as a spark of hope ignited from deep within her. Keane had told her there were other Criedans alive beyond Yulsa, Criedans who were fighting to get their people out. *I'm right here*, a voice within her shouted. As a tear fell from her eye and onto her cheek, she gave a quiet sigh. With hope alive in her heart, she turned to the path that led down the wall and descended to have another stone placed upon her split back.

19

The walls stared quietly at Reina as she moved swiftly down the halls toward where she thought the entrance to the palace was. The size of the building, coupled with the maze she shuffled through, made it hard to know exactly what direction she was moving in. The entrance to the palace had faced Den Zei when she had been dragged through the doors. Which meant the entrance was north. If she could only figure out which way north was.

The clanking of armor echoed from a hallway to her left, and she tiptoed straight until she found an opening in the wall she could duck into. She held her breath as she heard the metal of the armor grow closer. Her heart pounded in her chest, and she thanked the gods she hadn't taken the prince's advice when he recommended she bring a torch. The light would have been the end of her escapade.

As the sound retreated into another hallway, Reina pulled herself from the wall and continued. She didn't know what her plan was if she managed to escape. She couldn't leave her people behind, not with so much at stake. Not ever.

She met a dead end and huffed in frustration. Maybe if she backtracked and took a left, it would open up into another hallway that would take her north. She spun around.

Light filtered into the hall from an open door, and Reina moved to sneak by it undetected, but as she came upon it, something caught her eye. Candles burned wildly from atop a pedestal, where the priestess stood hunched over a book. She was alone.

Without the king or guards by her side, she looked less frail. Her wrinkles sagged around her face as she stared down into the pages, her eyes sharp and her shoulders pulled tall. A shiver ran down Reina's spine as she wondered what the strange woman was doing alone in the palace at night.

It sounded as if the priestess were muttering to herself as she skimmed the words, and Reina leaned closer to try and hear what she said. Her shoulder bumped against the wooden door, and a faint creak filled the air.

The priestess's head snapped up, her eyes alert. Reina pulled back against the wall and willed her breathing to settle. Silence gave way to footsteps as the old woman moved toward the door. Reina flattened herself as she saw a shadow stretch away from the light.

She closed her eyes tight as the seconds ticked by. If she was caught, that was the end. She was done. Her door would never be left unguarded and unlocked again. There would be no escape from the palace. There would be no helping her people. There would be no seeing Keane again.

The door clicked shut. Reina peaked out at the world, but the priestess did not stand before her. The priestess hadn't seen her. She loosed a breath and sagged forward in relief. Quickly, she passed the door and froze.

Goosebumps rose on her skin, and eyes drilled holes in the back of her head. The shadow was back. She didn't bother to turn around; she just ran. It was right behind her. She could feel it.

She took a left into another hallway, then a right. Adrenaline pumped through her veins as the shadow began to cackle at her heels. The noise was deafening but silent. Her head ached with the volume, but her ears didn't hear it. Water filled her eyes at the pain, and she took another left.

And collided with the prince.

"Exercising?" He asked, the corner of his mouth curled.

"What?" She breathed and turned to look behind her. The shadow wasn't there. The hallway stretched on, empty and quiet as it had been before. "No, I-."

"I thought you weren't going to come." He crossed his arms.

"I got lost," she offered, and the prince snorted.

"Then it's lucky you quite literally ran into me. This way." He motioned with his head, and Reina gave one last look over her shoulder before she begrudgingly followed.

The prince led her through the palace, and Reina paid attention to where they were going. As they continued down a long hall, she watched as the windows became scarcer and the walls turned from golden to stone. Reina realized why the prince had instructed her to bring a torch as darkness settled around them. The prince raised the small flame to illuminate their path, and Reina's skin crawled at the shadows just beyond the light.

They came upon a sharp right turn and took it before ducking into a room on the left. The prince walked over to a desk in the center and placed his torch into the sconce beside it. A book sat open as if the prince had been reading it before he had set out to find Reina.

He turned back to the book without another word, and she crept up behind him. Something felt weird about the air within the archive. Dust floated around them in a quiet complaint of being disturbed from its rest, and books lined shelves that went far back into the room. It had obviously been abandoned long ago, but the way the prince held himself made Reina think the room held much more importance to him than she knew. "Why did you bring me here?" She whispered, afraid to disturb the space around her.

His shoulders rose and fell evenly as his fingers ran over the edges of the pages within the book he flitted through. He was obviously searching for something specific, and all of his concentration went into scanning for whatever it was he deemed so important. She watched as the black shirt that stretched across his smooth back rippled in the dim flickering light of the torch.

"I needed to show you something," he responded and motioned with his arm for her to come closer.

She hesitated. She was already alone with him in an abandoned part of the castle. The least she could do was see whatever he has brought her there for. She gave a half-hearted shrug of apology to herself and stepped closer to Ferix. He moved his shoulder out of her line of sight, and she found herself staring at a page of the book.

"Why would you sneak me out of my room in the dead of night to make me read up on the gods?" She asked, annoyance in her tone. "Are you afraid I haven't gone to a chapel in a while? I mean, you wouldn't be wrong on account of me being enslaved for the past eleven years, but-." She had begun to ramble at the absurdity of it, but a sharp look from him cut her off.

He rubbed his temples for a moment before he pointed to the picture of the god upon the page. "Do you recognize this god?" He asked, and Reina gave him a blank stare. Her family had never attended a chapel back in Crieda, her father had always been in the mines in the mornings, and Reina's mother didn't like going without him. So they would instead stay home and tell stories as they waited for her father to return. It wasn't that her family didn't believe in the gods; they simply didn't speak of them much. They appeared on Albur don Gracos to give their thanks once a year, then wouldn't mention them again. Reina knew of their existence, but she wasn't able to point out any god by name. She shook her head at Ferix, and he sighed.

"This is Werthes, the God of Prosperity. He was an original god, one of seven that helped to build our world. Many stories speak of the power he had and the promiscuity he practiced with human women. That is until he fell in love with a Criedan princess many centuries ago."

"You brought me here to tell me a love story?" She interrupted.

"Hold your questions until the end, please," he told her, and she rolled her eyes. "The princess was beautiful, fair, and kind. Werthes decided he needed to meet her, and when the princess saw him, it was love at first sight. Werthes lived by her side and helped her brother, the king, run the kingdom of Crieda smoothly. He used his powers to ensure Crieda would want for nothing and did so out of love for his princess."

"How sweet," she muttered.

Ferix ignored her. "Slowly, the princess grew old. He watched as her mortal body gave out on her, and she died. Heartbroken, he decided he could not live without her. As her brother had died by that point, he went to her nephew, the new king, and explained what he wished to do. He gave the king an orb filled with his power and told him to hide it within the highest room of the castle to keep Crieda prosperous. He warned the king that if any man were to dare try to claim it for their own, the orb would shatter, and the power would escape into its rightful heir, the next of his bloodline. As the orb shattered, it would curse whoever had broken it with a strange illness that could not be cured. Werthes then ended his immortal life and was laid to rest beside his princess. The king took the orb and hid it within the palace. Only the Criedan prince was allowed to watch over it to ensure its safety."

Reina looked from the open book to Ferix, then back to the text. Her eyebrow quirked up in amusement, and she couldn't help but chuckle into the still air around them. "That's a beautiful story and all, but I'm not quite sure that it was worth my adventure through the palace to find this place." She crossed her arms across her chest and went to give him a smirk, but his eyes flared in frustration, and her mouth fell flat.

"It's not just a story, Reina. It *happened*." He ran his large hand over the short crop of his hair and looked to her, begging her to understand what he was saying.

She shook her head in apology, and her eyebrows drew together in confusion. "Let's say it did happen. What does any of it have to do with me?"

"It has everything to do with you, Reina. The day Yulsa attacked Crieda eleven years ago, it wasn't because my father wanted your people. They were just a consolation prize. What he really wanted," he paused and pointed his finger to a small picture of a glass sphere on the paper, "Was that orb. The priestess had been feeding him stories about it for months before the attack. She told him how it would make him all-powerful, that he would be rich beyond his wildest dreams, and that his kingdom would thrive for years to come. She baited him into going after the orb with the only thing my father cared about: the promise of more power. He became hungry, obsessed with the idea of finding that orb." Ferix looked to the ground, and his eyes held haunted shadows within them. He looked as if he were reliving the story as he told it, and Reina watched on in disbelief as she wondered if the prince had gone mad.

"So, did he find it?" She prodded, unsure of what else to say.

The prince sighed. "The day Yulsa invaded Crieda, I was there with my father. I was just a boy, but he forced me to go with him. He was too paranoid to allow anyone besides the priestess, and me, accompany him inside the palace to look for the orb. The priestess led us to it; she insisted she was drawn its essence and could feel as it called out to her. When my father threw the doors open, only the prince stood inside." His eyes flashed with saddened wonder as the scene replayed through his words. "My father was so power-crazed that he simply pushed the young prince aside. He couldn't have been much older than I was. My father grabbed the orb, and it was wonderful, a ball of golden light. The whole room had a golden glow, almost like the first rays of the sun. When my father touched it, the orb shattered into a million pieces. The power left it, and my father became enraged. He declared that all surviving Criedans be taken as slaves for the kingdom of Yulsa. It was his own form of retribution, I guess." Ferix leaned against the desk. The veins on his hands popped out as he tightened his grip against the wood.

She stood with her mouth agape. There had been no orb in Crieda; magic hadn't kept the kingdom prosperous. King Speranta had simply been a great king. He had ensured the land stayed fertile and healthy to provide them with food. Everything he had done had caused Crieda to prosper, not some make-believe orb. She shook her head vigorously at Ferix, and he closed his eyes against her denial. "When were you able to start healing yourself, Reina?" He asked calmly into the room, and Reina's head stopped moving. She clenched her fists at her sides and felt her fingernails as they dug into her palms.

Silence filled the space around them, and the prince snapped his eyes open and looked right through her. "*When?*" He demanded, and she flinched.

"The day Crieda fell," she responded fiercely. "What are you implying exactly?" Her voice was low, a warning. She was at the end of her patience and wouldn't listen to the stories of a mad prince much longer.

"Reina," he started, "You are the heir to the Werthes bloodline. When the orb broke, the power went into you. You are descended from a god, which is why you have the ability you do." His eyes were sincere as if he only wished to give Reina the truth.

She abruptly took a step away from him, "That's impossible," she stated as she slowly backed toward the door. "I don't know how I can do the things I do, but I am certain I am not descended from gods." She shook her head.

The prince observed her as she moved toward the hallway. "When you wish to talk, know I will be available to do so," he proclaimed.

The invitation was one Reina didn't want. She looked at him with wide eyes before she turned around and darted into the dark hall.

20

The weeks dragged by for Malyssandra, and she her skin began to grow tight around her bones. Lack of nutrition was affecting her body, but she had become stronger from the labor. Her back healed slowly, and she imagined herself to have ugly scars on her skin.

Malyssandra slowly began to understand the inner workings of Den Zei, and the guards had eventually given her the uniform of the slaves. She had become one of them.

She grew used to waking up before the guards ran their keys down the bars of the aisle. Occasionally, she and Keane would whisper in the darkness of the third level about letters he had received and what he believed the next move would be. She began to realize that although Keane was told basic things, he was still kept at arm's length. He was slightly frustrated by the vague words but clung to the hope that there was a day in the near future where the rebellion would fight for them.

Malyssandra tried to connect with Ivanka, but they were never given the same placement. She would see Ivanka's distinct hair in the crowd, but before she could approach her, she would be gone. Frustration tugged at Malyssandra as she realized the two things she had gone to Den Zei to do were pointless. Keane already knew about the trade, and there was no prayer in her talking with Ivanka.

"You know," Keane said one night in the quiet of the cell block, "Reina used to get irritated at me when I tried to get her to play it safe." His back faced Malyssandra.

She shrugged. "I don't really know her that well, but from what I've seen," Malyssandra paused, "she doesn't seem like the kind to play it safe." Her words were soft, and Keane turned his ear in her direction.

She saw a quick glint of moonlight flash across his teeth. He was smiling. His head shook, and she heard a small chuckle from within his cell. "You have no idea. As children, we used to be very close. We would look out for each other. Over the years, though, something changed. I still looked out for her, but she just... didn't seem to need me anymore." His head drooped, and she imagined he was staring at the floor with lidded eyes and a somber expression. "I couldn't help myself though, I kept pushing and pushing for her to be safe. I didn't even realize how far away I had pushed her until it was too late."

Malyssandra took in his words. She thought back to the strong woman within the palace who had given her a crazed grin as she removed all the hair from her head. The beautiful woman who had survived eleven long years in the third level of Den Zei and kept an impossible secret from the guards. She had sold her soul to the king to keep Keane alive. "I don't think you pushed her nearly as far away as you believe," Malyssandra reassured him. "She was worried about you when I saw her."

Keane's head bobbed up and down in the darkness. "Before she was taken away, we had been in an argument. It seems ridiculous considering our circumstances, but we were fighting." His laughter turned harsh, and the shadow of his hand rubbed at his chin. "I wouldn't tell her about the damned rebellion. I didn't think she could know about it and not do something drastic. I convinced myself she would ruin the whole thing," His head fell back and lightly tapped against the bars before it settled there. His shoulders rose and fell rhythmically, and Malyssandra stared at them in silence.

"You did what you thought was right," Malyssandra whispered. "Maybe you were wrong, maybe you weren't. We'll never know."

A loud sigh came from his mouth, and he climbed slowly to his feet. "The rebellion has been nothing but an excuse for me for a long time. When they started sending me letters, I felt important again. I hadn't been able to help my people for so long, and suddenly I could. I don't think Reina would have done anything to jeopardize their plans. I just liked that I was needed, that I could do something within the rebellion. I didn't want to share that with her. It was selfish." He pulled his shoulders back in the darkness, and Malyssandra scrambled up to her own feet to match his level.

"Possibly. Or maybe you're just a good guy in an impossible situation. Everyone makes mistakes; everyone is a little selfish."

Malyssandra chewed on the inside of her cheek before committing to what she said next, "I'm the reason my parents died that day." Keane's face reappeared from the darkness. She didn't have to say what day she was talking about. They both knew.

"Don't say that," he said as he settled back against the bars.

"It's true. My brother's snuck out to go to the festival, and they told me I couldn't come. I was mad. We were supposed to be working the harvest that day, and they just left me so that they could go have fun. I told my parents, and my father went after them. When the soldiers came to my house, he wasn't there to protect my mother. They killed her while I hid under my bed upstairs." A lump formed in her throat as her eyes began to burn. "If I hadn't told on my brothers, my father would have been there. He could have done something. But I was selfish. I couldn't go, so I wanted my brothers to be punished. Now they're all dead, and here I am." She choked on the last sentence, and Keane stared in silence.

"That's not your fault," he whispered, and Malyssandra let out a sad laugh.

"Maybe not directly. But if I had known-."

"There was no way you could have known what was about to happen. None of us did. Not even the king." He lowered his gaze to the floor.

She didn't know what else to say, so she stayed quiet. She walked over to the bars that connected their cells looked at him. She gripped a bar in her hand and pulled herself closer to their divide. Nothing but silence filled the air as they looked at each other. "Before I left the palace, I heard Reina didn't know how to take a bath." Malyssandra broke the quiet that had settled in the air, and she offered Keane a small smile.

His eyes lit up in amusement, and his shoulders bobbed quietly in suppressed laughter. When he was done, his eyes were lined with tears. He rested his forehead against the bars above Malyssandra. "That sounds like her," he mumbled, and a shiver ran across Malyssandra's body as his breath collided with her skin. She looked up through long lashes and found him staring down at her thoughtfully.

"What?" She breathed into the air between them, and his face fell serious for a moment.

"I was just wondering how different life would be right now if we had never been taken from Crieda." His words were soft.

She pondered it for a moment. The thought had never really crossed her mind. She couldn't even imagine a world where she hadn't been taken from her home. Where her family hadn't died. She might have had nieces and nephews; her parents might have grown old. The world could have been brighter, and her room wouldn't have been a damp cell. But those possibilities were gone. There was no use in dwelling on what might have happened.

Her eyes met his. "Maybe you should start wondering what life will be like when we get back.

21

REINA

Reina sat on the floor of her room with scissors in her hands. She had tried over the weeks to replicate what she had done to the brush, but nothing else dared turn to gold. Her eyes strained as they bulged at the scissors. The metal glinted back, taunting her with its silver blades. Frustration overcame her, and she threw them across the room.

The weeks had passed by quicker than Reina thought possible, and she had begun to fill out more. Skin that had spent most of her life pressed harshly against her bones relaxed as she received healthy amounts of food. Her appetite had grown slowly, and she could eat more of what was brought to her at mealtimes. Disgust still tugged at her insides as she remembered how those in Den Zei were treated, but she had gone too long without decent food to turn it away.

Her bed was another story. It sat untouched, the centerpiece of her exquisite room. The idea of sleeping upon it felt as though she would be crossing a boundary. She did not wish to become too comfortable within the confines of the palace. It was not her home, and she refused to pretend it was.

She pulled herself to her feet, prepared to spend the rest of her day roaming the palace. She had healed the king the day before, which meant she wouldn't have been called upon anytime soon. Their healing sessions had become habitual, and as the priestess stood at the king's side, Reina stayed silent. The king had mistaken her behavior for compliance and granted her the ability to explore the palace escorted by two guards.

She tried to make her walks seem as innocent as possible as she scoped out escape routes. If she acted distractible and sporadic, the guards didn't think anything of it. So, she flitted about the palace hectically while they silently judged her childish behavior.

Reina opened her door and greeted the guards stationed outside with an exaggerated smile. "Ready to go on an adventure?"

They stepped aside in response, and she marched by them. As she moved down random hallways, she felt déjà vu. She stopped dead, and she heard the guards behind her grunt as they tried not to run into her.

"Is there a problem?" One of them grunted deeply in annoyance.

"What's down there?" She asked, pointing at the open door near a dead end.

"The chapel. It's where the high priestess gives her sermons."

Reina nodded as if she were intrigued by the answer, but her heart thundered at the memory of the old woman as she leaned over an open book. She had no interest in seeing the priestess more than she had to. Her body whipped around so fast that the guards stepped back.

"What's over there?" She asked excitedly and ducked into another hallway.

The people who hustled about used to stop to stare at her as she walked by. But each day, the number of people who found her of any interest had dwindled. Nobody cared anymore about the woman from Den Zei. She had unknowingly been accepted as one of them, and her stomach clenched at the thought.

She avoided the eastern sector of the palace as she made her way through the maze of hallways. There was nothing within her that wanted to see the dark, dusty space again. Even as curiosity swirled beneath the surface of her mind. She hadn't seen the prince or the shadow since that night, and she wondered when her luck would run out.

In all her time at the palace, she had only seen the queen that first night. She thought it odd that she was never around, but she figured the queen was simply introverted. Years spent in a palace with that many people would have made Reina feel the same way.

As she pulled herself back from her thoughts, she noticed she had stumbled upon a wall made of glass. It looked out into a large garden, and Reina marveled at how lively the plants were in the blistering heat.

"Has it rained recently?" She asked the guards in awe, and they looked at each other before turning back to her and shaking their heads.

The familiar feeling of guilt tugged at her as she found a door that led out to the garden. She pushed it open and walked into the familiar heat that had tortured her only weeks ago. It felt as though an old friend embraced her, and a smile tugged at her lips. She hadn't been outside since she had been brought to the palace, and she hadn't realized how much she truly missed the sun.

The sound of the guard's feet as they hit the ground behind her caused her smile to falter, and she scowled in annoyance at the tall tree that stood healthily on the right of the dirt path. The garden was in a large courtyard, yet the guards still followed closely behind her as if she might escape at any minute.

What am I going to do? She thought to herself. *Scale the walls with my bare hands?* Her sigh was loud enough that she knew the guards heard it as she started down the path.

Benches sat beneath the ample shade of large trees, and flowers blossomed in the light. She took it all in as she slowly walked through, and she inhaled the floral scent that collided with her nose. It was miraculous to see the plants as they thrived in such harsh conditions, though she wondered how much water was wasted to keep them alive. The knowledge that many people struggled through the drought so that plants could live made her sick, and her mood instantly darkened.

As she gloomily made her way down the path, an unopened bud caught her eye. It sat within the shade, blue petals folded up in the shape of a bulb. She looked around and noticed many littered the garden, but each one had been planted of the sunlight. She shuffled closer and looked on in interest. She had never seen a bud such a vibrant shade of blue, and her hand reached forward to touch it.

"The cursed flower." The familiar voice sounded from behind Reina, and she abruptly stood up and spun around to face the prince. He was clean-shaven, and his eyes sparkled at her in the sunlight. She squinted at him, and a small dimple appeared as he pulled his lips wide to give her a smile.

Her eyes rolled dramatically in her head, and she spun around to continue down the path away from Ferix. "They're magic, you know," he casually mentioned, and Reina stopped suddenly. Her ear tilted in his direction as a sign to continue talking, and he obliged. "They're called sun-frosts, and they're my mother's favorite. That's why there are so many throughout the garden. She has them planted every year, always in the shadows of the trees." She could hear him move closer to where she stood, and she turned around to face him before he got too close. Half his face was clouded by the shade, and the other half basked in the light of the sun. The guards walked back to the doors through which Reina had entered the garden, and they watched from a distance.

Ferix crouched down beside the bud, and Reina allowed herself to lean down beside him as he caressed the shadowed flower. She watched curiously as he continued to speak. "The flowers hold a secret very few know about," he paused and gave Reina a pointed look, "their magic only lives when they're brought into the light." He gently pushed the bud into the sunlight, and Reina's eyes widened in wonder as it began to bloom.

The pedals expanded as if they were stretching after a long slumber. The blue-tipped ends faded inward to a frosty white center that looked as if it had been splattered on by a paintbrush. The green stem which held the proud petals turned white, and the prince plucked it from the ground. He twirled it between his fingers for a moment as he looked down in thought, then he passed it to Reina. She took it gently and stared at the beautiful petals in awe.

"Why did you call it the cursed flower?" Reina asked softly. There was nothing about it that seemed cursed to Reina. It was marvelous.

The prince shook his head as if she had missed something important, and he gave a small sigh. "They are easily the most beautiful flower in all the kingdoms, but many overlook them as all they see is what's in the shadows. If nobody thinks to move them into the light, their beauty is never seen. They live their lives in secret and die without having ever been truly seen." His eyes turned sad as he spoke, and he looked out to the garden at the other buds that littered the ground. "My mother loves keeping them a secret, knowing something that few others do. She keeps them where they will never see sunlight."

The world became quiet around them as Reina looked to Ferix in wonder. Despite the people who had raised him, he was thoughtful and gentle. Pride did not live in the storms of his eyes. It didn't make sense how he could have been in such a powerful position without being consumed by it.

His head turned back to face her, and his face fell serious as his voice dropped. "Have you given any thought to what we spoke about last?"

Her eyes scanned his face, but she saw no signs of a crazed man who wished to preach absurdities at her. Instead, she found his familiar sincerity. Slowly, she gave him a nod. "I have," she whispered into the heat, "and I have some questions."

"Well, hopefully, I have the answers," he retorted, and the blues of his eyes danced in the sun. "You know where to find me, and I do hope you won't get lost this time around. It seems as though you've done quite enough gallivanting around the palace to be able to find your way without issue." He gave a coy smile before he turned to walk away.

Reina watched him disappear back into the palace, and as the guards strutted across the dirt path to her side, she wondered if the prince had heard the way her heart thundered in her chest.

22

MALYSSANDRA

Malyssandra was awoken from a deep sleep and jolted up to look around in surprise. Her heart pounded within her chest, and her breathing immediately quickened as she expected to find a shadow before her. Instead, she turned to see Keane staring at her from his cell. Her heart rate slowed slightly, and she took a second to regain her composure before she glared at him through the bars.

"You nearly scared me to death!" She exclaimed harshly into the darkness, and she imagined the smirk that likely spread across Keane's face.

"For a moment, I believed you might have *been* dead. You sleep like a sack of potatoes." He chuckled, and Malyssandra stuck her tongue in his direction even though she was almost certain he hadn't been able to see it. She climbed to her feet and gave a slow stretch before she moved over to where Keane stood beside her cell.

Someone within the cell block muttered for them to quiet down, and she dipped her head as if that would have helped quiet her voice. "Whatever you revived me for better be good, I was having a great afterlife." Keane quietly laughed before it trailed off into the space around them. His demeanor shifted subtly, and Malyssandra's ears perked up in anticipation of what he was going to say.

"I just received a letter from the rebellion," he explained, and Malyssandra quirked an eyebrow in disinterest. He had received many letters over the week and had alerted her to each one as it arrived. Malyssandra thought he did so out of guilt for having not told Reina anything. As if he were afraid he might have pushed her away by keeping her in the dark.

Malyssandra frequently thought he was oversharing, as most letters he received simply stated there was no news yet. Still, she listened, and Keane seemed to enjoy the time they spent together discussing the lack of information. Their conversations would sometimes digress into stories from Crieda, but it was always Malyssandra that was asked to share her own experiences. Keane never told her any of his, and although she found that odd, she never pushed for him to share.

"Still nothing?" She asked, her voice low enough so that only they could hear it. She placed her hands against the bars and gripped them as she pulled herself against the metal.

Keane shook his head quickly, and Malyssandra noted the excitement that seemed to reverberate from his body. Her curiosity spiked, and her eyes widened as he spoke. "No, it's something," he breathed, and Malyssandra tilted her head up to look at his faintly illuminated face. "I think they have a plan." Malyssandra looked on expectantly as he began to pace the bars.

"I don't know exactly what it is, but it has to be something. The Prethans are arriving at the palace next week."

Malyssandra's heart stopped. She couldn't believe that much time had passed since she had been sent to Den Zei. When she had gotten there, the Prethans weren't set to arrive for over a month. She had been there for longer than she had realized, and the loss of time made her anxious. It was almost as if the darkness of Den Zei had swallowed her whole and spit her out weeks later. "So, what does that mean for us?" She inquired, her voice filled with fear.

Keane stopped pacing and looked sharply in her direction before he wandered back to the bars. "We'll be okay," he reassured her, "They have a plan."

"Which is?" Her voice rose a decimal above her usual whisper, and she flinched as she took a deep breath to force herself to relax.

"I'm not entirely sure. They want us to riot, though." His words were casual as if the very idea of a riot didn't terrify him. Keane, the man who preached safety and following orders, insinuated that they should throw caution to the wind and create chaos. Her jaw dropped, and she looked to him as if he were mad.

"*Riot?*" She exclaimed, and the volume of her voice showed that her deep breath had done nothing to relax her. Her hands released the bars, and she became the one who paced along their divide. "They want us to *riot? Now?*"

"No!" He interjected and threw his hands up, his palms facing her. "No, not now. The day the Prethans arrive, they need us to create a distraction. If we riot, the guards will be too concerned with us to be alerted by whatever they are doing."

"And what," Malyssandra pushed out, "Are they going to be doing?"

"*I don't know,*" Keane declared, and Malyssandra stopped her pacing at the desperate tone of his voice. "I don't know," he repeated and slid to the ground next to the bars, "I just know what they tell me, and that's all they said. But if this is real, and they have a plan, we have to do whatever we can to help. If we don't, we might as well give up now." He sounded defeated, and he hung his head in his hands. Malyssandra looked to him hesitantly before she sauntered over and placed a cautious hand on his shoulder through the bars.

"You know," she started, her voice settled and quiet, "If you had told me a little over a month ago that I would be in Den Zei talking about magical letters and riots, I would have told you that you were insane." A whimsical chuckle escaped her lips, and she looked down at the top of Keane's head. "I mean, come on, me? All I've done the past eleven years is reset rat traps alone in the dark." Keane's head tipped upwards, and she felt the muscles by his shoulders as they tightened.

"That's not all you've done," he whispered, "you survived. So many haven't, but you did. That's why we have to do this. If we don't, then so many more will die. Everything we've done up to this point won't matter. Every single day of survival will amount to nothing when we're dead on a boat somewhere within the Carnavan Sea."

Malyssandra's hand tightened on his shoulder as the weight of his words hit her. She knew he was right, that they had to do something. It had been a fairytale that the rebellion would simply swoop in and rescue the slaves without any effort from them. Logically it made sense that the slaves would have to fight back, but Malyssandra hadn't realized it until that moment.

"So we riot," she stated bluntly and released Keane's shoulder. Her heart ricocheted throughout her insides at the thought, but she was confident in her answer.

Keane relaxed at her words and spun to face her in the trickle of moonlight that lightened the space. His eyes looked hopeful, and he rubbed his hands along the wet fabric of his pants. "We riot." His smile was bright and contagious, and Malyssandra wondered if they had gone crazy. He laughed and climbed to his feet. "They'll send me another letter before the Prethans arrive with more details. I will let you know when I receive it."

Malyssandra's smile faltered as a question rose up within her, and she wasn't sure why she hadn't been curious before. "Keane?" Her voice hitched on his name, and his eyebrows shot up as he took in her furrowed stare. "Why you?"

His face dropped in confusion. "What do you mean?" He asked, unclear as to what she implied. Silence stretched between them as Malyssandra debated the question. She wondered if the answer was something obvious she had missed along the way. Her mind trailed back to the conversations that had happened between them over the past few weeks, but nothing came to light. She had never asked, and he had never offered up a reason.

She became more confident, "Why does the rebellion send letters only to you? Why doesn't anyone else get them? It just seems so random. You had to of been... thirteen when the Yulsans invaded? No offense, but I just don't see why they chose you. A thirteen-year-old boy just doesn't seem like the obvious choice for a rebel group to communicate with."

Keane's eyes flashed in the moonlight before his face retreated to the shadows as he turned away. He looked at the ground, battling something within himself, and Malyssandra thought he would ignore the question and wander off into the dark corner of his cell. Instead, he stood stone still in the shadows, and she could see the hesitation in his breathing. "Keane?" She whispered softly, and she leaned in his direction.

He flinched at the sound of his name, and as his head turned back into the blue light, sorrow deepened his eyes. "Because," his voice wavered as he fought to get the words out, "I am the Criedan prince."

23

Ferix had ensured the guards were not stationed outside Reina's door as she made her way beyond the threshold and into the palace. She was free to roam the halls without their watching eyes, and she faintly pondered escaping. The way out was clearly marked in her mind, but she knew the northern door held too many guards. If she tried to escape and failed, then she would have lost any possible chance she had at finding another exit. Besides, she wanted to hear what the prince had to say.

Although she had only been to the eastern sector once, she knew the way. After weeks of having avoided the dark hallways, her mind had marked out which path to avoid. She led herself down the beautifully adorned sections of the castle and watched as decorations began to turn to simple stone and the windows dwindled. She had heeded Ferix's advice and brought a torch. The light cast twisted shadows along the walls.

She inspected the darkness in search of anything that could have been deceitfully hidden within. Nothing moved, and she felt no eyes on her as the sound of her feet padded gently against the floor. The corner came into view, and she quickly darted around it and into the archive room on her left, where the prince stood underneath the light of his own torch.

"Record timing," he teased, and Reina scowled as she set her torch into a sconce by the door. She looked around the dusty old room.

If it had been another life, she might have enjoyed the space around her. When she was young, she used to love when her father read her stories before bedtime. She had sat above the covers and begged for him to read another until her mother stepped in to tell her it was time to go to sleep. The archive room was filled with stories she was sure she would have loved.

Maps lined the room, and Reina wondered if any showed faraway lands of which she would never see. She inched toward the old paper, and she felt as Ferix's eyes followed her curiously across the torch-lit room. Her fingers fluttered over an aged drawing of mountains.

"That's northern Ildris," Ferix spoke, and Reina looked back at him in confusion.

"Ildris?" She asked, and he blinked.

"The land we live on, Ildris." His words were slow as if he were explaining something to a child. Reina glared at his tone and shook her head to show she still didn't know what he was talking about.

"We're in Yulsa," she declared, and Ferix rubbed his forehead.

"Yes, you're right," he started as he came to stand next to her, "But Yulsa is in Ildris. Ildris is the mass of land we are settled on. Crieda was in Ildris as well. Many kingdoms are." Reina stared at him, puzzled by what he was saying. "You weren't taught this as a child?" He asked.

"I didn't get a chance to be taught much of anything as a child. Den Zei doesn't really offer classes on geography." Her voice was flat, unamused by the look he was giving her. "When I was young, I was taught to read and write, not about the land beyond Crieda. There was no reason to know much more. Nobody ever really left the kingdom. There was no reason to. Until your father destroyed it." Ferix flinched at her words and drew himself away from her side.

"People should know about the world they live in. Perhaps the naivety of your people helped in the downfall of your kingdom." He was passive, and Reina spun on him in irritation.

"Or perhaps your soldiers did that," she spat, and the prince shook his head.

"There's no use in rehashing the past, Reina. You told me you have questions, and I am here to answer them. Let's not waste time discussing things neither of us can change." He was right, and Reina knew it. The past was locked in stone while their present hadn't been yet. Annoyance still sat heavy in her chest, but she ignored it.

"What happened to you?" She asked, and the prince's eyebrows shot up at the question.

"What do you mean?"

"You are nothing like how I thought you'd be. I grew up in Den Zei, imagining the Yulsan royals to be harsh, cruel. Your father is, but not you. Why? What happened?" Their gazes locked, and Reina watched as the storms in his eyes froze over.

His jaw clenched, and he turned away from her. "Ask another question."

"I don't want to ask another question. That's what I want to know. How can I trust you if I don't even know why you're helping me?"

Reina watched as his head fell back, and he stared at the ceiling. It fell quiet as she waited for an answer.

"Yulsa has not always been this cruel, Reina." He spun to face her. "The day my father invaded Crieda, I knew what he was doing was wrong. But I couldn't do anything as he slaughtered your people, as he bound them in chains and tore them from their homes. I was just a boy, and he was my father." He took a step toward her. "My mother has never been a very present woman. She spends her days locked in a room, only coming out when she needs something. My father knew this and assigned a maid to keep an eye on me. Many lords and ladies in the kingdom do the same with the maids they were assigned. Too powerful to be bothered with raising their own children." His eyes flashed.

"She followed me everywhere and reported back to my father on if I had been studying long enough or training hard enough. At first, I hated that I had been assigned a babysitter. Then, I got to know her." He looked down at Reina. "She had two children of her own and a husband she missed dearly. He had been killed trying to protect their daughter. She was the only survivor in her family, and she had been broken because of it."

Reina thought back to her own parents. She knew what it was like being the only one left. The heartbreak, the hopelessness. It was a black hole of pain that threatened to pull someone through, never to be seen again. Her heart clenched.

"I began to enjoy having her around. She was the mother I never had, and I tried to help her as best I could. I knew I could never replace what she had lost, but she seemed to like caring for me. So, I let her boss me around and fuss over me as I got ready for the day." He took a deep breath, and his demeanor darkened. "Then, my father intervened."

"He didn't like that we had grown so close. He thought it was inappropriate that his son had developed a relationship with a slave. Even though he had assigned that slave to replace my mother. My father summoned me to his chambers one morning, and I went. When I got there, she was in his bed. My father had forced her to lay with him to teach me a lesson." A tear trailed down his cheek. Reina fought the urge to reach out to him as her own eyes watered. "He owned her. She was not a person to him but an object. Something he could do with as he pleased. He wanted me to see her the same way, but the only person I saw differently that day was him."

"What happened to her?" Reina whispered, afraid of the answer.

"She killed herself," he said bluntly. "After my father was done with her, she was never the same. She hung herself a few days later, and I swore I wouldn't watch as my father did that to anyone else."

"What was her name?"

"Myra," he breathed.

Silence settled around them. The prince dipped his head to stare solemnly at the ground. Reina watched as dust danced in the air, unsure of what to say.

"The day my father invaded Crieda was the day Yulsa broke," the price blurted, "I think you can help me fix it."

"Me?" Reina sputtered.

"You're a miracle, a human with the power of a god. If we can prove that to the Yulsan people, then we might have a chance. The priestess may have their ears now, but if they knew that you were gifted with the actual essence of Werthes, then maybe they will listen to you." His eyes were serious, and his jaw was clenched tight with emotion.

Reina scoffed. "People won't listen to me. I'm not a leader. I spent my life in Den Zei being constantly broken down by guards who got their jollies off torturing me. There is nothing about me that screams inspirational, and half these people view me as nothing more than your father's pet."

"You weren't broken, though," Ferix retorted, "You came out of Den Zei very much *alive*. Your story is something many people will look up to. You're not only miraculous for what you can do, Reina. You're miraculous for what you have done."

Words evaded her, and she sputtered as she tried to find something to say. "What if there are more like me?"

She didn't want to be alone. She wanted him to tell her that there were others that he knew about. Being the only one of her kind within their world scared her more than anything, and she wanted him to understand that.

He shook his head in confusion, and she pushed on. "What if I'm not descended from gods?" The words sounded strange on her tongue, but she ignored the absurdity of it all. "What if I'm just a witch, like the priestess?"

"You're not a witch," he stated.

"Why not?" She crossed her arms.

"Witches spend years honing what they do. They do not simply awaken one day with the ability to heal others. Even the most seasoned witches cannot do such a thing. It's impossible. They can only do trinket magic; it's petty and merely a parlor trick. Even those who practice dark magic cannot do even a fraction of what you can. It's unheard of." He was disinterested in the turn the conversation had taken.

"Can they see into the future?" She asked, and Ferix showed slight interest in the question.

"Now, why would you ask me that?" He mused, and his bright eyes signaled for her to continue.

"Someone I know can see things before they happen. She saw me with your father before I ever stepped foot in the palace. Is that something a witch can do?" Her voice came out louder than she intended, but she didn't care. She was desperate for an answer.

The prince leaned forward. "Who is this someone?" He drew out slowly, and Reina debated how much she could share of Malyssandra's secret. She shook her head to signal that she wasn't going to tell him, and he shrugged as if the answer to that question hadn't mattered much to him anyway. "Alright then, how do you know she can see into the future?"

"It happened when I touched her," Reina explained, "I grabbed her arm, and she had a vision."

He pondered her words for a moment and leaned back against the wall behind him, "Witches cannot see into the future. The amount of magic they can summon is too small. It is possible, however, that you could have drawn the ability out of this person."

Reina didn't like how his explanation had been brought back to her own abilities, and she huffed. "How is that even possible?"

Ferix was too enraptured by his own line of thought to notice Reina's frustration. "Gods are promiscuous beings, and there are descendants from many different gods within this world. But it has been so long since the gods have walked among us, the power within their bloodlines is likely quite faint. That being said, you absorbed the entirety of Werthes' abilities when the orb broke. Meaning you are basically carrying the absolute power of a god within you. If you were to touch someone with dormant bloodlines, your power might be able to awaken whatever lies within them. Hertes was the god of omens; he could see the future for what course it was set to be. It sounds like this maid could be descended from his bloodline, which is why she can see what is yet to come."

Reina's heart stopped in her chest as she looked to the prince with hope in her eyes. "So there could be more people like me out there?"

"Following that line of thought," the prince debated, "Yes, it would be likely there are many more people like you out there in the world. If only you can get to them."

Reina nodded, and she felt relief as it spread through her body. A smile stretched at her face. After years of having felt alone in the world, she realized she didn't have to be. "I can turn things to gold," she breathed, and the prince raised his eyebrows at the random confession.

"Excuse me?"

"I don't know how I did it, but I turned a brush to gold. It just kind of happened, and I thought I was going crazy." She looked at him wildly. "If there are people out there like me, I need to find them." A whirlwind of emotions swept through her, making her want to both laugh and cry. But before she could do either, a chill ran down her spine.

She froze as she recognized the feeling, and a cold sweat started at the base of her neck. The prince noticed the change in her, and his eyes narrowed, "What is it, Reina?" She stared at him in horror.

Goosebumps rose along her flesh. "It's here," she stated quietly, and she searched around the room for what she knew hid within the darkness.

"What's here?" He asked and pushed off the wall so that his tall frame stood before her. She swallowed at the dryness in her throat and blinked hard. Her torch by the doorway went out suddenly, and she jumped away from it and toward Ferix. A low growl started in her chest as she swiveled in place, attempting to locate the creature.

"The shadow." As soon as the words had exited her mouth, laughter picked up on her left. She turned as the laughter grew in volume, and she swallowed as it stretched upward toward the ceiling and towered over her.

"Dark magic," he muttered, and Reina swiveled her head so she could see him in her periphery. "I can't see it. Whoever it is doesn't wish me to. Only those who practice dark magic can cast themselves into the shadow realm. It's the most powerful thing a witch can accomplish. Although, it comes at a price. It's corruptive magic, and they cannot hold it for long." The laughter became too loud for Reina to hear the rest of what Ferix had to say, and she brought her hands to her ears. The noise burned within her mind, and no matter what she did, she could not quiet it.

She felt the prince's hand at her back as she hunched over, and her jaw clenched so tight that she thought her teeth would splinter from the pressure. *"Reina,"* the shadow whispered to her, and her vision blurred.

Then, it ended. The room grew quiet, and Ferix's voice came back to her. "It can't hurt you. It's okay." Her body was trembling, and she wondered when she had fallen to the floor. She removed her hands from her ears and looked around, disoriented. The shadow had left. She no longer felt eyes on her, and her trembling began to slow.

"It's gone," she stated flatly, and the prince pulled her to her feet. He looked her over and gave a curt nod before he let go of her and took a step back. "You said it was a witch?"

"Dark magic," he repeated and looked at her cautiously. "Very few practicing witches use it as they know of the dangers. Some do, though, and it's obvious when someone picks it up."

"How so?" Reina cleared her voice and stood taller. She didn't like how the prince looked at her like she was about to crumble.

"Their personality becomes... different. They become darker, almost manic in a way." He pulled his eyes from her as if he could sense her annoyance at his stare, and she felt more confident at the disappearance of his prying gaze.

"Why would a witch wish to follow me around?" She pondered.

"Have you seen the shadow before?" The prince pushed, but Reina ignored him. Her mind ran wild with what she had just learned. The shadow wasn't a creature but a human who was simply toying with her. She set her jaw and thought back to the priestess. The shadow had chased her moments after she had seen the woman in the chapel, her unnaturally green eyes planted in an open book.

"Could it have been the priestess?" Reina put her thoughts into words. Her heart pounded within her chest as she realized the severity of what had just happened. "If it was the priestess, could she have heard everything we said?" She wondered how long the shadow had been in the room. She had been distracted, lost in her need to find people like her. She hadn't been paying attention.

"I don't know," the Prince admitted and watched Reina carefully as she worked her way through her hectic thoughts.

"If she did... How long until she tells your father?" Reina asked.

The prince's face darkened at the question. He grew quiet, his lips thinned. His eyes glared into the darkness behind her, and she could see ice in his stare. In the faint light of the single torch, he looked sculpted from stone. His fists were clenched at his sides, his jaw was set in determination, ready for war.

Suddenly, he softened, and his eyes looked back to Reina in exhaustion. No longer was anger the primary resident within him. He let out a small sigh. "Take my torch and go back to your room," he stated, and Reina opened her mouth to protest. "Now. I'll deal with whatever is to come."

Reina's mouth snapped shut, and she looked at him for a moment longer before she gave a quiet nod. She walked over to the sconce which held his torch and carried it over to the doorway. Before she left, she hoisted the flame to the torch that had been put out by the shadow. She watched as it reignited.

"Ferix?" She whispered over her shoulder. Silence answered her, and she took a deep breath. "I had one more question."

Her ears rang from the lack of sound before the prince responded, "Go ahead."

"You said that your father pushed the prince aside in Crieda before he took the orb," she paused and chewed on the inside of her cheek as she looked out at the dark hallway, "What happened to him?"

"I told him to run."

She looked over her shoulder and gave him a soft smile. "You truly aren't what I thought you'd be." He blinked at her. "Thank you," she added softly before she exited the room and walked shakily out of the eastern sector.

24

MALYSSANDRA

"You are the *what*?" Malyssandra's words reverberated off the stone walls and around the cell block. Keane flinched at the volume, but she was too shocked to notice. She felt as if all the air had left her lungs. That hadn't been the answer she expected.

The third level was filled with shushes from other people within their cells, and Malyssandra's head looked around. She had momentarily forgotten where she was. Keane looked on cautiously as he monitored her reaction. *He must be joking*, she thought, but the serious set of his face made her feel as if what he had just said was true. Or at least, he believed it to be true.

She had never seen the prince when she lived in Crieda; not many had. There was no memory for her to compare the man who stood before her to, no way to see if he had any similar features. Her eyes squinted. *He's gone mad.* Eleven years within Den Zei had broken his mind.

He could have simply believed himself to be the prince as a way to escape his situation and buried himself into the ludicrous thoughts. Perhaps nothing he had told her during their time together was true. In fact, Malyssandra hadn't even seen any of the famed letters he had supposedly been receiving. She had only ever heard of them after they had disappeared back to wherever they had come from in the first place. *He knew about the trade though, how else could he have known?* She groaned in frustration at her thoughts and looked at him doubtfully.

"I know," he sighed, "it sounds crazy." He grabbed at the bars between them and drew himself tall. "I don't know how the rebellion found out I was still alive, but somehow they did. They aren't sending letters to a random slave. They're sending them to their prince." Malyssandra scanned him over and shook her head.

"How are you not dead? I thought the royal family had all been killed that day." His eyes flashed with sadness at the question, and he turned from her. His long hair rocked slowly behind him at his movement, and Malyssandra could see for the first time the weight he held on his shoulders. She wondered if what he said was true. If he really was the Criedan prince. The idea was insane to her, but the past month had been nothing but insane. She figured it wasn't as farfetched as healing others with a simple touch or seeing into the future. Although, the unexpectedness of it had completely caught her off guard.

"My parents were." His voice was soft and laced with a regret that Malyssandra couldn't understand, "I was in the palace, a boy at the time. I was tasked with defending something in the palace that was of great importance to our kingdom. My father went down to the town square to commence the festivities and left me to guard it. He had grown careless, confident in the safety of our kingdom. Nobody had ever attacked Crieda, and he had only ruled throughout an era of peace. Same as his father before him. When the Yulsans attacked, I stood alone. I knew something was wrong when the screaming started." His shoulders hitched as if he were reliving that horrible day, and her hands clenched at her sides. "I wasn't strong enough to stop what was happening. I was pushed aside as if I were nothing more than an inconvenience. I wanted to fight back, but I was scared. If I had, I know damn well I wouldn't be alive today. There was nothing I could do, and when someone told me to run, I did. I was a coward. I ran from the palace and into the streets. When they began to round people up, I went without a word. Nobody recognized me. I had spent my life within the palace protecting something that nobody was even supposed to know about. I was too afraid to tell anyone who I was, and I've kept it a secret all these years. If the king were to find out I'm here, he'd kill me. The royal family is supposed to be dead. *I'm* supposed to be dead." Malyssandra watched as his breathing quickened and his words became harsh. She worried at her bottom lip as what he had said registered slowly in her brain.

"So, Reina…?" She trailed off, and he turned around with a heavy expression on his face.

His head shook. "She doesn't know." The answer didn't surprise her as much as she thought it would. He had admitted before that he hadn't trusted Reina with the letters and that he hadn't trusted her not to be impulsive with the information. Her heart ached at the idea of him having held in such a secret for so long. She couldn't imagine how hard it had been and how lonely he had felt.

She finally broke her stillness and walked back to the bars that divided them. "I've been having visions," she blurted, and his posture snapped to attention at the absurdity of what she had confessed. Her eyes held his as she unburdened herself, "That day that I came here to deliver clothes to the guards. When Reina touched me, I had a vision of her with the king. Then a few days later, I had another one of you and me in these cells. I thought I was insane until I learned what Reina could do. If she can truly heal people with just a touch, would it really be so impossible that I can see the future?"

"Reina said she felt something. I didn't believe her; it just didn't make sense." He looked lost. "How is that possible?"

"I don't know," she murmured. "I have never felt anything like it. It was... intense. Like she had fixed me, made me whole. It wasn't like she gave me something, more like she woke something up that was already there."

Keane nodded, his hand resting on his chin. "Have you had any visions since you've been here? Anything that hasn't happened yet?"

Malyssandra hadn't expected him to accept her confession that easily, and it took her a moment to collect her thoughts. "No," she drew out, "my mind has been quiet. I can't control when I see things or what I see. At least, I don't think I can. I'm not really sure. I haven't tried."

"You should."

"What?" She pulled back in confusion. "But you told Reina not to experiment with what she can do."

"And if I hadn't, maybe we could have been out of here by now. If Reina sparked something inside you, maybe she could have done the same with the others. Maybe if she had tried to better understand her ability, things would be different. If you can really see what's going to happen next, then we have an advantage. We can plan for things that haven't yet happened." What he said made sense, but Malyssandra didn't even know where to start.

"I can't," she faltered, "I don't know how."

"Then try to figure it out," he insisted. "If you've done it before, you can do it again."

"Keane…"

"Just try it, okay? It doesn't have to be right this second, but promise you'll at least try." He was begging her. She had never had anyone beg her for anything, and she grew uncomfortable under the scrutiny of his gaze.

If she tried it and let him down, she didn't know what she would do. The thought of failure scared her, and her throat began to close up. Telling him had been a bad idea. She wanted to ignore that part of her, not embrace it. Her silence must have lasted a beat too long because Keane cleared his throat.

"Promise me," he urged her.

She didn't have a choice. Keane wouldn't drop it. He would push her every day until she gave in if she didn't say what he wanted to hear. She gnawed on her lip as she avoided his pleading gaze. Finally, she nodded. "I'll try."

His mouth stretched wide, revealing straight teeth and crinkling his eyes. Malyssandra didn't feel like speaking anymore, and her shoulders drooped forward. There was a pit in her stomach at the sight of his excitement. "Am I excused?"

His smile dropped. "What?"

"Am I excused, your majesty?" She asked with a curtsey, falling back into old habits.

"Mallie, you don't have to-."

"Am I excused?" She demanded, her eyes glued to the floor.

"You're excused," he answered.

She dipped her head in acknowledgment and turned away from him. As she settled onto the floor of her cell, she wondered if she'd ever be able to do what Keane had asked. Or if she'd fail her prince.

...

Malyssandra climbed on the wagon headed to the stone yards. The heat smothered her, and it was nearly unbearable for her to attempt to draw in breaths of the smoldering air. She didn't know how long she could survive on such little water in such intense heat. The supplies had run low, and the slaves within Den Zei were not a top priority to receive much of anything. Water breaks had slowly become lighter in the way of liquid, and even their food had been cut substantially. Moisture in the third level had also dwindled. There wasn't much relief from the uncomfortable thirst that dried her mouth.

She was distracted by what Keane had asked her to do and almost didn't notice a blonde woman moving to sit beside her. Familiarity made her head turn, and her eyes widened as she laid them upon Ivanka. In her time at Den Zei, she had nearly forgotten her friend. She looked ragged and tired, even as she offered Malyssandra a small smile.

"Ivanka," Malyssandra breathed, "I-."

Ivanka shook her head once, aggressively, and looked over at the guards that rounded the wagon to climb in front. Malyssandra understood and stopped speaking but scanned her friend's boney frame intensely. She had lost so much weight, and although her skin was usually pale, it looked unhealthily so.

Malyssandra's hand reached out to cover Ivanka's sharp knuckles and chipped nails, but Ivanka pulled away before she could do so. Her eyes were shrouded in fear, and her hair had lost the healthy shine it had held within the palace. The blues she had grown used to staring into looked dull, nearly grey in their lack of hope. She was not the woman Malyssandra had grown up with.

"Just hold on," Malyssandra whispered, ignoring the warning Ivanka had given her moments earlier. "Something is coming; you just need to hold on a little longer."

Ivanka shifted away from Malyssandra, and her heart shattered in her chest. She remembered Ivanka as a small girl within the palace. Before the king had chosen her as his favorite plaything. Happiness had followed wherever she went, and she had refused to pay any mind to the horror they had been forced into. All she had cared about was that they were within the palace and not Den Zei. She had done what was asked of her and more, and Malyssandra had been jealous of her friend for having been able to stay so positive back then. That little girl had been crushed under the wheel of the world. She no longer existed. She had grown into the woman who sat beside her, silent and hopeless, crouched over on a rotten wagon.

The wheels rolled forward underneath them, and those within rocked slightly at the motion. Malyssandra's hand reached out again to try and console her friend, but as her hand made contact with Ivanka's skin, the world faded away.

Chaos was everywhere. Fire scorched the city and headed toward the palace at an alarming rate. Malyssandra imagined she could feel the heat of the flames as they licked into the skies above. People ran around her but paid her no mind as she stood invisibly watching the carnage that fell upon the kingdom of Yulsa. Mouths opened to scream, and Malyssandra flinched even though she heard no noise escape their mouths. The fire ate at their clothing before it devoured their skin. Malyssandra turned away and was presented with the palace ballroom.

Many people sat within, confusion riddled their faces. Reina sat to the right of the king's table. She wore a beautiful golden gown, and her blue eyes swiveled around the room. Her hands were pressed flat against the white tablecloth beneath, bracing herself.

A man was standing at a table filled with men in green and blue robes that swept against the floor. The Prethans. It had to be. Malyssandra had never seen anyone in Yulsa don those colors. They had arrived, and they looked terrified.

The priestess slid out a side door, and Malyssandra watched as the queen was ushered away, but the prince stayed at the king's side. His gaze clung to Reina, and something unfamiliar clouded his eyes.

The ground shook, and the room exploded in panic. Malyssandra couldn't see Reina or the prince anymore, and as she spun around in search of them, she teleported yet again.

The yard of Den Zei was ravaged. The gates around the area were burned to the ground; both slaves and guards ran from the blaze surrounding them. A figure bolted through the wreckage and deeper into the fire. Malyssandra looked at the fallen gates before she ran after them.

There was something familiar about the person that she couldn't quite figure out. She watched as they threw their head back, and her heart twisted at the untamed coarse black hair that appeared. Malyssandra crept closer. Her heart was in her throat as she once again stared out at herself.

Tears streamed down her cheeks, and she looked frantically about as if she had lost something. Then, she watched as her own body sprinted through a wall of flames.

Malyssandra gasped as her vision disappeared, and she was presented with Ivanka once again. Ivanka looked at her quizzically, and Malyssandra shook her head at her as words refused to come. Ivanka blinked as if she wanted to say something but turned away from her instead.

Malyssandra's breathing came fast and short, and she looked around at the other slaves who seemed unbothered by her outburst. Sweat ran from her brow, and she raised a shaky arm to wipe it away as she tried to settle down.

If her vision was correct, then whatever she had just seen took place on the day the Prethans were set to arrive. They had less than a week until their world would go up in flames.

25

When the king summoned Reina the following morning, she couldn't help but wonder if he knew of the meeting she had with his son the night before. Her skin buzzed with anxiety, and sweat moistened her palms as she entered the throne room. She swallowed as she came to stand at the steps which led to the throne, and the guard backed away as she ascended. The king watched her with hungry eyes, and it took every ounce of her willpower to withhold the grimace that tried to grow on her face.

The priestess wasn't at his side, but the queen was. Her raven hair spiraled down from atop her head, and her blue eyes scanned Reina over. She seemed different than the last time Reina had seen her. There was something sharp about her stare and something off about the way her heart-shaped lips pulled up at the corners. She looked cruel, a harsh contrast to how she had looked the night Reina had been brought to the palace.

The king's eyes raked her up and down, inspecting the womanlier shape she had adopted due to the healthy amount of food she had devoured since she had arrived at the palace. The way he looked at her made her feel exposed, and her cheeks heated in anger.

"You should be careful running around like that." The king looked pointedly at her bare feet. "It'd be a shame if you stepped on something sharp and sliced your foot open."

"I'd heal," Reina spoke passively and flicked her wrist by her ear to signify the thought of cutting her foot really wasn't that daunting to her.

"I suppose you would." The skin beside the king's eyes pinched as he gave Reina a possessive smile. She clenched her teeth. "Speaking of," he said pointedly, "I believe we have business to attend to."

Reina wiped the sweat from her palms onto her trousers. She couldn't keep doing it. Each time she healed the king, she found it a little more impossible to live with herself. After hearing what he had done to the maid Ferix spoke of the night before, Reina could no longer pretend she wasn't helping a monster. Keane would be okay. He had to be. There was no way the king knew it was him she had saved. There were so many people in Den Zei, the guards would never remember it had been Keane crushed beneath a beam. Reina was ready to call the king's bluff.

"No."

The word echoed across the room, and Reina pulled her shoulders back in defiance. The queen's eyes glinted, intrigued. She didn't seem shocked or upset, not like how Reina had expected. Instead, she seemed aloof, unfeeling. Nothing like the woman who had looked to her in a plea to save her dying husband. Reina narrowed her eyes.

"No?" The king's voice rumbled from beside her, and Reina turned her attention to him. His stare was hard, and Reina fought the urge to pull away from it. She would not be weak in the eyes of the man who had enslaved her people.

"No," she repeated, certainty rang in her voice.

"Do I need to remind you of what will happen to your friend if you refuse me?" He settled back in his chair, convinced his words would have shut down any fight Reina had. They didn't.

"I remember. I just find it odd," she remarked.

"Odd?"

"Yes, quite odd. If you truly knew who it was that I cared for in Den Zei, why would you have ever risked leaving them inside? Why wouldn't you have lorded them over me, taunted me with them?" There was a challenge in her voice, and the king rose to it.

"I know who he is," he snarled.

"All you know is that he is a he. You don't know his face. There are many men in Den Zei. If you wish to find him, then happy hunting. But I am certain you'd have no luck." She smiled as the king's eyes flashed in rage. "I am not your pet. I am not your toy. I will no longer help you. It's time you realize you have no true ownership over my people. We do not belong to you, and you will suffer for what you have done."

The sound of the guard as he moved across the floor to the base of the stairs made Reina's head swivel. As he lifted his foot to ascend the stairs toward Reina, the king thundered, "I have this under control!"

Reina snapped around and looked the king in his eyes. *"You have no control!"* Her shout ricocheted off the walls. The king's face morphed, furious, as he climbed to his feet.

He opened his mouth to speak, but the soft laughter of the queen cut him off. Reina and the king turned in unison to the beautiful woman as her laugh turned into a cackle. The sound grated against Reina's ears, and she pulled away from the noise. As it died down, the queen sighed and wiped the tears from her eyes.

"My darling, my king." Her voice was high, light. As if she were sharing a fond memory. "Are you truly arguing with this imp of a slave?" Her arm darted out and grabbed Reina by the chin. Reina tried to recoil, but the woman's grip was firm.

She felt something build up inside of her, and her eyes darted around as her heart felt ready to explode. As the power began to trickle out of her, the queen's blue stare brightened. "There she is," she marveled, then pushed Reina's head back forcefully. Reina tried to steady herself as her feet stumbled backward. Too late, she remembered the stairs.

Her arms flailed as she stepped into the open air, and her world turned upside down. She felt as she toppled over and her arm snapped. Her hip bounced off a step. Blood filled her mouth as her teeth bit down on her tongue. Her neck whipped back, and her ankle twisted. Then, she was at the base of the steps.

She watched through hooded eyes as red pooled around her. The ground was cold. She watched through her lashes as the queen and king discussed something at the top of the steps, and she heard as the guard came up behind her.

"What would you like me to do with her, your highness?"

The king gave one last look to the queen before he marched down the steps. He stared down at Reina for a moment, an angry satisfaction in his eyes.

"You might have been right," he admitted begrudgingly, "I don't know who the man was that you healed." Reina's chest expanded with relief at the words. But her victory was short-lived. The king crouched beside her. "One thing you miscalculated was that I *do* know who your people are." Her heart sank. "When the Prethans arrived, I was going to offer my own people for the trade. They are less experienced. It's why I gathered them up in the first place. I wasn't going to trade my most skilled slaves. But now," he whispered harshly into her ear, "Now I will make sure you are the only Criedan left on all of Ildris. Your people have you to thank for what is to come." He stood up and spoke to the guard, "Take her to the prison. And make sure she's not conscious when you get there."

The queen descended the stairs and exited the room with the king. Reina reached for her power within her in an attempt to heal herself before the guard could do anything. As her arm snapped back in place, she spun to face the man and watched as he brought his boot down on her face.

26

MALYSSANDRA

The kingdom was going to be nothing more than ash in under a week. Malyssandra couldn't get the hellish flames out of her head. Everything was going to burn.

Keane had wanted her to have a vision that they could use to their advantage. They couldn't use fire. It was unpredictable, dangerous. It didn't matter that she had seen it before it happened. There was nothing they could do to stop such a thing. To utilize it. So many people would die, innocent people that had done nothing wrong.

She thought back to the day she had visited Den Zei. The kingdom had been so full of life. There had been children, families. The king and his soldiers could have burned in eternity for all she cared. But many Yulsans hadn't done anything wrong, who didn't deserve such a painful end.

"Keane," Malyssandra whispered into the darkness. "I need to tell you something." No moonlight shined down the stairwell that night. The clouds had smothered the sky. She hoped that meant rain was set to arrive soon, but deep down, she knew that wouldn't happen. The world had been as dry as ever in her vision, and the dangerous speed of the fire could have only meant the earth was parched. Keane's breathing grew closer in the darkness as he made his way to her, and she tilted her head to better project the softness of her voice. "I had another vision today."

Keane's breathing stopped. "What did you see?"

"The yard, the city, the kingdom, all of it. It was on fire." Malyssandra choked on the words as if the smoke were already in her lungs.

Keane was quiet as he slid down beside her against the bars, and she felt his hand reach through a gap to settle over hers. "When?" He finally asked after he had a few minutes to think through what she had said.

"The day the Prethans arrive. They were in the ballroom with Reina; everyone looked so scared, Keane," Her voice grew strained and faint. She rubbed her free hand over her mouth before she continued, "It was chaos, utter chaos. Do you," she paused, and her voice hitched on the words before she swallowed and pulled herself back on track. "Do you think the rebellion starts it?"

He sighed in response, "They might. We're in a war, Mallie. People are going to die; that's just the truth of it. Look what they did to Crieda. People died there too. Innocents died in the streets that day, and innocents will likely die when the rebellion arrives."

Malyssandra pulled her hand away from Keane's and rested it in her lap. "If innocents have to die, then we are not righting a wrong, Keane. We are simply trading one wrong for another." Her mouth tugged downward. "I was within those flames, and I don't think I was able to get out. I think I'm going to die, Keane. If they truly do set the kingdom on fire, I don't think I'm going to make it." Her voice broke, and she wiped at her eyes.

"I'm not going to let you die," he assured her. "If you had a vision, maybe there's something we can do to change it. If everyone here knows about the fire, then maybe we can plan for it. That's why I wanted you to see something in the first place, so we can prepare." His words were confident, and Malyssandra shook her head as tears slid down her cheeks in the darkness.

"There's no preparing for what I saw," she pushed out, "It was so hectic. People were everywhere, scared, lost, burning. Burning *alive*. Gods, Keane. It was worse than anything I could ever imagine. Nobody deserves that." She hugged her legs to her chest and began to rock back and forth.

"They do," he insisted.

"Who are you to decide that?" She turned on him, even though she couldn't see him in the darkness. "These are *people* we're talking about."

"And what are we?" He growled, "Are we not people? Is it okay that they killed *our* families, *our* children? That they threw us in chains and locked us in cells?"

"I didn't say that!" She argued, "It's not fair what the king did to us, but it was the king that did it. I've seen his people, and although they are ignorant, not all of them are bad." She remembered the man who had stood up at the king's party the night he had announced his trade deal with Pretha. He had known what the king was doing was wrong. She wondered how many others felt that way. How many Yulsans had laid awake at night thinking of those who suffered in their kingdom? How many had wanted to throw a knife at their king's head? How many were afraid to do so.

"Yes, they are. They're *Yulsans*, Malyssandra," he huffed.

"You know how I got sent here? How Ivanka got sent here?" Silence answered her, and she continued, "The prince. The *Yulsan* prince."

"The prince?" Keane asked, a strange tint to his voice.

"Yes. When the king summoned Ivanka to his chambers, the prince tried to help her. He sheltered her. When he couldn't, and the queen caught Ivanka in her husband's bed, the queen almost killed her. But she didn't because prince Ferix stepped in. He had her sent to Den Zei so she could live. When Reina asked me to be sent here, I asked the prince. I told him I needed to make sure she was okay. He didn't want me to go. He didn't want to put me in such an awful place, but I begged him. I threatened to do it myself. He agreed. He is a good man, and not just any man, the *Yulsan prince*. So do not tell me they are all bad." She spat the final words before she settled down. Her back faced him.

Keane was quiet, and she could have sworn he would not speak again for the remainder of the night. She wouldn't have minded. Malyssandra was angry at how closed-minded he was. In no world could Malyssandra ever imagine that the place of someone's birth depicted whether they were worthy of life or not.

"The prince saved my life," Keane whispered, and Malyssandra tipped her ear in his direction, sure she had heard him wrong.

"What?"

"The day the Yulsans invaded, the prince was the person who told me to run. He let me go." His words grew quiet, and Malyssandra hardly heard the last part, "I never understood why."

"Our war is not with the people of Yulsa. Our war is with the king and his guards. Or do you think the prince should be punished for saving your life?" Her voice was harsh, cold.

Keane sighed. "If I have to choose between the Yulsans or my people, innocent or not, I will choose my people every time. Whatever the rebellion decides to do, I cannot stop it. I will not stop it. It's time we were let out of these damn cages." He stood.

"Can you at least get a message to them?" She blurted the question, grasping at straws.

Keane froze. "What message?"

"Ask them if their plan involves fire. Please. If it's not them, then maybe we can figure out where it starts." She blinked into the darkness, blind as to what Keane was thinking. "Please."

"If they send me another letter, I will ask."

"Thank you," she whispered.

He began to walk away, but his footsteps halted. "But if it is them, we have to stick to the plan. We have to riot. If we don't," he paused, "then it's all been for nothing. People will die, and we'll die with them. You do understand that, right?"

Malyssandra didn't answer. She didn't want to think about what would happen to them if the fire spread to Den Zei and they hadn't managed to escape. Her skin itched with phantom heat, and she crawled from the bars to lay her body against the earth beneath.

27

REINA

Darkness stretched around Reina as she opened her eyes. She bolted upright, disoriented. Then, she remembered her meeting with the king. Her stomach clenched, and she crawled along the floor until she felt the familiar coolness of metal in her hands. Bars. They had really thrown her in a prison cell.

Her body had healed while she had been unconscious. There was no more pain in her joints, and she flinched as she remembered her fall down the stairs. She rested her forehead against the bars. Her people were damned because of her. If she had just done as the king had expected and kept her mouth shut, she could have tried to escape. She could have at least tried to free her people. She hoped Malyssandra was having more luck than she was.

She wished desperately for Keane to appear beside her like he used to. It felt strange having her face against cell bars again, but nobody to speak to. He would have been angry with her for how she had acted. He would have called her brash, reckless. He would have been right.

He had always been right.

She wondered what her father would think of who she had grown to be. Trapped within a cell after she failed their people. She was certain he wouldn't have been proud. He had been a hero. Someone who had risked his life to save his people. He wouldn't have egged on the king like she had. He wouldn't have provoked the man who held the lives of all the living Criedans in his hands. No, her father had been smarter than that.

She wasn't sure what her mom would have made of her, either. She wanted to believe she'd understand. Reina was tired. Eleven years had grated at her heart, and she couldn't take it anymore. The very man who had ordered her people dead- had caused her father's death- had been pulling Reina's strings for a month. She had to see him, had to lay her hands on him. It had been too much. Her mother might have understood, or she would have hated her daughter for what she had become.

Ultimately, it didn't matter what her parents would have thought about her. *They're dead*, she thought humorlessly. They were gone, and she was there. They could chastise her for the decisions she made when she met them in the afterlife, but there was no room for the thought of them among the living.

Her breathing halted as she heard the creaking of a door. Someone had entered the prison, and she wondered if they had come to drag her away. She hung her head as she waited for her punishment. She deserved it. Whatever they threw at her, she would take it.

But as the torchlight settled on her cell, it was not a guard she turned to see.

"Ferix?" She croaked.

"Gods, Reina," he breathed as he pulled a ring of keys from his pocket and pulled the door open. "What were you thinking?" He moved to crouch beside her. His eyes searched hers for an explanation that wasn't there.

"I wasn't," she admitted and pulled her gaze to the floor.

He reached out and put his finger under her chin to turn her head back to him. She jerked away from his touch. The memory of his mother as she grabbed her chin flashed in her mind. He let his hand drop.

"They could have killed you." His face hardened in the flickering light, and Reina blinked.

"I'm fine."

"Only because they stopped!" He shouted, and Reina pulled away from him.

"I healed," she mumbled and glanced at the open door.

He sighed and ran his hand over his face. "You should have told me what you were going to do. I would have stopped you."

"I didn't know I was going to do it. Not until I got there. He was just so smug, so sure that he had complete control over me. I couldn't do it again. I thought I could win." Her lip twitched as her eyes welled up with tears. "Ferix, he's going to send the Criedans to Pretha. They're going to die on those ships."

He spun and sat down beside her, his back against the bars. "I know."

"No, you don't," she sniveled, "He was going to trade your people, the ones he rounded up. He never planned to actually trade the Criedans. But then," she gasped, "but then I told him no. I refused to heal him. And it's all my fault, and I'm the reason the rest of my people are going to die." She broke down, sobbing into her hands. Ferix reached out and pulled her into his chest.

"Your people aren't going to die," he asserted, and Reina shook her head against the soft fabric of his shirt.

"Don't do that, don't lie to me. My people are going to die because of me." She went to pull away from him, but he held her tighter.

"Reina," he sighed, "I promise you that your people will be fine."

She peaked up at him through her moist lashes. "How can you possibly know that when everything points to the contrary?"

He pulled his arm away and spun to face her. His blue eyes turned silver in the light of the fire. "Because," he stated, "I haven't told you everything yet."

She ran her hand across her nose to stop it from running and looked at him uncertainly. "What do you mean?"

Ferix looked to the ceiling. "Remember last night when I told you about Myra?" Reina nodded. "After she died, I began searching Ildris for people willing to fight for you. I wrote under an alias to many different kingdoms, but nobody dared to go against my father. They were too scared of him, of what he might do to their people if they rose up against him. I kept trying though, even as I got back declination after declination, I kept looking." He reached out and grasped Reina's hand in his. "I never stopped. I told them of what was happening here, of the atrocities he was committing against your people. Then, one day, I got a letter back."

Reina squeezed his hand. "Someone is going to help us?"

"Not just someone." Ferix smiled. "*Criedans.*"

Reina's heart fluttered in her chest, and her head spun. "That's impossible," she breathed, "All the Criedans are either dead or in Yulsa."

Ferix shook his head. "Not all of them. So many escaped, and after they received my letter, they answered the call to action. They pulled together to free their people, *your* people. They started a rebellion, Reina."

She gaped at him. "Why didn't you tell me this before?"

His eyes dropped down. "After you arrived, we didn't really have a plan anymore."

"What? Why not?"

He pulled his hand back and rubbed behind his neck. "When I told them my father was becoming ill, they planned to wait until he died. At that point, they knew who I was, and they knew I was next in line. They thought it safer to wait a few months than to risk more Criedans in a battle. When my father died, I was going to release the Criedan slaves and reinstate Crieda as a kingdom."

"But then I healed him," she breathed.

Ferix nodded. "When Malyssandra told me about how Ivanka had-."

"You know Ivanka?" She asked in shock.

"I know Ivanka," he affirmed, "And once Malyssandra told me Ivanka had spoken of a girl who healed her in her cell and that she bore no marks from the whips, I knew who you were. I knew what you could do. And I knew my father would hear about you sooner or later. I sent a letter to the rebellion and told them my father would be better soon. They needed to start planning something, and they needed to come get their people out of here."

"What are they going to do?"

"I don't know," Ferix admitted, "I told them not to send any more letters. It was too risky. If the wrong person were to read their letters and discover their plans, then there would be no hope. All I know is that the day the Prethans arrive is the day of their attack." He dipped his head so he could see her face. "They're coming for you, all of you."

Reina blinked at the tears in her eyes and stared at Ferix in wonder. All those years that Reina had been locked in Den Zei, Ferix had been trying to help her people. He had fought for them, pushed to regain their freedom. "But you told me you wanted me to appeal to the Yulsans. That if I could get the Yulsans to believe I am part of Werthes bloodline, they would listen to me. That we'd have a chance. Why did you say that if you knew there was a rebellion coming for us?"

"Even though there is a decent amount of Criedans in the rebellion, my father's soldiers still outweigh them greatly. I thought if we could get the Yulsan people on our side, that we would have better odds." He cocked his head and looked around the cell. "That doesn't really seem to be an option anymore."

"I suppose not," she said, "Unless you let me out...?"

"If I let you out, my father will put this kingdom in lockdown until he finds you, Reina. You really managed to piss him off today. He wants you to attend the party when the Prethans arrive. He wants you to watch as he sells your people. You need to act as if you're truly upset. If you don't, he'll be suspicious." He gave her a serious look, and she gaped at him.

"How did you do all this? How did you manage to go years gathering information about gods and the rebellion without getting caught? I don't understand." She shook her head, still not believing what he had told her.

He smirked. "I pay attention."

Reina lunged forward and planted her mouth on his. His eyes widened in shock, and his muscles grew rigid before he melted into her. His arms wrapped around her back, and his hand caressed the nape of her neck. She closed her eyes as she leaned closer, throwing her arms around his shoulders.

He rocked backward onto the ground, so their flesh pressed together. She felt his heartbeat through his shirt, and it matched the desperation of her own. He moaned into her mouth, and her lips curled upward in a smile before she pulled away.

He sat up, dazed. His eyes were glassy, and he gave her a baffled stare. "What was that for?" He asked.

"For paying attention," she remarked.

He flashed straight white teeth at her. "I should pay attention more often."

She chuckled, and her cheeks warmed as their eyes remained locked on each other. "They're really coming," she breathed.

"They're really coming," he repeated before he climbed to his feet and walked to the door. As he locked it behind him, his face changed, and he gave Reina a stern look. "I have a feeling it's going to happen quickly, and it's not going to be pretty. With the difference in numbers, the Criedans know they have to do something big and messy to get the advantage." Reina nodded. "Be ready." With those words, he turned away from her and exited the prison.

As Reina fell back into the darkness, she couldn't help but smile. Out there, somewhere, was a group of Criedans. *Free* Criedans. And they were coming to save their people.

28

MALYSSANDRA

In a day, the Prethans would arrive in the kingdom of Yulsa to finalize the trade deal they had struck with the king. Malyssandra's nerves had grown exponentially over the week, and she couldn't get the sight of the burning kingdom out of her mind.

"I received another letter." The words were flat.

"Send it back. Ask them." She crossed her arms. The glare she shot him strained her eyes, and his jaw ticked.

"They aren't starting a fire," Keane insisted.

"How do you know that?" Doubt radiated from her question, and Keane shook his head.

"Because they just told me."

"Show me," she demanded.

"I can't. The letter is already gone. They're going to send more to everyone in Den Zei, telling them to wait for the signal tomorrow. They're going to take down the walls." Keane watched her closely for a reaction, and she looked at him in disbelief.

"The walls?"

"An eye for an eye," he muttered.

"What about the fire?" She asked abruptly, and Keane snorted humorlessly at her question. She clenched her fingers around her biceps as she glowered at him. "I saw a fire, Keane. If the rebellion doesn't start it, then we're in big danger of dying tomorrow if we don't know where it comes from. It could just sneak up on us at any moment. We need to talk about it."

"Maybe your vision was wrong. Maybe there is no fire."

"The other day, you were begging me to have another vision, saying it could help us know what was going to happen. Now you're saying, after I had another vision, that it's wrong?" She threw her hands in the air.

"I'm not saying it's wrong. I'm saying it could be. Besides," he stated, "even if it was right, and there's going to be a fire, what do you want us to do about it? Call the guards over and nicely ask them to let us out so that we can save their kingdom? Don't be ridiculous."

Malyssandra bristled. But his tone didn't sit right with her. Even if they couldn't do anything about it, Malyssandra still felt guilty. She had seen it happen, and she was helpless to stop it from coming to fruition.

She shook her head at him in frustration and felt something in the palm of her hand. Her eyebrows scrunched together as she looked down and saw the letter there. The paper was wrinkled and yellowed with age. The words were written in chicken scratch letters, telling her that she would be liberated the following day and that when the walls fell, they would riot.

Whispers filled the cells as the other slaves received their letters, and Malyssandra was skeptical such a tactic would work. Those people had been locked inside cages for eleven years, terrified of the very people they were to riot against the following day. Did any of them have enough life left to do as the letter asked? Malyssandra wasn't sure.

She wondered if the maids in the palace had received letters. Or if they had been forgotten by the rebellion. Even though they were slaves, they were different from those in Den Zei. Their lives weren't as dark, as hopeless. She thought back to their gossip circles and their dedication to doing as they were told. Malyssandra shivered.

She had been like that not too long ago. She had been so willing to do as she was told, to keep her eyes to the ground and her voice quiet. For years she had gone unseen. Keane was right. There was nothing they could do about the fire, but they could do this. They could break free.

Malyssandra glanced up at him as the letter disappeared from her hand. "Are we really doing this?"

Keane relaxed and flashed her a smile. "We're really doing this."

Her lips tugged down. "But *if* there's a fire…?"

Keane's eyes softened. "I won't let anything happen to you."

She nodded solemnly before she grinned. "Then let's start a riot."

. . .

They stayed in their cells the rest of the day. No food or water was given to them, and Malyssandra looked up at the faint sliver of the moon as it passed by the top of the stairs. In less than a day, she could have been dead. She didn't want to settle on that thought, but it kept coming back to her.

The image of her lost between walls of flame was imprinted behind her eyes. She had been searching for something. The fallen gates had been so close, but she had gone deeper into the fire. Why would she have done that? Why wouldn't she have just escaped? She loosed a breath.

"Can't sleep?" Keane's voice rumbled from the darkness, and she shook her head. "Me neither."

Malyssandra blinked at the moon. "The day Crieda was invaded, you said your father left you to defend something. What was it?" She had started the question as a distraction from her own thoughts, but as she finished it, she realized she was actually curious. Prince Ferix had been in that room with him, had told him to run. There had to be a reason both princes were there; it couldn't have been a coincidence.

Keane shifted. The sound of his skin as it scraped against the floor made her flinch. "It's a long story," he murmured.

"You said you can't sleep?"

"Yeah," he grunted as he pulled himself to sit against the bars.

"Then we've got time." She turned to see his outline and listened as he inhaled deeply.

As he loosed his breath, he began, "Do you believe in the gods?" His head swiveled so he could see her nod. "So then you know of Werthes, the god of prosperity." It was a statement, not a question. Still, she nodded again.

At that, he launched into the tale of Crieda. The kingdom which had inherited the power of a god. He told her of the curse and how when the king had touched the power-filled orb, it had shattered. She thought back to the sickly king and wondered how long he had been falling ill. How long it had taken to get him on his death bed.

Keane explained that he had been tasked with guarding it for most of his childhood. It was why the people of Crieda rarely saw their prince and why it had been so easy for him to go unnoticed in Den Zei. He complained that his father should have been prepared for such an attack but that he had been a naïve man. King Speranta had only ever known peace, and even with such a powerful secret, he had never even thought an attack on Crieda was possible.

"Then why did you even have to guard it?" Malyssandra interjected.

Keane shrugged. "It was tradition. The prince guarded the orb until he became king and the new prince took on the role."

"What happened to the orb's power when it broke?" She whispered as sweat rolled down her back and made her shiver.

"It went into Reina."

"What?" She barked, and her mind sharpened. "What do you mean *it went into Reina?*"

"The orb was created so that if it was ever destroyed, the power would be absorbed by the next in Werthes' bloodline. That was Reina. What she can do, that is his power. That's why

I was so adamant for her to keep her power secret. She is the key to reviving Crieda, to bringing it back to its former glory." He stood up and faced Malyssandra. "I never told her. I thought about it, but I didn't think she would take it well. She was always so afraid of being alone, of being the only one left. When she got hurt, she healed. But nobody else could do the same. It's why she always wanted to help people, to save them in whatever way possible. If she knew that she was the only one of her kind, she would have lost it." He ran his hand through his hair and pulled at the knots as they snagged his fingers. "I couldn't do that to her. She already felt different. There was no point in solidifying that she was."

Malyssandra remembered the day she spoke with Reina in the palace. She had been so insistent that Malyssandra go to Den Zei and warn the others of what was to come with the Prethans. She had agreed to heal the king so she could save Keane. She had healed Ivanka, even with the risk of being found out. Keane was right. Reina was so afraid of being the only one left that she had done whatever she could to ensure it didn't happen. Malyssandra's chest constricted.

"Do you know what she did to me?" She asked.

Keane shook his head. "No, I don't. I didn't know she could do anything like it." Malyssandra nodded. She had expected the answer. "We should try to get some sleep." He stated, and Malyssandra slid down until she laid on the floor.

As silence settled back into the world around her, she closed her eyes and dreamed of flames.

29

REINA

The morning of the party arrived. Guards collected Reina from her cell before the sun had risen and dragged her back to her room. She tried to appear distraught, even as thoughts of the upcoming liberation made her insides tremble in anticipation.

She hadn't slept the night before. There had been too much on her mind. Her lips tingled at the memory of Ferix's mouth against hers. She had kissed him. She had never kissed anyone before, and she didn't know what she had been thinking. With so much on her plate, she shouldn't have risked alienating her only ally in the palace. She shouldn't have complicated their relationship. It had been an emotional moment; Ferix had to of understood that. He had told her that there were Criedans free in the world, and they were coming for their people. They were coming to set them free.

Her heart clenched as she was thrown into her bedroom, and she barely heard the door lock behind her. The room looked like a warzone. Dresser drawers were pulled open, and clothes were strewn across the floor. The bedsheets had been thrown to the base of the mattress, and her pillow sat on the ground. Reina blinked.

The brush was gone.

She jumped as laughter sounded from with the closet, and a gaggle of handmaids emerged. They were in the middle of a conversation about palace drama when they noticed her standing there. The laughter stopped as they saw the disgruntled shape Reina was in.

"Did one of you touch my bed?" She asked accusingly, and each one of them slowly shook their heads.

If the king knew of her ability to turn things to gold, she would be in trouble. Not only could she heal his illness, but she could have made him the wealthiest king alive. It didn't matter that she didn't know how she had done it; he would try everything in his power to ensure she did it again. If he had unlimited wealth at his disposal, what would that have meant for the world?

She shook her head. The Criedans were coming, and whether the king knew or not, it didn't change anything. The rebellion would succeed; she was sure of it. She would be free, and the king would never have her at his disposal again. He would die of his illness without her, and that would be the end of his reign.

"Excuse me, miss?" The small voice broke through Reina's thoughts, and her head darted off to look at a small woman with kind eyes. Her feet stopped as she realized she had been furiously pacing along the edge of the bed. The handmaids all stared at her, and she brought her attention back to the small woman before her.

"Yes?" She rasped.

The woman smiled warmly at her. "It's completely natural for you to be nervous. Although, I do wish you had come a little more... prepared." Her eyes raked Reina up and down and scrunched her nose at the dirt that clung to her skin.

Reina looked at her in confusion. "You do know I spent my night in a prison cell, right?" The woman brushed off the comment with a wave of her hand.

"No matter, we will have you looking better than ever in no time. Ladies?" She looked over her shoulder at the other handmaids. "Please do tell me the bath has been filled. We have work to do."

The sun slowly rose through her window as the handmaids fussed over Reina's appearance. There was no time to protest as she was stripped of her clothing and pushed into the warm bathwater. Her cheeks heated while the women scrubbed her naked body until her skin was raw and ushered her out of the tub to be dressed. Reina felt exposed, undignified. She tried to take control of the situation, but the handmaids paid her no mind. They were in charge, and no matter how much Reina argued, they pushed on.

She felt as if she were drowning in fabric as layers of clothing were yanked down over her head. Their laughter started up again as they fell into a rhythm, and all Reina could do was gasp for breath as a corset was tightened over her ribs.

When Reina was fully dressed, the small woman reappeared in front of her. She chewed on her cheek as she sized Reina up, then gave a nod of approval. "Almost done," she promised and reached for a pair of blue heels a handmaid held out to her.

Reina's face scrunched up, and she shook her head vigorously. That was where she drew the line. "I'm not wearing those," she objected.

"You have to wear shoes!" The woman insisted and went to lift the skirt of Reina's dress up to put the heels on her feet.

Reina hastily pulled away and glared at the woman. "I will not, and if you try to put those things on my feet again, you will leave here with a broken nose. Do you understand?" The woman faltered. Her kind eyes looked up at Reina through dark lashes before she gave a slow nod. She was silent for a moment before she plastered another smile on her face.

"Time to put on your face, dear!" She clapped as if it were the most exciting thing she could have ever imagined and pulled Reina over to a chair. The women approached her with brushes and caked thick liquid over her face. They traced her eyes with charcoal and extended her lashes with brushes. She tried to pull back, but someone held her head in place. They finished by putting pink powder on her cheekbones, and the small woman once again looked her over.

"I'd say we're done here!" She stated and looked around to the other women, who nodded in agreement. "I would have liked to have done something with your hair, but... there's not enough of it to mess with." Her words sounded disappointed, and Reina rolled her eyes in response. "Wouldn't you like to see yourself?" The woman asked, and Reina almost said no. But her curiosity got the better of her, and she gave a hesitant nod.

She stood from the chair and slowly made her way into the washroom. The woman followed excitedly behind her, a proud smile plastered on her face. Reina secretly hoped she would hate how she looked, but as she stepped in front of the mirror, she gaped.

Her short golden hair accentuated her cheekbones and gave her neck the illusion of being of length. The black rings around her eyes made the blues look deep and mysterious, and the pink tint on her lips made them appear larger than they were.

The dress showed off the delicate tops of her collarbones and pointed downward at the center of her chest. It hugged her upper body and elegantly rounded out at her hips before it cascaded to the floor. No gems adorned the fabric, but there had been no need for them. The golden shine that radiated from it was enough, and Reina felt as if she wore the sun itself.

She turned back to the woman behind her and begrudgingly gave a nod of approval. The woman obnoxiously clapped again and motioned for Reina to follow her out of the washroom. "I just can't wait for the king to see you!" Her overly enthusiastic voice grated along Reina's nerves, and the guards collected her at the door to escort her down to the king's party.

. . .

The image of herself in the mirror would not vacate Reina's mind as she walked with the guards down the palace hallways. She looked so much different than she had two months ago in Den Zei. Her skin looked healthy and no longer stuck to her bones. The hair on her head was short but shined brighter than she could ever remember. She had been transformed throughout her time in the palace, and she looked almost normal. It was a strange realization to have as she made her way to the party. She had never paid any mind to her appearance before. There was nowhere for her to see her reflection inside Den Zei, so she hadn't seen her grown self until she had been locked within that room. In her mind, she had always looked like the child who had been taken from her home, when in fact, she had become a woman.

At that moment, she was a woman who had been dressed up as if she were a doll. Her mouth twisted into a scowl at the thought, and the dress fluttered with each step she took. The king had dressed her in the Yulsan colors. It was a statement. Even if she refused to help him, she was still in his kingdom. She was his to dress up and his to show off. His to torment, but not for much longer.

The world seemed to pass by her in slow motion as her heart beat rapidly against the tightened garment around her torso. She yearned to pull the dreaded thing off but ignored the uncomfortable feeling as she watched the golden walls slip behind her.

They turned down a hallway that had a deep blue rug laid upon the ground. As they stepped onto it, Reina looked up at two large doors that sat at the end of the hall. They were propped open, and within the room, she could see people as they moved around excitedly. Gentle music wafted from inside and played in Reina's ears. The doorway grew larger until it loomed before her, and she took a deep breath before she stepped off the blue rug and onto the porcelain tiles of the ballroom.

The chandelier was the first thing she noticed. It was so large that it fell close to the dance floor, and Reina felt as though she could reach up and touch it if she so wished. Light reflected off of the diamonds and painted the world beneath with small inklings of gold.

Reina expanded her gaze and realized there were at least a hundred tables within the ample space. Flowers bloomed from vases set in the center of each, and Reina felt disappointed that they were ordinary petals and not those of the sun-frost. A large open space filled the middle of the room and marked where the dance floor would be when the party neared its end. She hoped she wouldn't have to dance that night and looked around in confusion for where she was supposed to sit.

"Your table is over there," a maid said from behind her, and she jumped. She hadn't known anyone was there. Her eyes followed where the woman pointed, and her heart sank as she looked at where the table was positioned.

Reina made her way nervously past the excited people in the room and heard them quiet as she walked by. Whispers filled the space around her as people noticed her. "Healer," some stated, "King's pet," others laughed. Her cheeks heated at the attention, and anger rose to the surface, but she ignored it as she arrived at her table. It was set up in front of the crowd beside a large table with a blue cloth atop it. She immediately knew who would sit at that table later in the evening.

Reina pulled out her chair and smoothed out her skirt as she sat down. It felt awkward and clunky underneath her, and she squirmed to try and find a more comfortable position to sit in. She looked out at the guests already there, noting that they must have been from Yulsa's high society. They held themselves confidently in their outrageously dazzling dresses and obscenely haughty coats and trousers. Their laughter echoed around the room, and Reina looked on in disgust at the people who benefited from the pain they had caused others.

Maids stood along the edges of the room and hustled about to fill water glasses as the arrogant guests guzzled them down. They were so attentive to those within the room. Reina wondered what life would have been like if she had been brought to the palace instead of Den Zei as a child. Would she have stood along those very walls and cowered as obnoxious men shouted for her to refill their glasses? She didn't know the answer, and she wasn't sure she wanted to.

As the high-born began to find their seats, more people entered the room. They were dressed nicely, but Reina noticed that their dresses weren't quite as dazzling as those of the wealthier women. The men wore scraggly vests and pants that looked as if they were too short for the legs within. She assumed they were of the middle class and didn't understand why they would have been invited to such a party. Although they still looked nice, they seemed out of place in the decadent ballroom. They didn't talk as much as the others had, and they quickly made their way to their seats. Their heads ducked down to look at their feet as they moved and contrasted the confidence she had seen only minutes before from the original crowd.

The music rose from its gentle melody to a thundering crescendo, and Reina watched as everyone in the crowd turned to face the room entrance. She expected the spectacle to be for the king but was shocked to see men dressed in green and blue enter the room. If no music had been playing, the world would have been silent around her.

The guests watched in awe as the foreigners strutted through the door. At first glance, Reina thought they wore dresses, but as she looked closer, she realized they were robes. There were no women with them, only small men with dark hair and even darker eyes. They looked annoyed at the attention, and a Yulsan guard led them to a table where they sat facing the king's table.

Maids darted forward and pulled chairs out so the men could sit, and after they had done so, the maids pushed them toward the table and backed away. There was movement at her side, and she jerked around to see the priestess sitting beside her. Reina looked at her in confusion; she hadn't seen the woman enter the room. Then, she saw a small door in the far back corner of the space that she hadn't noticed before.

Her attention moved back to the priestess and found her green eyes staring deep into Reina's soul, and her wrinkled face stretched grotesquely into a toothy grin. "You've come a long way, little one," she observed.

Reina opened her mouth to reply, but the woman shook her head assertively as if she refused to hear any words from her. Before she could protest, the music changed into a powerful staccato of notes. The priestess stood and turned to face the far side of the room, and Reina looked back to the guests to notice that they had done the same. She followed their gazes and watched as the king marched in, followed by Ferix and the queen. Reina stayed in her chair.

The king gave Reina a predatory grin before he turned to face the room. She looked to Ferix, and their eyes clashed. Her cheeks heated at the memory of what had occurred the night before, and the prince gave her a secretive smile. Her heart skipped a beat, and she cast her eyes to the floor.

The king raised his hand, and the music stopped. He motioned for everyone to be seated, and Reina knotted the fabric of her dress in her hands. Silence rang around the room for what felt like an eternity before the king spoke. "The day has come for us to welcome the Prethans into our kingdom. I understand it was not a short journey and would like to thank you for the time spent coming to our corner of the world," the king paused and looked to the Prethans, who nodded in response. "I hope you will find what we have to offer to be to your liking. We have many slaves for your choosing who have been trained to do anything you desire. They have helped to make Yulsa into the kingdom you see today, and they can do the same for Pretha." Reina's stomach churned at what she heard, and she looked around at the excited faces that filled the room around her. "It is my understanding that in exchange for these slaves, I will be inheriting a large number of trained soldiers to do with as I please, is this still correct?"

A single man in a green and blue robe cleared his throat and stood from the table filled with Prethans. He looked thoughtful for a moment, but then his face hardened. "The offer has changed," he declared, and his voice boomed across the space.

The guests pulled back in unison, shocked at how the man spoke to their king. Reina whipped her head around to see the king's face as it fell into an expression of confusion, followed by annoyance. "What do you mean the offer has changed?" He asked as he raised his voice to match the other man's intensity.

"We no longer want your slaves," the man stated, his dark eyes steeled and ready for a negotiation.

The king regained his composure and plastered a smile on his face. "Well then," he politely asked, "What is it that you want?"

The man smiled darkly at the king and lifted his chin. "We have heard stories in our kingdom of a woman you are said to have in your possession. A woman with golden skin that can heal any ailment. If you give her to us, you can have your army."

Everyone in the room turned to look at her. She sat rigidly in her chair as her heart raced within her chest. Her eyes were so wide she felt as though they would fall from her head as she turned to look at Ferix. He stared at her in shock and shook his head slowly to signal for her to stay put. Her hands were flattened against the table to keep them from trembling as she swallowed the dryness in her throat.

The king laughed, "I can assure you that is nothing but a story. We have no such woman here. Who would have fed you such an absurd lie?" Although the king's face remained relaxed, his eyes betrayed his rage.

"The world has heard of the miracles this woman can accomplish, and I can assure you my resources are incredibly reliable. In fact, I am certain I can pick this woman from the crowd." The man sneered at the king before he looked to Reina. "She is quite beautiful as well, and my king would be very pleased to have her in his court."

"This is not what we discussed!" The king barked, and the man turned back to face him. The Prethans sat around their table with smug smiles on their faces and watched the king expectantly.

"Do you want an army?" The man nonchalantly inquired. His dark eyes glinted in the light of the chandelier.

"I want the deal that was agreed upon months ago!"

"Well, we don't always get what we want, even if you're royalty. My king wants the girl; it is up to you if you wish for an army or not," the Prethan sneered.

The king's face twisted in an ugly fit of rage. In a few weeks, he would be bedridden again and unable to rule his kingdom. There was no way he would have let Reina leave the palace. He needed her, even if she was uncooperative. He would die without her.

Despite the circumstances, Reina felt her lips pull up into a snide smile. He had lost at his own game. The king had planned to trade Reina's people, had forced her to appear at the party so she could watch it happen, only to have it thrown back in his face. The Prethans wanted her. Not the other Criedans. And Reina knew, if it came down to it, if the rebellion didn't show, she would go. She would have made that sacrifice a thousand times over if it had been asked of her.

The king opened his mouth to respond. Reina tensed in preparation for whatever he was about to say. Before he could release the words, the ground shook violently beneath them.

30

MALYSSANDRA

The air in Den Zei was charged that morning. Keane paced the bars, and Malyssandra listened as he mumbled softly to himself. She wondered again if the plan would even work. If only some slaves rioted, they would be forced back into their cells to die in the flames Malyssandra knew were coming.

She wrung her hands in front of her as she watched the guards make their way down the aisle. They didn't seem to notice the buzz in the air; they were too distracted by their orders. A key jingled at her door, and Malyssandra turned as it swung open.

As she went to leave her cell on shaky legs, she spared one last thought to those who would perish that day. She sent a prayer up to the gods to comfort the innocent as their souls entered the afterlife. There was nothing she could do for them, and she had accepted that. Her people were her first priority. Eleven years had been long enough.

She had lost her family and her life to the kingdom of Yulsa. She refused to lose anything more.

Anxiety tore at her insides, and she steeled herself for whatever was to happen. She gave one last look over her shoulder at the cell she had been forced into. Malyssandra had only known it for a short time, but it still left a scar on her soul. It had been the worst part of her life, and she prayed she would never have to see the inside of a cage again.

Keane came stood beside her and gave her a soft nudge to show that he was with her. He had been a prince in another time. He had been destined to rule a kingdom and live in a world of riches. The Yulsans had taken that from him. They had put him in chains and tossed him into the shadows, where he was forced to hide who he was. She wondered if Keane was even his real name; she couldn't remember what the prince had been called in Crieda. It had been so long ago and had faded from her mind.

"What's your name?" She whispered to him as they stared at the daunting steps in front of them.

"What?" He asked, taken aback.

"What's your name? Your real name. Is it actually Keane?" She turned her head so she could look at him, and he must have seen how close she was to losing it because he answered without protest.

"Leven," he stated quietly, "My name is Leven."

She gave a small smile as they looked into each other's eyes for what could have been the last time. "I think I like Keane better." He laughed softly and shook his head before he began to ascend the stairs. She watched him go and wiped her sweaty palms on her pants.

Slowly, she made her way up and into the blazing sunlight that beat down relentlessly on the poor souls beneath it. The ground was hard and dry; dead grass covered the surface and crunched loudly under her feet. As she looked around, she noticed the slaves were lined up along the edge of the fence and wrapped around the yard. She turned her head and blinked at the piles of chains that sat in the center.

A guard pushed Malyssandra from behind, and she stumbled forward. "Get in line!" He snarled and placed his hand at the butt of his whip. Malyssandra backed away and squeezed into the line. If they were to be chained together, they had no hope of starting a riot. They had no hope of escape.

Her eyes scanned the yard for Keane and spotted him down the line. He had already found her, and his expression showed that he had already made the same conclusion. Her heart rolled beneath her ribs, and sweat pooled at the base of her neck.

She began to look for Ivanka in a panic but couldn't find her in the lineup. A speck of pale hair flashed on the distant side of the yard, but she was too far away to see who it belonged to. Ivanka had to of gotten the letter. Would she fight back? Was she ready to do what had been asked of them? Malyssandra hoped her friend would make it out of Yulsa and start a life somewhere. She remembered the deflated woman she had seen on the wagon. Ivanka deserved to find happiness, all of them did.

Malyssandra's attention shifted to the commander's tower as he appeared at the top to look down on them. "Quiet down!" He snapped, and the yard halted as everyone looked up to the commander. "Guards, start chaining the Criedans. They're supposed to be ready for the visitors in a few hours. The others can go." He passively flicked his wrist in the air, and the guards began to move toward the chains.

The Yulsan slaves shuffled around, unsure of what to do. Malyssandra swallowed nervously as the guards pulled them from the lineup and placed them into a separate group. She didn't know if they had received the letters. They had been in Den Zei, locked within a cell just like the rest of them. It was only fair that they were given the opportunity to fight for their own lives.

The guards began to pull chains from the pile. Malyssandra's eyes darted around in search of anything that could cause a distraction, anything that could put off the guards for a moment longer as the slaves waited for their signal. There was nothing.

Her mind ran wild; she didn't know when the walls would fall. She didn't know where the rebellion was. They were about to lose their chance at freedom. The chains rattled closer to the edges of the yard. Then, Malyssandra opened her mouth and sang.

"In golden rays of light, may red and silver fly." The words felt weird in her mouth. She had only hummed the tune throughout her time in Yulsa. But she knew the song by heart and hoped others remembered it.

The slaves beside her turned and stared at her, their eyes wide in wonder. She continued, *"As we all work together, to live freely and thrive."* Her heart pounded in her chest as guards marched toward her. She looked pleadingly at those around her, and tears welled in their eyes as they puffed out their chests and joined her.

"*From wall to wall, we will stand tall.*" She met Keane's gaze, and his face stretched wide in a smile as he bellowed, "*Criedans! Through and through.*" The guards faltered, unsure of who to reprimand as each Criedan joined in on the anthem of their kingdom.

"Quiet them down!" The commander shouted, and the guards nodded as they burst forward in all directions.

Malyssandra flinched but kept going. "*Oh Crieda, oh Crieda, we owe our lives to you. Oh Crieda, oh Crieda, we owe our lives to you.*" As the guards hit the line of Criedans, everyone surged forward.

Battle cries echoed in Malyssandra's ears as she dodged around armed men, and she watched whips crack in the air. She didn't know how long it would be until the guards drew their swords, but she hoped the rebellion was almost there. The riot had started early, and if they didn't have backup soon, it was over.

Something barreled into Malyssandra's stomach, and she fell to the ground clutching her ribs. She looked up at a guard who stared maliciously into her eyes. Her body heaved to regain the air forced from her lungs, and the guard pushed her onto her back. As he pulled his whip behind him, prepared to slice open her flesh, the ground shook beneath them.

Everyone froze. The guard lowered his whip as he locked eyes on the horizon, and Malyssandra twisted to see what had happened. Part of the northern wall had exploded. Malyssandra watched as the stones at the top began to rain down in the distance when another explosion shook the ground. The wall began to crumble.

A shout rang out from across the yard, followed by another. As explosions shook the very ground they stood on, people continued to fight back against the startled guards. The screams of Criedans were loud enough to reach the heavens, and Malyssandra looked to the falling walls with a smile on her face. *Now they know how it feels*, she thought, then she pulled herself to her feet and charged the guard in front of her.

31

REINA

The room fell silent as Reina pressed her hands harder into the table. There had been something familiar about the way the ground shook, and it had thrown her back into the body of a terrified child. The king laughed it off in the background of her terror, and she turned her head slowly to look at the priestess. She was shocked to find an empty seat beside her.

"Do not be so alarmed; it was likely just thunder. Perhaps we are set to finally get some rain," he stated before turning back to the Prethans. "Now, I want to make this clear-," he was cut off as the world trembled again. The guests began to stand up. "Stay in your seats!" The king growled, and those who had stood quickly buckled back into their chairs. The king looked at the Prethans accusingly. "What is the meaning of this!" He shouted, and the Prethans looked to him in confusion.

"I can assure you, this is not our doing. Do you not have a handle on your own kingdom?" The man asked, and Reina noted a small amount of fear within his wide-set eyes. The king's jaw clenched at the question, and a guard slowly approached the throne.

As the guard leaned in to whisper something in the king's ear, Reina watched as his skin turned paler and his eyes bulged. He pushed the guard away from him and stood up. "Gather up the guards and head to the walls. Now!" Reina looked to Ferix, who stared at her intensely. The rebellion had come.

The guard sprinted from the room while the ones stationed at the door waited for orders. The guests began to stand once again, and the king swiped his arm at them. "Nobody is to leave this room!" The guards at the door pushed together to create a human wall, and Reina watched as the queen stood and quickly shuffled out the side door the priestess had come in from earlier. Ferix stayed seated and continued to look over at Reina.

The Prethans stood and turned to exit; the guards pushed them back. The man who had spoken to the king started to say something, but his words were drowned out as another explosion rocked the palace. The guests began to rush the guards in their panic. The smell of smoke wafted into the room, and Reina's heart stopped. It hadn't rained since she had been in the palace, which marked two months of the scorching sun. The fire would devour the ground quickly as it ate up the dead earth beneath.

She pushed herself to her feet, and the chair toppled behind her. The room had delved into chaos, and she watched in horror as the guards refused to let anyone leave. She turned to find Ferix, but he wasn't at the table. The king still was, though, and he looked irate as he watched the crowd panic below him. Reina took advantage of the distraction and backed toward the door the queen had gone through.

The smell of smoke was pungent, and Reina's eyes watered violently as she continued to scan the area for Ferix. She wondered if he was within the hoard of terrified guests or if he had simply left.

When she felt the door press against the skirt of her dress, she spun and bolted from the room. The hallway she entered was small and dark, with no torches to light up the space. She placed her hand on the stone to feel her way through the corridor and noted the cold rock. It was a good sign; it meant the fire wasn't close enough to heat it. Her days in Den Zei had taught her that stone warmed quickly in the sunlight. It made sense that it would heat up quickly if a fire was near as well.

Her feet padded quietly through the darkness until she reached another door. She placed her palms against it and pushed. It was heavier than she had expected, and she put all of her weight into it. As it slowly creaked open, she squeezed through the small opening and allowed it to slam behind her.

She looked around to get her bearings and realized she was in an old chapel. A stand lined with unlit candles sat in front of her. Quickly she skirted around it and stumbled down the few steps behind it toward an open door.

As she walked into another hallway, she realized she was in the eastern sector of the palace. The archive room was on the other side of the hall. Relief filled her. She knew how to get out of the castle from there.

She turned and lifted her skirt to run down the hall and around the corner at the end. As she ran, a strange feeling built up within her. Goosebumps rose along her flesh, and she felt as though she were being watched. She looked to the shadows suspiciously but continued her sprint through the eastern sector. "Not now," she huffed. The tightness around her chest made it hard for her to catch her breath as she ran, and she began to feel lightheaded from the lack of oxygen.

The scenery began to change around her as she entered a different area. The paintings on the walls taunted her as she bolted past them. As she went by the windows, she looked out to see the sun was clouded by smoke. It looked eerily orange in the sky as if it were the end of days.

Reina snapped her attention forward to focus herself as she came upon an area split into three hallways. She stopped and tried to remember which one she was supposed to take. The one in the middle led to her room, but that was deeper in the palace. She wanted out, not further in. The hairs on her neck began to stand on end, and she jigged her leg impatiently. "*Please* not now," she begged to whoever might have been listening, and she darted into the hallway on her right. If she were coming from the eastern sector, then the right hallway should lead her north.

As she became more confident in her choice, her speed picked up. Sweat ran down her skin and soaked the layers of fabric she had been dressed in that morning. The black liner on her eyelids burned her eyes, but she forced them to stay open. Smoke was everywhere she looked, and the palace was in chaos as she flew by the terrified people within.

Her foot landed on something sharp, and she winced as she continued to run on it. She felt as the object pressed deeper into her skin. The floor became slick beneath her as blood leaked from her wound. The power within her churned as it fought to be released to do what it was meant to do. She couldn't let it out, not with whatever it was still embedded in the pad of her foot.

The hallway let out into a large room that broke off into many different paths. Reina spun quickly as she tried to pick out which was the correct route to take. Panic clogged her memories of trips around the palace. She didn't know where to go. She couldn't remember. Reina shook her head; she didn't have time. She took off toward the hall in front of her.

When she was mere inches away from the hallway, a shadow filled the space in front of her. She slipped on the blood beneath her foot in surprise and fell to the ground. What little air had made it into her lungs was knocked out of her as she stared into the swirling mass of shadows.

It was larger than the one she had been seeing and much darker. The hallway was not visible through it, and it grew to the top of the room. It leaned over her, and she pushed herself backward on the floor. Smoke burned at her eyes, and urgency ripped at her insides.

Screams sounded from within the palace, and Reina didn't know how close the fire was. If she were caught inside when it made its way to the castle, she was afraid she wasn't going to be able to make her way out. The idea of burning alive made her jump into action. She pushed herself to her feet and spun on her heel to run down a different hallway.

The shadow moved and stood before her once again. She stared up at it defiantly. The swirling mass seemed to anticipate her next move as she turned to try another hallway. Everywhere she tried to go, it blocked her path. She clenched her jaw and felt as the room grew hotter. It was toying with her. The shadow was playing a dangerous game Reina knew she could not afford to lose.

32

MALYSSANDRA

The rebellion had set the world on fire. When their explosives had gone off, the ground beneath had been showered with sparks. It was all it took for the world to be thrown into a blazing inferno.

Malyssandra struggled to see through the smoke. Flames ate at the yard around her, and she gagged as she failed to get air into her lungs. Guards screamed as they were cooked alive in their armor, and Malyssandra squinted as people ran by her, the fire scorching their skin.

She choked in mortification as the smell of burnt flesh filled her nose. Explosions continued to rock the ground beneath her, but she could no longer see the walls as they fell. All she could do was brace herself against the dry earth and pray.

She tried to find Keane in the throng of people, but he was nowhere to be seen. People fell dead before her as she shuffled in a daze through the heat around her. A creaking noise sounded above her, and she looked up to see that fire burned at the gate's metal. The sound grew louder, and Malyssandra watched in horror as it crashed to the ground. People were crushed as they failed to move out of the way fast enough.

When people saw the gate had fallen, they rushed it and clamored over the hot metal. Their hands blistered, but they didn't even flinch as they raced toward their freedom. Malyssandra scanned the faces of those who ran, but Keane wasn't one of them. She watched as guards threw the metal armor from their bodies and charged to follow the slaves who had escaped.

Tears ran freely from her eyes and marked small paths down her soot-stained skin; she didn't know where to go. She hadn't seen Keane leave. He could have still been in the yard, trapped within the flames. Her eyes turned away from her chance at escape and immediately caught a flash of pale blonde hair.

"Ivanka!" She cried and pushed deeper into the blaze. Her lungs protested as she breathed in the poisonous air, and her skin felt as if it were going to melt from her bones. She looked down, but no blisters had yet appeared, and she carefully tried to avoid the maze of fire that grew around her. "Ivanka!" She shouted again and stopped in place before she began to spin around. The flash of hair had disappeared, and she had no idea where she was. Behind her, the path she had just taken closed up. She couldn't turn back.

Adrenaline pulsed through her body, and she shook as she pushed onward, deeper into the orange light. "*Ivanka,*" She coughed out and brought her elbow up to cover her mouth. A stray flame licked at her leg, causing her to jerk away in pain. Her eyes squinted in an attempt to keep the smoke at bay, but she couldn't see anything. She needed to open her eyes, but her body fought the command. Water pooled between her eyelids and evaporated quickly as they traveled down her skin. The heat was unbearable, and she didn't see anyone else that deep in the flames. She was alone, and she realized that had been what she had seen in her vision.

A soft sob escaped her lips, and she fell to her knees on the hard ground. The air was a little cooler down there, and she could breathe a little easier. She greedily devoured the oxygen around her and slowly opened her eyes to try and see again. The world was hazy around her. She began to crawl through the flames, flinching as her hands landed on hot rocks.

She saw another flash of pale blonde hair and pushed her feet beneath her. As she came upon the owner of the hair, she realized there had been no reason to move so quickly. They were sprawled out face-down on the ground, their small arms and legs splayed about awkwardly, and their face pressed into the dead earth beneath. Malyssandra slowly reached forward, grabbed the woman's shoulder, and pulled so she could see her face.

She knew who it was before she even saw her. Not many people had hair like that. Her body fell beside Ivanka's as her hands lightly shook her. There were no burn marks on her skin; she didn't look hurt in any way. But she wasn't responding. She wasn't moving.

The ground shook again, and Malyssandra folded herself over her friend to shield her from the chaos around them. She felt a soft gust of air against her cheek. Malyssandra pulled her head up and looked around in confusion. There was no wind. She blinked at the brightness of the fire and turned back to Ivanka.

She lifted her hand to Ivanka's mouth and waited. Another gust of air hit her palm. Ivanka was breathing. Her heart rate grew even more rapid, and over the crackling of the fire, she shouted, "Help!" The word was swallowed up quickly, drowned out by the noise around them. She cleared her throat and steeled her voice as she hugged her friend to her chest. "Somebody, *please*," she begged and hooked her arms underneath her friend as she began to crawl toward an opening in the flames with Ivanka in tow.

Suddenly, a figure jumped through the deadly wall of fire. Malyssandra looked up in confusion at the stranger that stood in front of her. He looked fierce in the harsh environment. There was no hair on his head, and his green eyes stared down at her in determination. Her mouth opened to ask him for help, but before she could say anything, Keane appeared at his side.

"Gods, Mallie," he breathed, reaching down to help her up. She jerked away from him with pleading eyes and tried to hoist Ivanka into the air.

"Please help her," she grunted, and Keane looked to Ivanka in confusion, then back to Malyssandra.

"She's dead, Mallie. We need to go." He tried to grab her again, but she wouldn't allow him to.

"No, she's breathing. I felt it. *Please*, Keane. Help her." Her eyes stared up at him, wide and pleading. He looked back in desperation, then looked to Ivanka. He sighed and motioned to the man beside him. The man pulled Ivanka up into his arms and sprinted into the flames. "Thank you," Malyssandra cried, "Thank you."

Keane frowned as he quickly reached down to grab her elbow and hoisted her to her feet. She stumbled on her trembling legs, and Keane stabilized her. "Can you walk?" His voice was raspy from the smoke, and Malyssandra nodded. "Can you run?"

Malyssandra stared blankly at the question, and Keane wasted no time as he bent down and hefted her into his arms. She looked at him in shock, but he paid her no mind as he began to run through the fire. Another loud creak filled the air as another fence fell. Keane pushed faster, and Malyssandra closed her eyes as she realized he was about to hurtle through a wall of flames.

She felt for a second as if the heat were going to burn them alive. It tauntingly caressed her skin with promises of torture. Her arms wrapped tightly around Keane's neck, and she held her breath in fear of inhaling the ribbons of flame. His chest rose and fell against her side as his legs pumped even quicker.

As he leaped into the air, Malyssandra felt as if time stood still. Her eyes flew open to look at the deadly wall before them, and her heart stopped in her chest. Keane's wide eyes betrayed his fear, but he held her tightly to him as he defied the danger around them. Nothing could stop him from escaping the yard. He had spent most of his life in anticipation of that moment. Freedom beckoned to him behind the flames, and he was determined to answer its call.

The fire broke around them as Keane's feet landed back on the ground. The fallen fence had been pulled out of the way to create a small opening, and Keane dodged through it. When they were far enough away from the yard, he set her down.

"Your friend is being taken to the western wall; I suggest you follow. There are people there waiting to help." His words were hurried and distracted as he turned to move away from Malyssandra.

"Where are you going?" She asked suspiciously, her eyes darting between him and the western wall. That was their chance. They could escape, be free.

"The palace. Reina is still inside." He threw the words over his shoulder as he moved away from her.

She is the key to reviving Crieda. His words from the night before echoed in her head. If they were ever going to rebuild their kingdom, they needed Reina.

Malyssandra looked at Den Zei, the yard destroyed by the fire Malyssandra had seen in her vision. She had been granted her freedom. Had been told to go. But she couldn't. They needed to find Reina. "I'll come with you," she declared.

"This is not your responsibility, Mallie. You're out; you're free. Turn and leave before you're dead." The words were final. He was not going to entertain an argument with her.

"It's my home too, Keane," she insisted, but Keane had already run off.

She stood there for a moment and stared into the smoke where he had disappeared. Malyssandra once again felt lost. She could have run, could have broken free, and been safe in the arms of the rebellion. Ivanka was there, and Malyssandra hoped she was still alive. She wanted to be by her side, to apologize for how caught up she had been over the past few weeks that she hadn't tried harder to be with her friend. But the truth was, her friend wasn't her only priority anymore. She hadn't been since the night she met Reina.

Ivanka would understand; Malyssandra knew she would. She gave one last look in the direction of the western wall before she sprinted in the direction Keane had gone. Toward the palace.

33

REINA

The darkness swirled, taunting her. People ran past her, oblivi-
ous to the shadow that stretched ominously to the ceiling, and
Reina watched as they disappeared through the creature. The
world baked around her, but goosebumps still protruded
proudly from her arms. She clenched her fists at her sides and
sucked in a deep breath.

"*What do you want?*" She screamed.

Laughter bubbled up from within the shadow's center and
echoed around her head. It didn't answer her question and instead snaked closer to her. It began to shrink in size until it stood
before her at eye level, and they stared at each other for what felt
like an eternity. Reina watched the ribbons of silken shadow
smoothly glide within its form. It looked like a patchwork of living darkness.

She stepped back, and it pursued her, forcing her into a hallway on her right. Ferix had told her that the use of dark magic
was corruptive, and she knew it to be true at that moment. It was
unnatural, almost painful on her skin. Her breathing

turned shallow as the oxygen became thin, and her arms trembled as she tried to reach out and touch the wall.

She felt the ground disappear beneath her foot, and she threw her weight forward to keep herself from falling. Her head turned to see a staircase led into the earth behind her. It wasn't anywhere she had been in the palace before; her explorations had never taken her there. She looked back at the shadow that continued to creep closer, and she swallowed all of the instincts that told her not to go down the steps.

Her feet carried her down warily, and she refused to take her eyes from the darkness that followed. The faint sound of laughter still rang in her ears and mixed with the soft sound of her nails as they dragged against the stone walls beside her. She didn't know where it was forcing her.

The steps ended, and she stood on level ground. A doorway stood beside her with no door upon its rusted old hinges. Reina gave one last look to the shadow before she turned and darted into the room beyond. The light from the stairway faintly lit up the dark space. Walls of solid rock cornered her in, and the smell of damp mildew and death reached her flaring nostrils. Her dress became heavy with moisture, and Reina shuffled as far away from the stairs as she could manage.

She saw where the smell of death came from as she took in the many sprung rat traps. There had to of been hundreds of dead rats down in the darkened room, locked between sharp metal and wood. She pondered what they had thought in their last moments before the traps ended their lives. Did they even know of the colossal mistake they had made? Did they not notice the other dead rats around them? Reina wondered if she had backed herself into a similar trap. *It hasn't sprung yet. I'm still alive,* she thought to herself and took a deep breath. Then, she spun around to face her pursuer.

There was nobody there. The shadow had disappeared, and Reina looked around wildly. If it were in the darkness of the room, she wouldn't be able to see it as it snuck up on her. As her nervousness grew, she realized that the feeling of terror from the air had dissipated. Eyes no longer raised bumps along her skin, and she felt she could breathe easier. Screams still echoed from those above her trapped within the palace, but the laughter had halted.

The smell of smoke had been reduced, and her eyes were no longer burning. It seemed as if the horrors of the world had faded away from her for a moment. She was just a girl in a dress underground, with the corpses of dead rats adorning the floor around her.

She desperately wanted to run up the stairway and make her way out of the palace like she had set out to do mere minutes earlier before her escape had been derailed by the shadow. But she was too afraid to move, terrified the shadow would return and finish whatever it had set out to do. The opening looked inviting, but whatever lay beyond was not something Reina wanted to see.

She wondered if the fire would even get to her down there. It was damp and cool; it reminded her of her cell back in Den Zei. Nostalgia filled her every pore as she gave the slick wall a soft touch. She didn't wish to return to Den Zei, but she missed the familiarity of it. In Den Zei, she had known who she was and what she was meant to do. Within the walls of the palace, she had become someone else. Someone she no longer recognized. The things she had learned while she had been there had torn her world to shreds. She wasn't even fully human anymore; she had the powers of a god.

Slowly, she reached down and removed the sharp object from the bottom of her foot. Her shoulder lit up and cast a golden light around the room. It didn't even burn as much as it used to. She had become more confident in the ability, capable of controlling it.

Her skin mended itself, and she looked to the piece of glass in her hand that had caused her pain. It was so small and insignificant, but it had made quite the wound in her soft flesh. She ran her finger along the sharp edges and watched as her skin opened up only to be closed seconds later.

Reina didn't want to die in that room. She didn't want to wait for the fire or the shadow to find her cowering underground. The rebellion had arrived in the kingdom. If she could just get to them, there was a chance she could be free again.

She threw the glass to the side and looked up in anger at the doorway. Determination filled her as she began to take a step forward. Her light faded from her shoulder, and the room became dark once again. She walked briskly toward the stairway, her hands ready to push through whatever might await her on the other side.

Before she could walk through the opening, the sound of feet as they padded down the steps filled the room. She ducked to the side and pushed her body flat against the wall. If someone walked through that door, she needed the element of surprise.

The steps came closer, and Reina sucked in her breath as she saw a shadow rise up from the light. It wasn't the living shadow; it belonged to someone. Her eyes narrowed as it stretched in the doorway. She refused to acknowledge the fear that rose within her and forced herself to maintain a tight grip on the determination she had felt seconds earlier.

As the sound came nearer, Reina's body tensed up in anticipation. When she saw a form in the doorway, she pounced, her fist pulled back and ready to force her way through whatever barrier had arisen in her path. She froze as her eyes locked with the unnaturally green stare of the priestess.

34

MALYSSANDRA

There was no way she would make it to the palace by foot, not before the fire did. She held her arm to her mouth in an attempt to block out the smoke. It was impossible to see anything, and Malyssandra feared she would never find her way out from the blackened air.

She spun, unsure of which way Keane had gone. Or even which way she had come from. Terror rose in her throat as she stumbled blindly about. The sun had disappeared from the sky, the smoke too thick for it to break through. She blinked through her tears as the world began to disappear.

The familiar darkness of the basement came into view. Dead rats littered the traps Malyssandra had spent eleven years resetting. She noted that nobody had taken up her task after being sent to Den Zei, but she wasn't surprised. Her attention turned to a woman who stood beside the doorway. It was Reina. She was pressed against the wall as someone made their way down the stairs beyond the room.

Malyssandra felt the unnatural weight of the air settle on her shoulders. Something was going on within the palace, something terrible. Reina's eyes were a mixture of determination and terror, unlike anything Malyssandra had ever seen.

Air brushed against the back of Malyssandra's neck, and she whipped around to see the shadow. She tried to tell herself it couldn't see her, but she knew that was wrong. The shadow wasn't in the vision; it was in her mind.

"Malyssandra," it whispered. She refused to be afraid. Malyssandra would not fall into the abyss of petrification that the shadow usually brought upon her. It couldn't hurt her; it was helpless to do anything but stare from its eyeless face.

Familiar laughter bubbled up from within it as if it could hear her thoughts. "I don't wish to hurt you," the feminine voice purred, and the shadow darted around her. "But I'm afraid you cannot see what comes next, my dear." With that, the shadow lunged at her.

The world was thrown back into view, and Malyssandra choked as she inhaled a mouthful of smoke. Reina was in the basement, and the shadow knew it. Keane had no chance of finding her in time, not without Malyssandra.

She forced herself to calm down. If she panicked, she would never escape the smoke that clogged her vision. She needed to focus. There wasn't enough time for her to waste meandering around lost. She closed her eyes and listened.

The loud crackling of the fire filled her ears, but she allowed it to fall into the background. There, in the distance, someone was shouting. Malyssandra opened her eyes and ran toward the sound. She hoped she was right.

Men began to appear beyond the smoke. They covered the ground from atop proud horses, and some barked orders. Their red and silver armor made her heart skip a beat. *Criedans,* she thought. Not just any Criedans, Criedan soldiers. She loosed a breath of amazement. They really had been out there all along, waiting for that day.

She waved her arms above her head to get their attention, and they turned to look at her. "The wall is that way," a man shouted and pointed to the west with his sword. She shook her head.

"I need to get to the palace," she breathed, "It's important." The men looked to each other, then back to her.

"We already have a team sent to the palace; you need to head to the wall. This place is going up fast."

"No!" She objected, "Where is Keane? I need to talk to Keane." They looked at her dumbly, and she shook her head as she realized her mistake. "Prince Leven."

The soldier's eyes lit up in understanding before he looked toward the palace. "Prince Leven has already commandeered his horse and his team. His majesty is likely halfway to the palace by now," he paused and looked at the approaching flames, "You need to get to that wall before the fire gets here."

Malyssandra's eyes flitted back to the flames in worry before she set her jaw. "No, what I *need* is to get to that palace." She pointed. "Prince Leven has gone on a mission that he will fail if I do not get to him in time. All I ask for is a horse. You do not need to follow me. But I will not go to that wall. Not yet." Her voice was strong, fierce. She had never felt more certain about anything in her life. She needed to get to the palace.

The soldier turned and seemed to have a silent conversation with his comrades. Malyssandra watched as the world burned around her until he finally looked back to her and nodded. Another soldier dismounted from his horse and handed Malyssandra the reins.

"She'll take care of you, and she'll get you there fast. You don't have much time before this whole kingdom is on fire. Ride straight and true." He hoisted her into the saddle, and she sat awkwardly upon the beast. She hadn't been atop a horse since she had been a little girl, and she had forgotten how to ride.

Before she could say anything else, the man raised his hand and slapped the animal on its hind end. The horse launched forward. Malyssandra bunched the reins in her hands and grabbed at its silver mane as they surged toward the palace.

The horse's gallop ate up the ground beneath it as it barreled forward at a neck-breaking speed. Her legs gripped at its narrow sides with all the strength she could muster up. The city loomed before Malyssandra, and her heart twisted as she remembered what she had seen in her vision. Within seconds she would be presented with the gruesome reality of it. Her fingers tightened in the mare's mane.

As she entered the city's outskirts, she refused to look at the people on the ground. The horse did not shy at the horrors that raged around them, nor did it falter at the flames. It was almost as if the animal knew it had a job to do and was determined to finish what it had started. Malyssandra ducked close to its sweat-soaked neck and stared ahead. If she focused hard enough, she wouldn't have to see the images around her. She could ignore the screams and only look to the horizon at the palace that loomed in the distance.

There was no plan in her mind of what to do once she arrived at the palace. She didn't know where Keane was. The rebellion would have been inside by the time she got there, and she knew they hadn't gone in to hold peaceful negotiations with the king. She wasn't naïve. There would be blood spilled within the palace, and she would walk right into the middle of it. For the first time in her life, Malyssandra wished for a weapon. She had never wielded one before, but she was painfully aware of how unprotected she was.

She was within the city's center before she knew it, and it became more difficult for her to ignore the world around her. The screams seemed louder as people crowded the streets. Beneath her, the horse barreled through the masses of panic. People were knocked down by the powerful animal, and Malyssandra watched in horror as they were trampled by the crowd around them.

The kingdom of Yulsa was crumbling, but Malyssandra felt no joy at the knowledge that the Criedans had gotten their revenge. Nothing was satisfying about the stench of burnt flesh around her or the shouts of lost children. Shame filled her at what her people had brought upon the innocents within the kingdom.

Her eyes closed as she dug her heels into the beast's sides, and she felt as its weight went back before it lunged forward even faster. The hot air whipped at her wildly untamed hair and pushed against the skin on her face. It felt apocalyptic in every sense of the word, and she wondered how many would lose their lives before the fires were quenched.

The horse's gait changed as the footing shifted from brick streets to flat stone. She knew it meant the palace was close, and she opened her eyes to see that it loomed in front of her. The entrance was surrounded by men dressed in Criedan colors. She pulled the mare to a halt and threw her leg over the side to dismount. Her muscles felt as if they had been liquefied by how hard she had forced them to hold onto the beast, but she paid the uncomfortable feeling no mind as she awkwardly ran toward the entrance. The men looked to her in confusion as she ran past them without a second glance. She had to find Keane and tell him what she had seen.

As she passed the threshold of the palace, she was presented with nothing short of a nightmare. The rebels plunged their swords into unarmed civilians that worked within the castle. Blood covered the porcelain floor and made it difficult to run without slipping. Pictures that used to stare at Malyssandra as she roamed the hallways were slashed to pieces. The gold that lined the walls was covered by crimson gore, and bodies littered the space with frozen looks of terror forever printed upon their faces.

Bile rose in Malyssandra's throat at the sight before her, but she didn't stop. She knew she would be haunted by the bodies in front of her for years to come, but she could do nothing for them. They were already gone, and she needed to get to Reina.

Her eyes scanned the scene for Keane. He was nowhere to be found in the crowd, and a slight tug in her heart was the only thing she allowed herself to feel as she hoped he was okay. Her body weaved through the chaos around her, and she wondered how anyone could have let it get that far.

They had to know that they weren't killing the people responsible for the fall of Crieda. Half of those within the palace had only done what they had been told. They had committed no crimes; they had done no wrong.

Her feet skidded along the bloody ground, and her eyes bulged as she watched a Criedan rebel slice his sword across the neck of a pregnant woman. The woman fell to the ground and clutched at the wound in shock. Malyssandra looked to the man in disgust and terror, but he had already turned to his next victim. She turned her head back to the woman and found her already dead. Her eyes stared up lifelessly as her blood pooled freely across the ground around her.

Malyssandra backpedaled in horror and spun only to run into a hard body behind her. She looked up in fear that she would be the next victim but found familiar blue eyes staring down at her. The prince breathed heavily; his chest visibly rose and fell from exertion. A blood-stained silver sword was clutched in his grip, and red spattered across his face. She glanced behind him to see that Criedan men scattered the floor leading up to where he stood. His eyes glinted in recognition before they widened in surprise.

"What are you doing here?" He breathed, and Malyssandra blinked dumbly at him. A man ran up behind him, and he spun around at the sound, skillfully blocking the killing blow before he delivered one of his own. His sword plunged into the soft flesh of the rebel's stomach and pulled upward. The man fell to the floor as the prince turned back to Malyssandra, waiting for an answer. When she didn't offer one up, he looked around anxiously. "You need to get out of here. The rebels have gone too far. They're attacking everyone in the palace; this is not the place for you to be right now." He reached for her arm as if he planned to drag her away, but she yanked her shoulder away from his grasp.

"No," she declared, "Reina is in trouble."

He froze and stared down at her in confusion, "How do you know-?" His voice was cut off as understanding dawned in his eyes. "You have visions." The words were blunt and left no room for Malyssandra to protest.

She recoiled at the statement. "What? How do you-?"

"There's no time for that." He looked around before he turned back to her urgently, "Where is she?" Terror raged in his icy eyes, and Malyssandra diverted her gaze.

"The basement." Her voice was raspy and harsh as she tried to hold back the urge to cough on the smoke. He looked over his right shoulder at the path they would have to take through the violence toward the basement. When he turned back to her, he gave a nod of acknowledgment and reached out to grasp her forearm.

"Stay close," he instructed her, and she shuffled as closely behind him as she could manage. He released her arm when he was sure she wouldn't stray and began to move powerfully forward into the deadly crowd around them.

35

REINA

The priestess stared at Reina, a frantic look on her wrinkled face. Reina's hand hung in the air between them. She knew if she wanted to, she could get by the woman with no trouble. But something in her eyes made Reina drop her fist. She pulled away from her.

"You shouldn't be here." Her old gravelly voice sounded concerned. She looked back nervously and walked away from the doorway. Reina was forced to take a few steps back, and she continued to stare at the woman. "You're in danger; you need to leave. There are dark forces at work in this palace, forces you don't understand."

"Dark magic," Reina stated confidently and nodded her head with the words. "I know."

"No." The interjection was loud, and Reina startled backward at the sudden outburst from the woman as she reached for Reina's arm. "It's not just dark magic. There's something new here. It's been awoken, and I fear it's after you."

Reina shook her head. "Why have you been following me? You've been harassing me for weeks."

The priestess blinked at her for a moment. "What do you mean?"

Reina scoffed and began to skirt around the woman, closer to the exit. "The shadow, I know you're behind it. You've been practicing dark magic to spy on me, and I want to know why."

The woman looked aghast. Her eyes peered straight through her. Reina squirmed under the scrutiny but refused to back down from her question. She needed to know what was going on, why the woman had been following her.

"My dear, I do not practice dark magic. Nor would I dare to harm a descendant of Werthes. You represent the very thing I have dedicated my life to. I do not know who has been tormenting you, but I do know it is not over. The energy in this palace has grown darker since you have arrived, and I fear for your life." She seemed genuine, but Reina stared at her in suspicion.

"I saw you in the chapel one night with a book. You were reading from it. Mere seconds after, the shadow appeared. Do not lie to me. Besides, how would you know I am the descendent of Werthes if you had not been the shadow within the archives that night?" Reina took another step toward the door as she awaited the old woman's answer. Her green eyes were etched with concern as she watched Reina's movement.

"Do you really think," she started, "That I wouldn't know? My entire life has been spent honoring the gods, studying their histories. That's what I do in the chapel at night. I read the books of the gods. The second I saw what you could do, I knew who you were. In the weeks since you've come to the palace, I have been trying to keep others from figuring it out for themselves. If I was against you, why wouldn't I have told the king the moment you healed him in front of me? I am not your foe, Reina."

Reina stopped inching nearer to the doorway as she registered the woman's words. It made sense that the priestess would have known who she was, but she had only gained more questions from the woman's answer. "Ferix said it was your idea to invade Crieda, to take the orb. If you had really been working for the gods, why would you do such a thing? You caused the destruction of the very thing Werthes created. That doesn't sound like someone devoted to the gods. That sounds like someone who wanted a power that didn't belong to them."

"Ferix is correct. It was my idea to go after the orb. But not for the reason you suspect me of. I respected Werthes' decision most of my life until I realized the power of the gods had faded from this world. The gods left long ago, and without them, the world was dying. I knew what would happen if the king touched the orb, and I believed it was time. The power of the gods had to be awoken, and Werthes' line was the only way to do so. You can awaken the powers of the gods again; you have the power of prosperity, my dear. When you learn how to fully harness it, you can truly make anything in this world prosper. Even long-dead bloodlines of the gods. You are the only hope to save this world before it plummets into something I'm afraid we cannot come back from. This drought we are in is not a coincidence; these angry men you see were not born this way. We all need you, Reina. You are the head of something that cannot fail. There are those who do not want you to succeed though, some thrive off of the dependence of others as the world falls to its knees. For that reason, you are not safe here. *Please* leave while you can." The words rang true to Reina. There was no reason for the woman to lie to her. Still, she couldn't heed her advice until she had her questions answered.

"Why do you preach to the king's people to follow him blindly if you think so poorly of those within this kingdom? If you stand for the world being healed, then why do you destroy it further by spreading such fear?" Reina motioned to the sound of screams that rang above them, and the woman sighed at the question.

"What do you not understand, child? *Everything* I have done has been for you. In order to stay by the king's side, I had to show I was utterly devoted to him. I knew one day you would be found and brought to his attention. Werthes' line had only ever been within the walls of Crieda, which meant a Criedan slave was the only possibility for someone to have his power. I waited eleven years for you, and I would have waited for eleven more. I did what I had to do to stay of importance in this kingdom so that when you appeared one day, I would be there." She looked around in paranoia as she spoke and stared back at Reina, shooing her with her hands. "Now go."

"*Everything you have done was for me?*" Reina's voice thundered around them in anger as she rushed toward the woman. The screams from upstairs were drowned out by the noise, and she didn't stop until she stood inches from the priestess. "You were the very reason the king invaded my kingdom. My parents were *killed*. I lived in Den Zei for *eleven years* and watched my people suffer. My life was ruined because you thought it was your decision whether the world needed to be saved. The world is not my responsibility; I did not ask for this. You threw this upon me against my will. Do not stand there pretentiously and act as if you have done me a favor. All I have known for the past eleven years has been loss and pain. At least now I know who's fault that is." Reina turned her back on the woman and made her way toward the stairs.

"You are stronger now than you would have been if the invasion had never happened. I made you into a person who should be feared, who could withstand the worst of humanity. You are a *survivor*, more so than you ever would have been otherwise. You may not see it now, but you will. What has happened to you over the years will do nothing but help you in the future." The words were harsh, and Reina snarled as she spun back around.

She opened her mouth to respond, but the air grew heavy around her. Goosebumps rose on her flesh, and her heart began to pound in fear. Her eyes darted around to see where the shadow was, but she didn't see anything in the darkness. She turned back to the priestess and saw that the old woman's face was twisted in mortification. Her green eyes stared past her to the open doorway, but Reina couldn't turn around. Because behind the priestess stood the shadow.

It stared down at her, a strange hunger radiating from it. It grew tall and filled the space behind the priestess as it stretched toward the ceiling.

Reina wanted to cry out for the woman to turn around, but the words wouldn't come. The woman seemed far away in her terror, and understanding lit up her eyes. Reina didn't know what stood behind her, but it couldn't have been worse than the shadow at the priestess's back. As the woman opened her mouth to say something, the shadow dove straight down and entered through her open jaws.

She choked on the blackness as its entirety forced its way into her frail old body. Her chest jerked, and her jaw cracked loudly as the creature continued to push its way inside her. Reina's hand covered her mouth at the scene before her as the last shred of the dark mass disappeared within the woman's throat. Her head snapped sideways, and her eyes faded into a duller green than they had been seconds earlier. She fell to the ground knees first before the rest of her body toppled sideways. She didn't get up.

The shadow slowly reappeared as it came out of her ears, nose, and mouth. Then, it dissipated. It was gone from the world, but Reina still felt a chill on her skin as she stared at the priestess's dead body.

Someone was behind her. Their eyes burrowed into her skin in the same way the shadow's did. She refused to turn around, unsure if she was ready to see who watched her from the exit.

"Well, that was quite an unfortunate sight." The voice was one she recognized. Her stomach clenched, and she closed her eyes as she took a deep breath to steel herself. Then, she turned around to face the queen.

36

The queen looked bored as she stared over at Reina from the opening of the doorway. A black cloak was draped around her slim shoulders, and black lines curved upwards at the corner of her eyes to give her the likeness of a cat. Her lips were stained red and pursed in a pout while she looked at the lethally sharp nails that extended from her fingertips. She seemed relaxed as if she hadn't just witnessed the gruesome death of the priestess moments earlier. Power like nothing Reina had ever felt radiated from the queen as she stood confidently before her.

"You?" Reina asked, astounded by the dark transformation of the woman before her. The memory of the queen pushing her down the stairs flashed before her eyes, and she flinched. She knew the queen could be cruel, but she had never expected her to be the puppet master behind the shadow.

The queen flashed Reina a predatory grin. "I've been following you for quite some time now, my dear. It's nice to have the veil lifted so we can speak freely with one another, don't you agree?" She peered at Reina through her long lashes, and Reina felt a chill go down her spine.

"Why me? What do you want from me?" Reina blurted the questions out as she became nervous under the weight of the air. The room was electric with tension, and she clenched her jaw tightly to ground herself.

"I've already gotten it." She opened her hand, and a shadow slithered out from the skin and snaked toward Reina on the ground. "You know, when the priestess showed up at the palace all those years ago, I believed her to be insane. I actually threw her into the dungeon when I heard her rattle on about magic and witches. She wanted to work for the king, reconstruct religion in our kingdom. I forbade it, but my curiosity got the best of me. One night, I went to see her, and she showed me what she was capable of. They were only small tricks, things barely worth my time. But when she warned me of dark magic, I knew I had to learn it. I had her released from the dungeon and made a part of the king's court, so she could teach me the fundamentals of what she knew."

Another shadow escaped from her palm, and Reina stepped away as they crept toward her. "When I was confident enough, I went off on my own. I studied old texts from within the archive room and failed many times before I was able to control the shadows. Before I was able to *become* the shadows." She smiled lovingly at the wisps of darkness on the ground. "I thought I had become the most powerful version of myself, until one day, I happened upon a ledger. On that ledger was the name of my great-grandmother. She was the last documented descendent of

Hecra, the goddess of chaos. Which meant that I, too, was descended from a goddess."

Reina's insides froze. She didn't like where the tale was going. The queen continued, "At first, I was infatuated with this knowledge. I believed it meant I should have a power within me that surpasses what I had learned with dark magic. For weeks I tried to force it out into the open, but it never amounted to anything. I was frustrated, to say the least. When the priestess mentioned the orb within your kingdom, I knew she was holding something back. She knew more than she let on, and my husband was too dumb to see it. I used my shadows to spy on her until one night, I saw her reading a scripture on the descendants of Werthes. It spoke of the abilities you would possess when the orb was shattered."

She pulled a golden brush out from underneath her cloak, and Reina's eyes bulged as she casually tossed it to the side. The queen had been in her room. She had been the one to take the brush. "It said you would be able to bring the powers of the gods back to this world with nothing more than a single touch. I'm happy to say I was not disappointed when I found that to be true."

Reina remembered when the queen had grabbed her face in the throne room. How Reina had felt a surge of power before the queen had pushed her away. Reina's face twisted in mortification. "How did you know it was me?"

"Well, I didn't at first. I knew the Werthes line had to be Criedan, so I spent many years searching for you. I followed a maid girl around for a bit; she seemed odd. Always wanted to be alone and seemed very withdrawn. I assumed she had a secret of some kind, but I was wrong. My shadows roamed Den Zei quite often, tucked away in the darkness and hidden from prying eyes. When one night, they noticed you in an argument with the prince, there was something about-?"

"The prince?" Reina interjected in confusion. She had never seen Ferix within Den Zei, of that she was sure.

The queen's eyes flashed in interest for the first time since the conversation had started. Her mouth quirked up in a smirk as she purred, "You don't know?" Reina looked to her in silence and furrowed her brows. The shadows halted their movements toward her and seemed as if they, too, found amusement in Reina's confusion. "Oh dear, always left in the dark in more ways than one I see. The man who lived in the cell beside yours, he's the Criedan prince. My shadows showed him to me long ago, and I believed there was something strange about him. At first, I believed he might have been who I was searching for, but it didn't take much digging to realize he was the son of King Speranta. He never told you?" Reina's head spun, and she gave it a shake to signify that she hadn't known. The woman gave a tsk. "Poor girl."

Keane was the prince of Crieda, and he had never told her? Even when he knew her deepest secret, he hadn't trusted her with his? Betrayal stung behind her eyes as she realized even at the beginning of their time in Den Zei, they hadn't truly been friends. She had been alone for longer than she had even thought. The queen watched happily as Reina worked through the storm of feelings that ravaged her mind, and the shadows started toward her again.

"I didn't want this," Reina whispered as she looked to the queen through tear-filled eyes. "I never asked for any of this. I just want to go home. That's all I've ever wanted."

"Unfortunately, we don't always get what we want. You were necessary in this world for a time. Though, you have done quite enough. With you gone, I will be the most powerful descendent in this world. Hecra was the creator of magic in this realm. She created the ability for humans to harness minuscule amounts of her power. Thus, witches were born. After all, magic is nothing but chaos. I can control the shadows so much easier now. I can create anything. Magic has become me, and I can do anything I please. Without you to awaken more dormant bloodlines, I will be everything to this world. They will worship me, or chaos will rain down on them all." Her voice raised manically, and Reina flinched as the shadows that had crept toward her retreated quickly back into the queen's hand.

"I'm not the only one!" Reina shouted quickly, and the queen lowered her eyes to glance at her. "I have awoken others; they're going to come for you." Her lie fell flat as the queen began to chuckle.

"You mean the maid girl who can see into the future? My darling, that's hardly a threat." She waved her hand in the air to brush off Reina's words.

Reina's lip pulled back in a snarl. "Your son." The queen recoiled at the words as if she hadn't thought of the fact that Ferix was her child. If she were the descendent of Hecra, then so was he. "Are you going to kill your own blood? Your own child? He *will* defy you. You were there that night in the archives; you saw him helping me. He will not stand by and allow people to suffer at the hands of Yulsa any longer. When he knows what you have done, what you plan to do, he will come after you."

The queen growled as she threw her hands downward, and Reina watched in horror as shadows poured out of her palms. They morphed at her sides, taking the shape of large beasts that roared ferociously into the space between them. As they opened their mouths, Reina saw sharp teeth that could easily tear through skin.

She swallowed and wiped the old tears from her face. Her shoulders pulled back so she could stand tall before the new threat as she challenged the queen with her own glare. The shadow darks barked and snarled aggressively as the queen held them back, and she gave Reina one last smirk. "I'll do what needs to be done." Then, she released the dogs.

Reina watched as they flew toward her, and the queen exited the room. She raised her hands to cover her face instinctively as they leaped at her. When they made contact, she was knocked to the ground painfully. The sound of her dress tearing filled the air as the sharp claws of the shadow dogs shredded the golden fabric and turned it red with her blood. Her power burned within her, but the injuries were coming too fast for Reina to heal.

She felt as the collar of her dress was gripped between one of the beast's mighty jaws, and her head was thrown back against the stone. Her vision blurred, and she felt as if she were going to throw up. Teeth buried themselves in her leg, and she screamed in pain as a chunk of her thigh was ripped from her body. Her hands pushed at the creatures, but they were too strong. There was no way for Reina to fight them off, and she knew it.

I'm going to die, she thought. A sharp claw raked against her midsection, and she began to taste blood in her mouth. *In a dark room, alone, I'm going to die.* She felt a sob rise in her throat, but as it went to explode from her mouth, it was nothing more than a weak cry. Her throat bubbled, and she began to lose feeling in her body. The numbness was soothing, and she felt sleep tug at her.

The sound of growling became muted as Reina began to fade within herself. She wondered if she would see her parents. If they would accept her even after all she had done. She hoped they would, that they would welcome her with open arms and tell her she had done the best she could. Eleven years of pain had been long enough, and it was time to go home.

You're so close, a little voice piped up from within her. *You can get out of here. You can be free. There are so many people that need you now more than ever. Are you really going to let them down?* Reina was annoyed by the intrusive thoughts and wished for them to disappear. She felt a distant tug and looked down to see one of the beasts had ahold of her arm and was dragging her across the room. Faintly, she could feel the hard stone at her back, but there was no pain.

Her vision faded to black, but she was still conscious behind her eyes. *I didn't ask for this*, she repeated to herself.

Maybe not, the voice grew louder, *but it's your responsibility now. Imagine how many people are going to die if you give up.* It was right; she knew it was right. She didn't want to keep fighting, though. If she let herself fade away, she would know no more pain, and if she stayed, she feared that would be all she'd ever know.

Let me go, she begged the voice. *I can't do this anymore.*

This is not the end, sweet child. Only the beginning. You can rest when you're done. With that, the voice vanished from her mind, and Reina was thrown back into a world of excruciating pain. Her head flew backward as she screamed in agony through the blood that clogged her throat. The dogs howled in excitement as they charged her once more. Her blood covered the floor, and she didn't know how much more she had left to lose. She should have been dead.

The feeling of teeth as they sank into her skin made her wail, and she begged for it to be over. Death wouldn't take her back though, it had already refused her once. She clenched her jaw in rage at what had become of her life. Her only friend had lied to her about who he was. The priestess had admitted Crieda had only been destroyed for Reina, and the queen had used and discarded her as if she were nothing more than a toy. She was tired, she was in pain, and she was angry.

She gave an enraged scream as the shadows tore into her once again, and she felt something burn in her. It built inside her body until she felt as if she were about to explode. The pain sharpened her vision and heightened her senses as the world around her began to glow golden. The dogs paused in uncertainty and turned to run away. But it was too late as Reina felt the power release from within her.

37

MALYSSANDRA

The fire had arrived at the palace. It felt as though Malyssandra ran through an oven as the prince led their way toward the basement. The smell of death mixed with smoke and sweat in the air, and her breathing was labored. She couldn't get any oxygen into her lungs. Her eyes burned from both the smoke and fear. The screams in the palace had become few and far between. Most inside had either escaped or been killed by the rebels. She thought back to the pregnant woman she had seen brutally murdered, and she wondered if anyone would remember her. There had to of been a father out there somewhere. Was he still alive? Would he miss his child?

Bodies became scarce as they traveled deeper into the palace. It was a ghost town. She couldn't help but remember the stories of the haunted eastern sector, and a shiver ran down her spine despite the heat. The whole palace had become haunted with the horrors of what had taken place there.

Lives had been forcibly taken from the world under the guise of retribution. Malyssandra hoped the rebels knew what they had done, and she hoped it tore them apart for the rest of their lives. The mission hadn't been to save the enslaved Criedans. It had been revenge, and the wrong people had fallen at their swords.

Malyssandra ripped her focus away from the desolation of the palace halls. It was not her fault, and she would not feel guilty for the wrongdoings of others. Although, her heart still weighed heavily at the knowledge of what had transpired at the hands of her people. She had thought they were better than that. The Crieda she had known as a child was not the Crieda that had stood before her that day.

She rammed into the prince's back as he suddenly stopped atop the steps that led to the basement. His breathing halted, and Malyssandra feared they were too late. She didn't wish to look but knew she must. Her weight shifted as she slowly brought herself to peer around the prince's side, and her heart sputtered in her chest. The stone stairs she had walked down many times in her life were not stone anymore, but pure gold.

Malyssandra couldn't see through the door at the base of the steps due to her angle, and she was nervous about descending. The prince gave her a sidelong glance as he took a step onto the golden stairs. She faltered at the top as he made his way down. Uncertainty rose up within her at the strangeness of the sight, but she refused to be left behind.

She expected the smooth gold to be slick beneath her feet, but it wasn't. There was an odd warmth to it, and Malyssandra stared at the steps. No sound came from the room below. Her stomach twisted anxiously as she tried to imagine what they would see as they entered the doorway. She picked up her pace and caught up with the prince as they landed at the base of the steps. He grabbed a torch from the wall, and they walked in together.

Her breathing hitched at the sight before her. The entire room had been turned to gold. Rats lay eternally trapped within golden traps, and their bodies reflected the flames Ferix held. The body of an elderly woman was slumped to the ground, and Malyssandra recoiled as she realized it was the priestess. Her eyes were unseeing, and her skin glinted as they walked past her. She wondered what had taken place in that room, what she had been blocked from seeing by the shadow.

Her head turned to scan the rest of the space, and a small shriek escaped from her mouth as she came face to face with fangs. She stumbled backward and tripped over her feet. The ground rushed up behind her, and she braced herself for impact, but the prince's hand darted out and caught her arm before she landed. He quickly tugged her up and waited until she regained her balance.

When she was standing on her own again, she looked more closely at the frozen creatures. They looked like mutts but much larger than any she could recall. Each one came up to her waist and looked like they had been bred to kill. As she inspected them, she noticed something odd.

Large masses of shadows whirled within the golden hounds and threw themselves against the encasement. They were trapped inside, and Malyssandra realized in horror that the creatures hadn't been real dogs. The shadows inside seemed frantic as they pulled back and rammed against their prisons in an escape to free themselves. The dark masses seemed less frightening to Malyssandra from within their cages, and her hand snaked forward to touch the gold around them.

"Reina!" The prince's loud voice startled her, and her hand dropped to her side as she turned to what had grabbed his attention.

Blood covered the floor around Reina's body as she lay slumped against the wall. Her eyes were closed, but Malyssandra could see that her chest still rose and fell beneath torn fabric. Bones emerged from her violently shredded skin. Her arm was twisted unnaturally, and she looked like a ragdoll discarded haphazardly onto the floor. Malyssandra's hands went to cover her mouth as her eyes widened in disbelief. It was a miracle Reina was still breathing.

Her eyes fluttered open at the sound of the prince's voice, and she gave a weak smile. She opened her mouth to speak, and the prince was at her side within a second. "What took you so long?" She croaked, and the prince cracked a pained smile.

"I got lost." He shrugged half-heartedly, and Reina let out a small laugh. She winced in pain at the sharp movement, and the prince's hands hovered frantically over the wounds on her body. He seemed almost afraid to touch her, and Malyssandra watched quietly from a distance. "You're hurt," he stated dumbly.

"I'll heal," she groaned as she tried to push herself to her feet, "we need to get out of here." The prince moved forward to support her, and her eyes widened. "Your mother, she's the shadow." As she blurted the words, the prince looked at her in shock. Malyssandra froze.

"The queen?" She whispered. Malyssandra had rarely seen the queen within the palace walls. The woman had been so withdrawn, so quiet. Malyssandra never would have expected the woman to be the phantom stalker that had tormented her and Reina.

"What? How?" He seemed lost in the questions, but the way he looked at Reina told Malyssandra that he believed her without a second thought. Malyssandra wondered what had happened between them in the time Reina had been in the palace.

"She's been practicing dark magic for years." Reina flinched as the prince brushed against her side. "She's been waiting for me; she knew about the orb's curse. She knew a Criedan would have the power of Werthes. Ferix, she's descended from Hecra. Which means you are too. Do you feel any different? Have you noticed anything strange?" Her words were breathy and uncomfortable as the prince helped her move toward the open doorway.

The prince shook his head, "No. Or at least, I don't think so. Maybe it skips a generation? I didn't... I don't know."

Reina nodded and gave a small sigh. "That's okay, we'll figure it out." Malyssandra shifted out of the way as they walked past. Reina gave her a quick glance and reached out to take her hand. "Thank you," she whispered.

"For what?" Malyssandra asked.

"For going to Den Zei, you didn't need to, but you did anyway. Did everyone make it out? Is your friend okay?" Reina blinked at Malyssandra in pain, and Malyssandra deflated.

She shook her head. "I honestly don't know. It happened so fast. The fire is everywhere up there. Ivanka is with the rebellion; she was breathing last I saw her." Malyssandra's stomach twisted. She hoped her friend was still breathing when she got to her side.

The prince's eyes darkened at the mention of the rebellion. Before he could interject, Reina stumbled, and he rushed to steady her. He looked her up and down in concern. "Why aren't you healing?"

"I think I'm just... drained. The wounds are deep, and I used most of my power on," Reina looked around the golden room, "this. Hurts like hell, but don't worry. Death isn't ready for me yet. You might need to carry me, though. I'm not sure how much longer I'm going to be conscious for."

The prince nodded and scooped her into his arms as they came upon the bottom of the stairs. He glared up at the dark smoke that billowed through the palace above and glanced over at Malyssandra. The fire had to be deep within the castle by that point, and she dreaded the journey they would have to make. She released a deep breath and began to ascend the golden steps with the prince behind her.

When they reached the top, her arm automatically went to cover her mouth. Her skin tasted of soot, but it was decidedly better than the feeling of inhaling smoke. She turned back to see that Reina had indeed lost consciousness in his arms, and his eyes stared forward confidently. Malyssandra steeled herself against the unbearable heat and barreled back through the palace. "We need to get to the western wall!" She shouted back at the prince, "The rebellion is waiting there to help."

His footfalls behind her were the only answer she needed as she pushed onward. Flames licked up the sides of the slashed paintings, and she watched as they crumpled inward and turned black as the fire devoured them. The blood-stained walls were being cleansed of their sins by the inferno around them. Bodies were blackened beneath her feet, and she took care not to trip over them.

The prince was close behind her through it all as she led them out of the destroyed palace she had once called home. When they made it through the threshold, Malyssandra spun around to see the smoke billowed from the windows above. The window Ivanka had stared out of for years had been blown out by the flames, and she backed away slowly.

The prince ran up beside her. "Keep moving!" He shouted. As they began to run toward the western wall and into the burning city, she could have sworn she had seen the tendril of a shadow whirl in the periphery of her vision.

...

The fire did not follow them to the western wall. They slowed their pace, and Malyssandra looked up at the moon's white face. The light wasn't necessary to see that night, but she felt comfort in its presence. Exhaustion tugged at her feet as she stumbled alongside the prince, who still held Reina in his arms.

She hadn't woken up, but at some point, she had healed. Blood still caked her body and made her a pitiful sight, but bones no longer peaked out from beneath her skin. There were no scars to show what had happened to her within the basement, but Malyssandra knew none of them would ever forget how broken she had been upon that golden floor.

People appeared in the distance, scattered about a large opening in the wall. Malyssandra wasn't sure how she felt about trusting the rebellion after what she had seen that day, but they needed a place to rest. They drew nearer, and the men at the wall became stiff as they approached. They raised their swords in the darkness.

Malyssandra lifted her hands as she approached. "I'm Criedan; my friend is injured. We need help." Her voice shook as she spoke, and they continued to walk up to the men until their faces were evident in the darkness.

They looked at each other uncertainly until one man stepped up. "Who is he?" He pointed his sword at the prince, and Malyssandra sighed at the idea of having to explain the situation to the man.

"Prince Ferix," he declared, and Malyssandra watched in confusion as the men at the wall lowered their weapons. "I need to talk with your commander."

Malyssandra looked between the prince and the Criedan soldiers. She felt as if she had missed something. Why would they lay down their arms for the Yulsan prince? Her head pulsed, overwhelmed by the day. "Is Keane here?" She asked abruptly, and the men raised their brows. "Prince Leven," she corrected herself. "I'm not sure if he made it." Her voice cracked as she remembered how the world had burned around them when she had seen him last. "But if he did, tell him that Malyssandra is here."

The men turned to converse quietly before the one that seemed to be in charge turned back to her. "Stay here." She nodded in response, and he turned to head through the hole in the wall.

As they waited, she turned to look at the burning city in the distance. It was beautiful in the way only a disaster could be. She had never seen anything like it, and she hoped she would never have to again. The image of children as they ran through the flames flashed through her mind once again, and she flinched. They were long dead by then, likely turned to ash beneath the heat of the fire.

"Mallie?" The voice was soft from behind her, and she whipped around to see Keane's broad form make its way to her in the darkness. When he saw her face, he rushed forward and pulled her into a hug. "Thank the gods," he whispered before he pulled back, "I told you to go straight to the western wall. Why didn't you listen to me?"

She looked to Reina's slumped form in response, and Keane's eyes followed and widened in shock. "You said she was the key to Crieda's revival, and I knew where she was. I had a vision." Her voice was tired, and it was all she could do to keep herself standing. "I knew you wouldn't find her by yourself, so I went to the palace. He helped." Malyssandra motioned to prince Ferix, and the men's gazes clashed against each other.

As Keane's stare darted between Reina's limp body and the prince's arms wrapped protectively around her, tension rose in the air. Keane's eyes narrowed, and his chest puffed out as he took a deep breath. Malyssandra tensed, afraid of what was about to happen between the two as prince Ferix watched Keane, daring him to make the first move.

Keane's hand darted forward and landed on Ferix's shoulder. "Thank you," he stated bluntly and gave a firm shake before he turned back to the men at the wall. "Let them through; they belong here." At his command, the men stepped aside as Keane led them through the wall.

Malyssandra marveled at all the people who had made it out of the kingdom, and tears welled in her eyes. They were free; they had made it. Wagons lined the area and were filled with sleeping people as the rebels stood guard around the camp. Torches lit a path that led them to an opening filled with large white tents and bustling Criedans.

Keane pulled back the flap on one of the tents, and Malyssandra realized it was an infirmary. Keane brought them to an empty bed and motioned for Ferix to set Reina down upon the white sheets. As Ferix did so, Reina opened her eyes. She looked around in confusion for a moment before her focus settled on Keane.

"Hey," he spoke softly and leaned forward with kind eyes. "You made it-."

Reina's fist came out of nowhere and collided with the side of Keane's face. He pulled back as she sat up abruptly, rage churning in her glare. "You're a godsdamn *liar*!" She shouted, and those in the area around them turned to look at the commotion.

Keane rubbed his hand along his jaw as he looked to Reina with a hurt stare, and she climbed to her feet. Ferix moved forward with her, likely afraid she would lose consciousness again. Reina ignored him as she stalked into Keane's personal space. "A *prince*? All these years, and you never *told me*? You knew *everything* about me, but you never thought to share that one small detail about yourself?" She pushed him, and he allowed her to do so. Her voice was shrill in her anger, and Keane looked as if he didn't know what to do.

"Reina, I'm sorry. I should have told you a lot of things, but I can't change the past. Please don't-." He stopped talking as a woman entered the tent. She walked briskly, power radiating from her. Her soft brown hair was pulled back tightly from her face, and her dark eyes stared fiercely forward as she moved.

Reina didn't see her as she continued to berate Keane. "Don't what? Be mad?" She went to push at Keane again, but he grabbed her by the wrists before she could do so. Everyone in the tent stood as the woman walked by them, and Malyssandra realized she must have been someone of importance within the rebellion.

The woman approached Reina and Keane, and Keane bowed his head. "My apologies for the disruption, commander.

My friend here is just upset. She was just about to calm down." He turned back to Reina with a warning in his eyes.

"See to it that she does," the woman spoke with authority. "There are injured in this tent, and they don't need any dramatics. Why don't you take this outside? There's no need for you to be in here." Reina spun on her heel to face the woman with wrath on her face.

As she opened her mouth to offer a retort, her expression fell in disbelief. She looked to the woman as if she had seen a ghost, and her skin turned pale. The woman's face registered shock as she stared back at Reina, and a strange emotional silence stretched between them. Keane looked down at the woman in front of him, and his eyebrows scrunched together.

Tears filled Reina's eyes as she reached forward and touched the woman's face. "Mom?"

38

Keane sat across from Reina at a round table as the rebellion leaders marched to their own seats. Reina looked at Ferix beside her, and his eyes glinted in the soft light of the tent. He had been waiting for that meeting since they had arrived at the rebellion camp one week prior. What the rebellion had done to the innocents in his kingdom weighed heavily on his mind, and Reina didn't know what she could do to soothe his guilt.

She hadn't been there when the rebels had infiltrated the palace. She hadn't seen the things that haunted Malyssandra's and Ferix's stares. Reina had been underground in her own nightmare. They were all different after what they had seen, and there hadn't been much satisfaction in their freedom. There couldn't have been, not when there was so much left to do.

Reina's mother entered the tent, and Reina and Ferix stayed seated as everyone stood. She hadn't spoken to her mother since the night she had seen her in the infirmary. The woman was a stranger to her, someone from a long-forgotten dream.

"You may be seated," her mother spoke, and the sound of chairs scraping against the ground grated against Reina's ears as everyone sat. Her mother looked around the table until her eyes fell on Keane. "My prince." She bowed, and Keane looked around uncomfortably.

Reina hadn't spoken to Keane since that night, either. She was livid with him for having kept his identity a secret from her for so long. He tried to explain himself many times over the week that followed, but Reina wasn't ready to hear him out yet. She wasn't sure she ever would be.

"So we have our people back, now what?" A large man blurted out at the table around him.

Reina's mother looked at him calmly before she said, "Now we recover."

"All due respect, commander, but I disagree. The king could still be alive in the palace; we need to attack while they're still down. If the king can get his feet back under himself, he will come for us. And his numbers far outweigh our own," the man stated and leaned over the table.

"The king will be dead in a few days," Reina interjected, and everyone turned to her. "He is ill, and without me to heal him, he will succumb to his illness. There is no need for more violence, not yet."

Her mother turned and stared at her as if she had forgotten her daughter was in the room. As if she had forgotten her daughter was still alive. Her eyes were shielded; no emotion came from within their depths. The child within Reina yearned for her mother to show that she cared, that she was relieved her daughter had survived.

"You have no right to speak here, *traitor*," the man barked at her. Ferix bristled at her side, and the man continued, "You spent weeks as the king's pet, supposedly healing him. Yet, when you arrive here, you can't even heal your own people. How can we trust a word you say?" Reina flinched at the harsh words.

She had tried to heal the wounded in the camp, but her powers were still strained from what had happened within the palace basement. She wished she could have done more, that she could have helped them. But the swell of power within her faltered every time she tried to use it.

"That's rich coming from you," Ferix growled. "When your people wrote me, I recall a promise was made that you would not raise your swords to the innocent within my kingdom. Tell me, how many innocent lives fell victim to your men?"

"That's not the same!" The man bellowed.

"Like hell it isn't!" Ferix slammed his hands down on the table and stood. "You were supposed to free your people, not murder mine! I expected you to go after my father, but you didn't even do that. Instead, the bodies of children littered the ground outside the palace. You didn't come to save your people; you came for revenge."

The man opened his mouth to respond, but the commander cut him off. "I apologize for how the rebels behaved, prince Ferix, but we did what was necessary to extract our people. If I recall, we promised we would *try* not to harm the innocent. We didn't know the explosions would result in such a blaze."

Reina scoffed.

"Do you have something to add?" Her mother turned to her.

Reina set her jaw. "We have been in a drought for months now. The ground is dead beneath our feet. My apologies if I don't believe you were stupid enough to truly believe your explosives wouldn't *'result in such a blaze,'*" she mocked. "You knew what would happen; you just didn't care."

The table stared at Reina, and Keane sighed in disappointment. "What would you have had me do?" Her mother asked, still no emotion on her face.

"It doesn't matter. What's done is done, and you are all too proud to admit that you were wrong." The rebels around the table had the audacity to look offended. "Regardless of whether or not any of you trust me, the king will be dead soon. But that is not the end of our fight. The queen will take the throne upon his death, and she plans to do much worse than her husband has ever done."

Another man at the table laughed. "I do not fear a woman in power." Reina and her mother turned to the man, their eyebrows raised in a challenge and their eyes hardened. His laughter died down as he shrunk back into his chair.

"Be careful what you say," Reina leered, "She could be watching you right now." The man's eyes widened as his face went white. Reina continued, "The queen is a descendant of Hecra, and the goddess's power has been awakened within her. There is no telling how much destruction she will bring to this world if she is not stopped. We cannot do this alone. We need others, people from the bloodlines of the gods. I propose-."

The first man stood up, anger on his face. "Do you think us fools? People descended from the gods? Powers? This is absurd! Commander, I-."

"She's telling the truth," Keane declared, and all eyes turned to him. His face heated under the scrutiny, but he finished, "Let her speak."

She gave him a sidelong stare before she cleared her throat. "I propose you allow me to gather a small team of people, and we will find these other descendants. We will recruit them and bring them back here. That way, we will have a chance against the queen." Reina looked around the room.

"Absolutely not," her mother interjected.

"I am only asking you as a formality," Reina informed her, "I will go whether you forbade me or not."

"She's right," Keane said, "I'll go with her."

Reina opened her mouth to argue, but her mother beat her to it. "I will not allow such a ridiculous expedition based off of fairytales. The gods are dead; they have not appeared to us in centuries. You will not take any of my people on such a wild goose chase."

Keane's eyes darkened. "I am your prince."

"And I am your commander," Reina's mother retorted, "While you've been locked in a cage the past eleven years, I have been leading your people. My apologies, Prince Leven, but you are nothing more than a celebrity anymore. I am in charge, and I say this is not happening."

Ferix stood beside her. "Are you really so daft that you cannot see what is right in front of you? We will all die if we don't do as Reina says. My mother is coming for us all, and you would rather argue on if this threat is real or not?" Ferix huffed. "If you don't want to believe us, then fine. Don't. But we are leaving, and that's the end of it."

Ferix stormed out of the tent, and Reina watched as he went. "We do not need any of your people," Reina muttered before she turned back to the skeptical eyes around her. "I have my own." She looked up at Keane, and even though she was still angry with him, she gave him a slight nod of appreciation. Reina went to follow Ferix out of the tent but turned back to the group one last time. "You know, when I first heard that there was a rebellion out there, coming for us, I was excited. But looking at you now," she paused as she looked at her mother, her eyes rigid as their stares met each other across the room, "I don't know what I was excited for." Then, she exited the tent.

Keane followed her and his voice piped up from behind her. "When do we leave?"

Reina spun on him, and he froze. "If you lie to me *ever* again, you're done. Understand?" Keane nodded, a small smile tugged at the corner of his mouth. "What?"

He chuckled, "I missed you, Rein."

She rolled her eyes. "We'll leave in the morning, go get packed. I need to tell Malyssandra."

39

MALYSSANDRA

Malyssandra had one last thing to do before she left that morning.

She walked slowly through the rebel camp, her mind wild with the possibilities of what they were going to find out in the world. Reina had told her about her ability to awaken the powers of the gods within their descendants. Malyssandra had the power of Hertes, the god of omens. It made sense, but she still struggled to come to terms with it. She wasn't entirely human.

Malyssandra pulled the flap of the tent back as she slowly walked inside to say goodbye to her friend. After they arrived at the rebel camp, it took her days of searching before someone pointed her to where Ivanka was staying. When Malyssandra first saw her, Ivanka had looked as if she had finally gained a small amount of peace in her eyes. She was healthy, and Malyssandra charged her and gave her a long hug. They had made it, the both of them.

Malyssandra smiled at the memory as she looked around Ivanka's small home. Her friend would be fine, she told herself.

Ivanka was strong; she would make a life in the rebel camp without Malyssandra. They didn't need each other anymore.

As her eyes settled on Ivanka's slim body, her thoughts halted. The woman turned around, a bag slung over her shoulder and a fierce look in her blue eyes. "I'm coming too," she stated defiantly before Malyssandra could say anything.

Malyssandra didn't want an argument, but she didn't feel Ivanka knew what she was getting herself into. "No," she stated, "You're not."

"Like hell I'm not, Mallie. All the talk in the camp is about what you guys are setting out to do, and I refuse to be left behind. I've been a prisoner all my life. I've never been able to make choices for myself. Let me have this," she begged Malyssandra.

Malyssandra shook her head. "It's too dangerous. We don't know what's out there, Ivanka. The queen will come after us eventually, and I don't want you caught in the crossfire. You got out; can't that be enough?"

Ivanka gave a harsh laugh, "*Dangerous*? Mallie, we grew up in 'dangerous.' I can take care of myself. As for the queen, she's the reason I'm going." Ivanka crossed her arms. "She had me beaten into an inch of my life and thrown into Den Zei. If I can have even the smallest hand in ruining her life, I want in. You can't take this from me; I won't let you." She stepped forward, refusing to be turned away.

Malyssandra took a deep breath and exhaled as she looked at her friend. Her long pale-blonde hair was brushed and pulled back into a low ponytail. Her blue eyes looked as if they were carved from stone, and her porcelain skin seemed to reflect the light around her. She was beautiful, even in the muffled light of the tent. Malyssandra knew she couldn't deny her, so she spun on her heel and strutted out without another word.

Ivanka trailed after her as they made their way past the tents within the camp and toward the hill where Malyssandra was supposed to meet everyone. They had taken enough supplies and coins to last them a few weeks, but after that, they would have to resort to scavenging for their food. She hoped that they would make it to another kingdom before they had to begin hunting. After what she had seen in the palace, she didn't want to hold a weapon in her hand. Much less kill something. The idea sickened her, and she cast a nervous glance to the rebels that inhabited the camp.

She was happy to be leaving. The images of the rebel soldiers slicing through civilians replayed in Malyssandra's head on repeat. There was no feeling of safety for her within the camp, and she didn't think there ever would be.

As they came over the crest of the hill, Malyssandra realized she had been the last to arrive. Reina and Ferix were huddled over a map as they discussed where their first stop would be, and Keane stood off to the side. His face lit up when he saw her, and he raised his hand to wave. Malyssandra gave him a small smile as she walked over to Reina.

"Room for one more?" She asked and motioned behind her.

Reina looked at Ivanka, recognition lighting up her face. She offered a warm smile and nodded. "As long as you know what you're getting yourself into, I'd love to have you. Nice to see you again." Ivanka nodded vigorously, and Reina turned back in the direction she had been facing. "Looks like we have a two weeks walk to our first destination. You guys ready?"

Keane and Ivanka mumbled their agreements, but Malyssandra felt a twinge of curiosity that made her speak up. "Where are we going?"

All they had been through over the past eleven years had led them to that moment. They had been shredded by the whips of unjust men, beaten at the command of a tyrant. Forced to hide the deepest parts of themselves from the world, taunted by chains and shadows alike. But they were free; they were alive. They were survivors.

But they weren't done. Something was coming, something worse than anything they had seen before. If they failed what they were set out to do, the queen would win. Chaos would rule the world.

Reina looked off into the distance in determination before she finally answered, "Wyverst."

ABOUT THE AUTHOR

Lauren is a young author who resides in Upstate New York with her rabbit, horse, and two cats. When she isn't writing you can find her binge watching comically awful TV shows, curling up with a good book, or manically drinking caffeine.

Since she was a little girl she would spend time jotting down stories as they entered her head. When she was in eighth grade she started and finished two novels that she still has in her possession to this day. Although she never published them, they each hold a special place in her heart.

If you wish to know more about her upcoming novels, follow her writing account on Instagram: @ld_writes. This is where you will find updates on what she is working on, as well as release dates.

Acknowledgments

Rachel, from the bottom of my heart I thank you for listening to all of my crazy ideas as they popped up in my head. For years you have been telling me to publish one of my stories, and I likely wouldn't have if you hadn't been there along the way to push me.

Peyton, you have been a huge support to me through all of this. Thank you for sticking by me through the late nights, and for turning your closet into a writing room for me to lock myself inside when the world got too loud. I couldn't ask for a better boyfriend, I love you.

Mom and Dad, you guys gave me the comfort and tools I needed to be able to accomplish my dream. You helped me grow into the person I have become, and believed in me every step of the way. Thank you for everything.

Reader, thank you for spending the time to read my first book *ever*. The fact that you are out there somewhere reading about this world that I have dreamed about for years blows my mind. Thank you for joining these characters on their journey, and I hope you enjoyed it.

To everyone else who has helped me through this process, I appreciate each and every one of you. Your feedback, your support, your listening ears, your help to bring this story to life.

Thank you.

www.ingramcontent.com/pod-product-compliance
Lightning Source LLC
Chambersburg PA
CBHW051327250626
47155CB00007B/2490